W9-BDH-329

Once Upon a Summertime

This Large Print Book carries the
Seal of Approval of N.A.V.H.

ONCE UPON A SUMMERTIME

A NEW YORK CITY ROMANCE

MELODY CARLSON

THORNDIKE PRESS
A part of Gale, Cengage Learning

Farmington Hills, Mich • San Francisco • New York • Waterville, Maine
Meriden, Conn • Mason, Ohio • Chicago

Thorndike Press, a part of Gale, Cengage Learning.

Thorndike Press® Large Print Christian Romance.
The text of this Large Print edition is unabridged.
Other aspects of the book may vary from the original edition.
Set in 16 pt. Plantin.

LIBRARY OF CONGRESS CATALOGING-IN-PUBLICATION DATA

Carlson, Melody.
Once upon a summertime : a New York City romance / by Melody Carlson.
— Large print edition.
pages cm. — (Follow your heart ; book 1) (Thorndike Press large print Christian romance)
ISBN 978-1-4104-8148-1 (hardcover) — ISBN 1-4104-8148-4 (hardcover)
1. Large type books. I. Title.
PS3553.A73257O54 2015b
813'.54—dc23 2015014223

Published in 2015 by arrangement with Revell Books, a division of Baker Publishing Group

Printed in the United States of America
1 2 3 4 5 6 7 19 18 17 16 15

Once Upon a Summertime

1

It had never been Anna Gordon's dream to work for a motel — certainly not the Value Lodge. And most definitely not in the same sleepy town she'd grown up in. But as her grandma had reminded her just that morning, "A job is a job, and I'm sure there are plenty of unemployed folks who would be grateful to trade places." Even so, as Anna walked the six blocks from her grandmother's apartment to her place of employment, she longed for something more.

As Anna came to Lou's Café, someone backed out the front door with a watering can in hand, nearly knocking Anna down. "Excuse *me*!" the careless woman cried as she slopped cold water onto Anna's good Nine West pumps.

As Anna caught her balance, she recognized the offender. "Marley Ferris!" she cried out. "What on earth are you doing here in Springville?"

Marley blinked in surprise. *"Anna?"*

"I can't believe it's you." Anna stared at her old friend in wonder.

Marley set aside the watering can and the two hugged — long and hard — exclaiming joyfully over this unexpected meeting.

"It's been so long," Marley said as they stepped apart.

"Way too long." Anna slowly shook her head.

"And look at you." Marley studied Anna closely, from her shoulder-length strawberry blonde hair to her shoes. "So professional in your stylish suit. And still looking way too much like Nicole Kidman's little sister."

Anna smiled. "Thanks."

"What're you doing in these parts anyway?"

"I was about to ask you the same thing." Anna adjusted her purse strap.

"I'm just home for a few days." She jerked her thumb over her shoulder. "Helping out with my parents' café. My mom's laid up after back surgery."

"Oh dear. Is she okay?"

"Yeah. It was a ruptured disc, but sounds like they got it cleaned up. She just needs to take it easy for a few days." Marley pointed at Anna. "Seriously, what're you doing back in Springville, and looking all uptown too?"

Anna grimaced, wishing for a better answer. "I'm, uh, I'm managing the, uh, the motel," she mumbled.

"Oh?" Marley's brow creased. "A motel? In *this* town?"

Anna tipped her head down the street with a somber expression.

"The Value Lodge?"

"Uh-huh." Anna glanced at her watch. "And I should probably get going."

"Oh yeah, sure." Marley looked doubtful, as if she was still processing this bit of news.

"It's great seeing you," Anna said. "You look fantastic."

"Hey, why don't you come back over here for lunch?" Marley said quickly. "Give us time to catch up. The Value Lodge does give you a lunch break, doesn't it?"

"Absolutely." Anna nodded eagerly. "At 1:00."

"I'll be right here." Marley picked up the can and began to water the large terra-cotta pot by the front door, which was overflowing with colorful pansies and red geraniums. "I promised Mom I'd keep her plants alive until she gets back. Can you believe how hot it's been? And it's only May!" She plucked off a dried bloom, tossing it into the gutter.

"I adore your mom's flowers. So pretty and cheerful." Anna waved as she continued on her way. And it was true — she did love seeing the café's flowers. It was a bright spot in her day. The blooms reminded her of the small hotel she'd worked at during her college years. Some students in the hospitality management program had disparaged the old Pomonte Hotel by calling it the *Podunk* Hotel. But compared to the Value Lodge, the thirty-six-room Pomonte was quite chic, from its cast iron flowerpots by the door to the bubbling fountain in the lobby. It was true what they said: you don't know what you've got until it's gone.

Anna felt a familiar wave of disappointment wash over as her destination came into view. The boring two-story motel had been built in the early eighties, and most Springville residents agreed it was an eyesore. Some more motivated citizens had even gone to the city council demanding improvements. Anna couldn't blame them. When she'd accepted the managerial job, she had convinced herself that she could make a difference in the humdrum lodgings — or she could move on after a year. Unfortunately, she'd been wrong on both accounts.

As she got closer to the building, her

general dismay was replaced by some ironic gratitude — she was thankful that none of her college chums could see her now. It was bad enough having to confess her lackluster vocation to a childhood friend this morning. But if her college acquaintances knew — like her ex-roommate who now worked in Paris, or the ex-boyfriend who managed a Caribbean Ritz — Anna would feel thoroughly humiliated.

She wasn't a big fan of social networking, but she occasionally sneaked a peek at friends' Facebook pages — not for long, lest she feed any jealous green demons festering inside of her. Naturally, she never posted a single word about her own personal or professional life. Occasionally she was tempted to fake some exotic photos and falsify her whereabouts, just for fun, but really that wasn't her style. Better to remain honest and simply suffer in silence.

From across the street, she frowned at the garishly painted Value Lodge. Not for the first time, she wondered what idiot picked out those colors. The bright yellow and red stripes had always reminded her of a fast-food restaurant; they looked like mustard and ketchup, but much less appetizing. In Anna's opinion, almost everything about this motel was unappealing, from the "free continental breakfast," which consisted of small cardboard boxes of cereal and cartons of milk and juice, to the kidney-shaped swimming pool in its varying shades of blue and sometimes green, to the lumpy queen beds topped with bedspreads with a texture akin to fiberglass. For the life of her, she could not understand why anyone would stay here on purpose. Well, except that the Value Lodge boasted the "lowest rates in town." She would give the motel that much — it was definitely cheap.

It was, in fact, the general frugality of this establishment that was the very bane of her existence. She'd suggested improvements to the owners, a semi-retired couple who were friends of her grandmother: relatively inexpensive perks like fresh floral arrangements in the lobby, upgraded linens, quality toiletries, or even a bowl of fresh fruit to accompany the continental breakfast. Every time, her ideas were politely but firmly declined. "Not in the budget," Rich Morgan would tell her. "Not in the budget," his wife Sharon would repeat like a trained parrot. And off they'd go on their merry little way.

As Anna walked across the motel's narrow parking lot, which had trash in it as usual, she made a mental note to herself to send Mickey out for litter patrol — again. Taking a deep breath, Anna forced a pleasant smile as an elderly couple exited the motel. They had checked in with her yesterday afternoon, for just one night, but they'd gotten her attention because they seemed like such sweet people. They were taking a cross-country car trip to mark their fiftieth anniversary.

"I hope you enjoyed your stay with us," she said cheerfully as the gentleman politely held the outer door for her and his wife.

"Yes, uh, thank you." He sounded hesitant as he followed his wife out. Almost as if something was wrong. Well, why should she be surprised? And why bother to inquire, except that was what a manager said to guests who were checking out. Still standing in the vestibule between the two sets of doors, Anna watched them hurry to their car. Wrinkling her nose, she peered curiously around the small space. Why did it always smell so doggone nasty in here? And even worse on warm days. It was as if someone had gotten sick and no one had bothered to properly clean it up.

She held her breath as she propped the exterior door open, wedging it in place with the rubber doorstop. Fresh air couldn't hurt! Second note to self: *Remind housekeeping to give this room a good disinfectant scrub during the night shift tonight.* With temps heading for the high nineties this week, this entryway needed to smell fresh — or at least not quite so disgusting.

As she continued into the shabby lobby with its faux marble vinyl floor and eighties wallpaper, she vaguely wondered why guests never complained about that wretched smell as they entered. Maybe she should put in a suggestions box. But as she stooped down to smooth a wrinkle from a worn area rug with a curling corner that would soon be a tripping hazard, she realized if guests ever paused to complain, there would be no stopping them.

"Morning, Anna." Jacob, the night manager, waved sleepily from the reception area.

"Good morning, Jacob."

He made a relieved smile. "You're early as usual." He'd already gathered his belongings, as if he planned to make a fast getaway. "Refreshing to see someone who takes her job seriously."

She heard the teasing tone in his voice but forced a smile. "A good manager is punctual, preemptive, and positive." She grimaced to think she had just quoted the three Ps from one of her least favorite college instructors. What a joke.

Jacob simply laughed. "Well, then I'll be preemptive and punctual by making a positively swift exit. If I get home in time, I might have a chance to see Maizie before Kendra carts her off for the day. See ya — wouldn't wanna be ya!"

"Not so fast." Anna held up a hand. Jacob had worked here longer than she had and was well aware that management was expected to "communicate between shifts." They were supposed to fill each other in about the goings-on of the motel. "You haven't even given me your update —"

"Nothing to report." He dropped his manager name tag into the top drawer. "Well, except a little excitement in Room 213 last night." He tugged off his tie, dropping it in the drawer as well.

"What happened?" She stashed her purse in the storage cabinet, locking it since they suspected someone in housekeeping had sticky fingers.

"Just the same old same old." He tossed the morning mail into the "In" box, then slipped his cell phone into his shirt pocket. "Some teenagers had an adult register a room for them last night. He slipped them in a back door, and of course, they decided to party a little too hearty. The family in

212 called to complain around midnight. Mickey had mentioned something about the kids partying down by the pool earlier but not that they had alcohol or were underage. Anyway, when I checked in on them, it was pretty obvious someone had pulled a fast one on me. So I called the cops. They found alcohol and weed in the room. Hauled all six kids down to the station. End of story."

She shook her head. "And it's not even the weekend yet."

"Yeah, but they feel summer in the air. And you know how kids in small towns can be when the weather gets hot." With his nylon lunch bag in hand, Jacob was on his way out of the reception area. "After all, you grew up here." He winked. "Bet you were trouble too, back then."

"That's a bet you'd lose," she called as he headed for the front door.

"See ya tomorrow, Anna. Same bat-place. Same bat-time. Same bat-channel."

Then he was gone and the lobby was quiet. As Anna shuffled through some checkout receipts that Jacob had already printed, she wondered about Jacob and his young family. He and Kendra had their hands full with eight-year-old Maizie and three dogs. Jacob was supposed to be finishing his business degree with an online university, but he was nearly forty now, and Anna wondered if he would really pull it off. Even if he did, would he look for other employment or, like her, would he settle here? And did that mean she had settled?

Anna sighed as she pinned the plastic name tag onto the lapel of her dark blue blazer, careful not to snag the fabric. It was a nicely cut Ralph Lauren suit and something the saleswoman had called an "investment" piece. "You should dress for the job you want," she'd told Anna with authority that seemed convincing, even if the young woman was simply working as a Nordstrom sales clerk. For her first year at the Value Lodge, Anna had been reluctant to wear the expensive suit. Into her second year, it no longer seemed to matter. At least she'd looked impressive when she'd bumped into Marley, she remembered. That was lucky.

After sorting the mail and tending to the usual reception chores, Anna noticed a mom with two small children exiting from the nearby breakfast area. Since she hadn't seen Shawna around yet and it was Shawna's responsibility to maintain "complimentary continental breakfast," Anna ventured over to check on the condition of the food area. As usual, the counter was messy and sticky and the glass coffeepot of regular coffee was empty and scorching on the bottom. She turned off the element and considered calling Shawna to remedy this situation, but seeing a young couple headed her way, she decided to do it herself.

After all, she knew a good manager was willing to do any or all of the tasks that she expected of her staff. Of course, she also knew that a truly good manager made sure that she never needed to. Grabbing paper towels and a fresh coffeepot from the storage cabinet, she quickly put the kitchen to order. As she gave the final swipe to the counter, she imagined how inviting a big bowl of fresh fruit would look. It didn't have to be extravagant or expensive — just oranges, apples, and bananas.

"Good morning," Anna said to the couple as they studied the selection of boxed cereals. They looked about as impressed as she felt.

"Good morning." The woman held up a box of toasted flakes with a creased brow. "Are we too late?"

"Too late?" Anna considered playing stupid but couldn't. "Oh, you mean for the continental breakfast? No, this is what we have to offer — cereal, juice, milk, coffee, and tea — that's about it on this particular *continent.*" She smiled stiffly. "Have a great day." She grabbed a few more paper towels to use in the reception area. When was the last time someone had dusted in there anyway?

As she cleaned the dark green plastic laminate countertop, she remembered how she used to bring a small bouquet of flowers with her every Monday. She'd pick them up at the Safeway store the night before and arrange them in a vase at Grandma's, and in the morning, feeling optimistic about the upcoming week, she'd place her perky blooms on the corner of the reception desk. She realized she probably appreciated the flowers more than anyone else. But after a few months, and after both the vase and flowers went missing one time too many, she gave up that habit.

With her regular chores done and the reception area tidier than usual, Anna was bored. Drumming her fingers, she stared at the clock. Because checkout time was 11:00, she didn't expect to be very busy until a quarter till when a few guests would trickle down to check out. It would pick up around 11:00, and sometimes there would even be a short line by 11:30. It amused Anna how guests seemed intent to stretch their stays at the Value Lodge to the very last minute, as if they couldn't bear to part with such luxurious accommodations.

Eventually the guests began checking out. She didn't feel too surprised when the dad from room 212 complained about the disruptive noise from the rowdies last night. She had expected this. Smiling, she pointed to his receipt — the one she'd already reprinted and adjusted earlier.

"I'm so sorry for your inconvenience, Mr. Ramsay," she said with a look of sincere concern. "As you can see, I've discounted your bill by twenty percent and included a discount coupon for your next visit with us. I hope that will help." She pointed to his kids, who were waiting with his wife. "Count your blessings that your children aren't teenagers yet." She smiled. "I'm sure they'd never be like that anyway." She slid the papers to him, and just as she expected, he simply nodded and thanked her. *Preemptive,* she thought as she told them all to have a great day. Now if she could only be preemptive when it came to her own life. Was there no action to take, nothing she could do, no way to change this dead-end route her life had taken?

2

Anna always took her lunch break at 1:00 because it was the last lull before check-in time at 3:00. Not that it would be particularly busy today since it was only Thursday. But since she'd promised to meet Marley, she promptly left at 1:00 and headed straight for Lou's Café. Despite her earlier embarrassment, she was looking forward to catching up with her old friend. They had known each other since eighth grade, and although they'd never been best friends, they had always been good friends. Anna hadn't actually talked to Marley since their five-year high school reunion several years ago, but as far as Anna knew, Marley was still living out her childhood dream by teaching foreign languages in an Indianapolis middle school.

"I reserved us a table," Marley said as she led Anna through the noisy café. "Right back there."

Soon they were seated in a corner booth that looked out the window onto Main Street. "Just like old times," Anna said as she set her purse on the seat next to her. "It's so great to see you, Marley."

"I know." Marley pushed a strand of short blonde hair behind an ear. "I was so shocked to see you in town. I'd envisioned you managing some posh hotel in Dubai or Martinique . . . not the Value Lodge. I'm surprised my mom didn't mention it to me."

Anna shrugged. "No offense, but I don't really come in here much."

Marley laughed. "What? You're not still into cheeseburgers and fries?"

"Not so much." Anna picked up the laminated menu. "But tell me about you, Marley. How do you like teaching? Is it everything you hoped it would be?" Anna had come prepared with a short list of questions for Marley, hoping to divert the conversation from herself and onto her loquacious friend for as long as possible. The last thing Anna wanted to do right now was to talk about her own dismal career.

"I'm not teaching anymore." Marley's eyes twinkled. "Those middle-school monsters drove me absolutely bonkers."

"Seriously? You quit teaching?"

"That's right." She nodded. "And you'll

never guess what I've been doing the past couple years." She waited as if she expected Anna to figure this out.

Anna tried to think of a clever response, but for as long as she'd known her, Marley had always wanted to be a schoolteacher. "I give up."

"I'm a flight attendant."

"No way." Anna shook her head in disbelief. The image of her slightly intellectual friend serving ill-tempered travelers soft drinks and peanuts was just too weird. This was the sort of job that someone like Marley would've made fun of back in their high school days. "Are you serious?"

"Absolutely." Marley nodded. "I know, I know. I'll admit that I used to think of flight attendants as glorified waitresses in the sky." She waved her hand to where Kellie Jo was balancing a large tray of food on one arm while unloading it with the other. "Not so different than working here. But it turns out I was wrong."

Anna was trying to absorb this. It almost sounded as if Marley's career track wasn't going much better than Anna's. "Well, I suppose being a flight attendant is just another part of the hospitality industry — only at a higher elevation." She imagined Marley wheeling a beverage cart down a tight aisle as she catered to disgruntled passengers. Maybe it really wasn't so different from Anna's job.

"Because of my fluency in languages, I passed up domestic and went straight into international. I'm getting to see the world, Anna. Going to all the exotic places I'd dreamed of seeing. It's been totally amazing."

"Really?" Anna felt blindsided. "You honestly *enjoy* the work?"

"I love it." Marley started to list all the countries she'd visited recently — and it was impressive. "International flights are far more civilized and cultivated than domestic. According to the other flight attendants, it's a whole different clientele." She laughed. "And, hey, it's not a bad place to meet eligible men."

"Interesting."

"Oh, I probably won't do this forever. Although there are attendants who work clear into their fifties and beyond. But right now I'm having such a great time, I have no intention of quitting anytime soon."

"Wow." Anna didn't know what to say. Part of her was shocked and another part was seriously envious. Imagine being paid to travel the globe! "It sounds really exciting, Marley. Very cool."

"The icing on the cake is that I'm based in New York City," Marley continued with enthusiasm. "It's a wonderful place to live. I share an apartment in Greenwich Village with three other flight attendants. I'll admit it's pretty cozy when we're all home at the same time, but thankfully that rarely happens. And our apartment is so close to everything. I mean, you've got Manhattan, SoHo, great shopping, world-class restaurants, and the subway will take you anywhere you want. Well, anyway, I don't want to go on and on. But I certainly can't complain." She beamed. "It's like I'm living my dreams."

"I'm so happy for you, Marley." But if she was that happy, why did she feel on the verge of tears?

Fortunately, as Kellie Jo came to take their orders, Anna got a brief reprieve to gather her emotions, but as soon as Kellie Jo left their table, Marley turned her full attention on Anna. "Okay, now tell me, what's going on with you, Anna? I mean, it's so weird, I can hardly wrap my head around it — *you* working at the Value Lodge." She shook her head. "Last time I saw you, you were dreaming about managing a five-star hotel in some exotic locale."

"Yes . . . Well, dreams can change."

"But you're such a smart, classy girl — I always felt certain you would go far." She made a sympathetic smile. "I assume this is just temporary, right? I mean, what are your plans after the Value Lodge?"

Anna bit her lip. "To be honest . . . I'm not really sure."

"But you always had such big plans. Bigger than mine. I just wanted to teach foreign languages. But you were going to travel and work overseas." Marley frowned. "What happened?"

"Well, my grandpa died right before I finished my bachelor's degree," Anna began slowly. "Grandma was so lonely. And you know how she took me in when I was a kid, back when things fell apart with my parents. Anyway, Grandma sold her little house over on Vermont Street in order to help me with my master's program, and I really felt like I needed that extra degree to land a good job in hotel management. So when she suggested I come back here to live and work for a while, well, it was hard to turn her down."

"You felt like you owed her?"

"Sort of. I was concerned about her being alone too. I could tell she was depressed. And really, I'm all she has."

"That's understandable." Marley nodded

sympathetically. "Very generous on your part, Anna." She reached over and patted Anna's hand. "But you've always been kind and thoughtful like that. Setting aside your dreams to help your grandmother, well, I get that. She's a sweet lady. How's she doing now?"

"She's doing great. She's actually made a lot of friends at her apartment complex. There are lots of retired singles living there. She plays bridge and bunco, and takes tai chi classes, belongs to a book club as well as a theater group. She's really made a great adjustment." Anna laughed. "To be honest, my grandmother's social life is way busier than mine."

"So why are you still there?" Marley looked puzzled. "And still at the Value Lodge?"

Anna explained about needing managerial experience, and about how she'd been able to pay back her student loans. "It seemed to make sense at the time. I figured I'd give it a year . . . and then it turned into a second year." She sighed. "Sharon and Rich Morgan own the motel, and they'd been friends with my grandparents for years, and I sort of thought I was going to have a more active role. They gave me the impression they were going to make some big improvements, and that was kind of exciting." Anna frowned. "But it hasn't really panned out."

"Back to my question." Marley leaned forward. "Why are you still there?"

Anna pressed her lips tightly together, slowly shaking her head. "I honestly don't know." As Kellie Jo set their drinks down on the table, Anna let out a long, sad sigh. Seriously, why *was* she still here?

"Look, Anna, I really don't like telling people what to do — well, unless it's a stubborn middle-school student who needs a swift kick in the behind." Marley took a sip of her soda. "But you seem stuck to me."

Anna just nodded. "I know."

"Have you talked about this with your grandmother? Told her how you feel?"

"She thinks I'm lucky to have a job. She hears all these stories about twentysomethings who've finished college but just can't seem to launch their careers. She's worried that's going to be me."

"But you're not like that, Anna. You've got initiative," Marley assured her. "You want to go places. You have drive."

"Do I?" Anna really wasn't so sure anymore. She watched as Kellie Jo arrived with their orders, smiling and making pleasant small talk as she efficiently arranged their food on the table. It seemed like Kellie

Jo had more initiative and drive than Anna. The truth was that in the last year, Anna had begun to feel as if she were settling. Like she just didn't care anymore. As much as that bothered her, she didn't really know what to do about it.

"You used to be such a dreamer. You wanted more," Marley said quietly after Kellie Jo had left. "I can't believe you've changed that much."

"Do you think working at the Value Lodge has impaired my reasoning skills?" Anna asked meekly. "Like there's something in the air there, or the water? Something that's messing with my brain, killing my ambition?"

Marley laughed. "Well, I suppose that's possible — in a sci-fi flick. But I don't think that's your problem."

"You don't think I've been brainwashed?" Anna gave Marley a wry smile as she squeezed lemon into her iced tea. She knew she was being silly, but sometimes it felt like all the Value Lodge employees had undergone a group lobotomy — making them unmotivated and complacent with their substandard work ethic.

"Well, I suppose you could feel that way. Still, it's not too late to escape. You could make a change. I mean, if I could quit teaching middle school, you ought to be able to walk away from the Value Lodge."

Suddenly Anna felt uneasy. She vividly remembered how helpless she'd felt when her father had abandoned her and her mom — and how her mom had fallen completely apart. As a result of her parents' issues and ineptness, Anna had been personally acquainted with poverty. She knew what it was like to be hungry or to spend a night in a car because no one had paid the rent. If not for her grandma's intervention, she might not have survived her childhood. Was she really willing to give up a dependable job that was slowly filling her savings account?

"You look like a deer caught in the headlights." Marley chuckled. "How hard would it be to quit your dead-end job?"

"But what would I do? Where would I go?"

"Oh, Anna, there must be dozens of great hotel jobs out there."

Anna could hear her grandmother's voice in her ear saying, "A bird in the hand is worth two in the bush." She slowly shook her head. "I don't know. I've heard the jobless rate is on its way up again."

"Have you done any online searches?"

"No . . . I wouldn't even know where to begin."

Marley stopped with her turkey sandwich halfway to her mouth. "I have an idea, Anna. Why don't you become a flight attendant? I can introduce you to my —"

"No thank you." Anna firmly shook her head. "I've only flown twice, and both times it was awful. I'm really uncomfortable in planes. I mean, it's a nice job for you, and I do believe in hospitality, but trust me, I would make a lousy flight attendant."

"Too bad." Marley frowned.

"I'm sorry to be such a buzzkill," Anna said. "I wanted us to enjoy our lunch and catching up, and here I am bringing us both down."

"You're not bringing us down, Anna. I just want you to see that the Value Lodge is not the end of the line. You can't give up on your dreams." Marley set down her sandwich and pulled out her smartphone. "Hey, I've got an idea."

Anna focused her attention on her beef and barley soup while Marley checked into whatever it was she was so interested in. Hopefully she understood that Anna had meant it — she could not possibly be a flight attendant. She'd rather put on one of those silly uniforms and start working right here in Lou's Café.

"There," Marley said as she set her phone

on the table. "I just texted my brother."

"Max?"

"Yeah. He lives in New York too."

"How nice for you."

"It is. Anyway, Max and his wife —"

"Max is married?"

"Yeah. Just last winter. I actually brought them together." She smiled with pride. "Max was already working in New York. A great job in an accounting firm. I had met this girl I knew would be perfect for him. Her name's Elsie and she's a doll."

"A flight attendant too?"

"No. Elsie has this great little shop in SoHo."

"Really? What kind of shop?" Anna had no idea where Marley was going with this, but she was relieved to have the spotlight off of her — and off of her sad little life.

"It's called Elsie Dolce. It's like a bakery, a chocolatier, a patisserie — all wrapped up in one little shop. Sweets and cakes and chocolates, oh my."

"Sounds nice."

"Yeah, you barely walk in the door and you are assaulted by all the calories just floating through the air. Decadently delicious."

"Yum. Suddenly I'm craving dessert."

"Me too." Marley laughed. "Elsie runs the

creative end of the shop — since it was originally her shop. But Max has taken over the business end. He handles the bookkeeping and office work and whatnot, which really frees Elsie up to be creative."

"What a nice setup." Once again, Anna felt a twinge of jealousy, and she did not like it. She wasn't usually an envious person. What was wrong with her?

"Aha!" Marley held up her phone victoriously, looking like she'd struck gold. "I was absolutely right."

Anna set down her spoon, moving her empty bowl to the side. "About what?"

"You see, Max is good friends with the couple that owns the building where the Elsie Dolce shop is located. It's in SoHo. Anyway, their names are Denise and Vincent Newman. And believe me, they are über-rich. I think Vincent was a real estate mogul, an associate of Donald Trump or someone like that. But for rich people, they are actually very down-to-earth. Anyway, Max has done bookkeeping for Vincent." She paused for a breath and a bite.

"Okay, I'm feeling a little lost here," Anna confessed. "Does this have something to do with me, or is it just a good story? It's fine if it's just a good story. I'm actually enjoying it." She didn't want to admit how much more colorful it was than her bland little world.

Marley swallowed her bite. "Here's the deal, Anna. Vincent Newman has been working on this cool old building, the same building that Elsie's shop is in. Naturally, she's on the first floor with a street entrance. Anyway, it's this fabulous brick structure, not too tall, probably about ten or twelve stories. It's called the Rothsberg, and it's about a hundred years old and has been renovated a few times. I've been through a lot of it and it's very cool. It even has a courtyard — a valuable asset in the city. And it still has a lot of its original architectural elements too. Big bay windows with carved cornices, high ceilings with intricate crown molding, and some gorgeous stone floors in places — like this fabulous mosaic in the foyer."

"Uh-huh?" Anna sipped her iced tea, trying to imagine this old building and wondering why Marley seemed so obsessed over it.

"For the past several years, Vincent and his wife Denise have been renovating the Rothsberg. Sparing no expense either. According to Denise, it will be the grandest building in SoHo — and she might be exaggerating, but maybe not. According to Max — and this is under the cone of silence —

the Newmans are putting a fortune into this building."

"Sounds like a very cool project. I've heard how much New York apartments can go for. Like in the millions."

"No. It's not going to be apartments. It's a hotel. A boutique hotel. The Rothsberg of SoHo."

"Oh . . . ?" Anna heard the pitch of her voice rising with interest. "A boutique hotel? Interesting." Anna used to dream of working in a boutique hotel in a big city.

"You can imagine how pleased Elsie was about this. She has a five-year lease on her shop space, so the extra traffic from the hotel will be a real boon for her. A local coffee roaster is vying with Starbucks for shop space too. Max and Elsie are rooting for the local. Although I must admit that I like Starbucks."

Anna sighed. "Can you imagine if Springville ever got a Starbucks?"

Marley laughed. "Yeah, like that's going to happen. Well, back to the Rothsberg. It will have about sixty rooms, plus a restaurant, a pool, a workout area, and some other amenities. But here's the best part, Anna. According to Max, it's scheduled to open this summer. He said they're just starting to furnish the rooms this week and the

Newmans are hiring employees right and left."

Anna felt an unexpected flutter of hope. "Did you say the hotel opens *this* summer?"

"Yes. And that's why I just texted Max. I asked him to check with Vincent to find out if you can send him a résumé."

"Really?" Anna took in a quick breath. "Do you honestly think this guy — Mr. Newman — would actually consider me?"

"Why not? You have a degree and some experience — even if it is at the Value Lodge."

Anna frowned. "That's not going to impress some rich New Yorker."

"But *you* could impress him." Marley pointed at her. "Anna, you are smart and motivated. I know you're a hard worker." She grinned. "You're not hard on the eyes either. Don't take this wrong, but the Newmans are really into appearances. It's not that they're shallow, but they like attractive people. I bet they'd love you."

Anna made a grateful smile. "Thanks. You're sweet, but you're my friend — you have to say that."

"Hey, I still say you could pass for Nicole Kidman's little sister."

Anna laughed. "Well, if I were, I might have a better chance of landing a job at a boutique hotel in New York."

"You could do it, Anna. I know you could."

Anna allowed herself to consider this. "Well, I wouldn't expect a top management job. I'd be happy to be an assistant manager or night manager or whatever. Do you think I'd really have a chance?"

Marley shrugged as she reached for her drink. "You never know unless you try."

"I know," Anna murmured.

"And you can't just give up."

"No," Anna agreed with more enthusiasm. "You're absolutely right. I can't just give up."

As Anna walked back to work, she considered the picture Marley had just painted for her. A gorgeous boutique hotel in SoHo, with a restaurant and a courtyard, not to mention a delightful bakery and a Starbucks on its way. It all sounded so perfect — so wonderful. Like a dream come true. Was it really possible that she would be considered for a position? Perhaps even a lower management position? And then she remembered her grandma's warning: when something looks too good to be true, watch out!

3

Despite a nagging little voice inside of her, reminding her of all the reasons this plan would never pan out, Anna's feet felt light as she walked back to work. Yes, she knew the chances of this New York real estate mogul and hotel developer being impressed by her sparse résumé were slim; even so, she felt hopeful. Sure, it was probably irrational, but somehow that whole conversation with Marley had given Anna real hope. Like she could almost see the light at the end of her long gloomy tunnel. And even if she didn't land a job in New York, like Marley had pointed out, there were other hotel management jobs out there. Why couldn't Anna land one of them? After all, she had put in her time — she'd paid her dues. Two years was long enough to waste away here.

After the registration "rush" passed and guests were settling into their rooms, making the usual calls to the desk, mostly requests that were passed on to housekeeping, the motel grew relatively quiet. Capitalizing on this calm, Anna pulled her own résumé out of the motel's computer system and, after giving it a few quick tweaks, emailed it to Marley just like she'd promised. As she hit Send, Anna sent up a little prayer too. Or maybe it was a plea — somehow she had to get out of this place.

With that done, she decided to make sure that Mickey had cleaned up around the swimming pool like she had asked him. Since it was a hot day, it wouldn't be long before some of the guests meandered on down there. The last time she'd passed by the pool, earlier this morning, it had looked like a wreck. Probably the remnants from last night's teenagers. She wished she could rely on the fact that she'd asked Mickey to handle it — but she knew that was no guarantee.

"Loretta," she called back to the office where the bookkeeper was working. "Mind keeping an eye on the reception desk for a few minutes? I need to check on something."

Loretta looked over the top of her glasses and waved. "No problem."

"I've got my phone if you need me," Anna

called as she headed toward the west wing. While she walked down the hallway, she called Mickey's number, asking him to meet her in the pool area. But when she arrived, not only was Mickey noticeably absent, but the back end of the pool deck was still trashed with bottles, cans, dirty towels, and fast-food packaging. Feeling exasperated at the reckless teens and her MIA janitor, Anna pulled out a pair of vinyl gloves — she always kept some handy because you never knew what you might find in a motel like this — and started to clean up.

As she picked up disgusting pieces of trash, she felt seriously irked at Mickey. This certainly wasn't the first time he'd neglected janitorial duties that were his responsibility. Nor was it the first time she'd stepped in and covered for him. Grabbing a nearby trash can, she proceeded to collect the debris, tossing it in. Thankfully, no guests had come to the pool yet. She tried not to imagine how disappointed the young couple with their two little ones would've been to find this garbage dump.

Before long she had removed all the rubbish, and since the pool was currently unoccupied, she decided to give the cement decks a quick hose-down. While she did this, she decided to arrange the white plastic lounge chairs all facing toward the pool in a nice line, as if this were a four-star resort. Spraying the decks and arranging the chairs, she imagined the ways this pool area could be spruced up. Just a few simple elements could make such an improvement, starting with some neutral-colored paint on the privacy fence over there, a few potted shrubs by the main entrance here, maybe some flowerpots with hardy petunias to add color.

"Hey, Anna." Mickey sauntered across the wet deck toward her with his usual cocky expression — like he thought he was still the football jock he'd been in high school a few years ago. "What's up? What're you doing?"

"Your job," she said tersely.

"Thanks." He made a sassy grin. "Wanna do a job swap? Then I can have *your* job."

"I told you to clean this pool area this morning, Mickey."

"I did."

She narrowed her eyes slightly. "No, you did not. I just did it myself."

"Hey, I cleaned it this morning." Averting his gaze, he squinted into the sunshine. "Can I help it if someone else trashed it since then? People can be such slobs."

Controlling the urge to spray him down,

she simply handed him the hose nozzle. "Go wash down the other side of the pool." She pointed at the lounge chairs. "And I want the chairs arranged just like this, three times a day. Once in the morning. Then again just before check-in time at 3:00. And again at the end of your shift."

His brows arched. "Getting all high and mighty, are we?"

She gave him a warning look. "By the way, did you clean the parking lot like I asked you to do?" She actually knew the answer to this already. She'd seen it on her way back from lunch.

"Yeah, sure. I did that this morning too."

"Right . . ." She was about to call him on this as well as his other lie, but she noticed the young family coming toward the pool gate. This wasn't the place for a showdown. Suddenly she remembered something else that had been bothering her since her conversation with Jacob.

Walking with Mickey as he went to the other end of the pool, she spoke quietly. "Jacob mentioned that you were still on duty when those teenagers were out here last night, Mickey. Is that right?"

"Yeah, I was here. The kids weren't acting too crazy then. Nothing worth calling the cops over."

She pointed to the trash can she'd set by the back fence. "Those bottles and cans I just picked up were not all soft drinks, Mickey."

He just shrugged as he sprayed the deck.

"You didn't notice any booze last night?" She pointed to the sign on the wall. "See the third rule? *No alcoholic beverages.*"

He shrugged again, adjusting the hose nozzle to a firmer flow so that the overspray splashed onto her shoes.

She stepped back. "And you didn't notice that the kids were underage?"

"What is this — the Spanish Inquisition?"

She just shook her head, then, seeing the family was inside the pool area and within hearing distance, she simply turned and walked away. If she were truly the manager of this fleabag motel, Mickey would've received his walking papers long before this. But she knew that wasn't going to happen. She'd already complained about him to the owners once, shortly after she started work here, nearly two years ago. That was when she discovered Mickey was the owners' nephew — and that his job as "head janitor" was probably more secure than her own.

"He's my brother's son and he's had a rough go," Sharon Morgan had confided to

Anna after the meeting. "Cut him some slack, okay? He just needs to know we believe in him. He'll straighten out in time."

Anna had cut him slack. It seemed like she cut him slack almost every single day. And unless she was imagining things, Mickey's slack was rubbing off on the other employees. It was like a disease of slacking had plagued this motel. Oh, certainly not everyone was affected. A few employees still took their jobs seriously. The Gonzales sisters, for instance — if Anna wanted something done right she would ask Rita or Consuelo to do it. She knew she couldn't depend on Shawna; although she was head of housekeeping, she was also Mickey's on-again, off-again girlfriend. Anna could never keep up with the couple. Since Shawna had been even less motivated lately, Anna would wager they were "off-again." Not that Shawna was ever particularly motivated anyway. Anna couldn't begin to count how many times she'd spotted Shawna and another maid lounging in a room with the TV on and just visiting as if they thought they were on vacation. Shawna's favorite response was, "Oh, it'll get done. It always gets done." Maybe so, but it was the way it got done that really made Anna want to pull her hair out.

Despite the training meetings Anna had held with housekeeping — trying to teach them time-saving tricks, build up their morale, encourage them toward excellence, and explain that cutting corners could lead to lost jobs — other than the Gonzales sisters and a couple others, the rest just returned to their old bad habits. And some of their bad habits were truly disgusting.

Anna had learned several things while working at Value Lodge — things she would never do if she were forced to be a guest in this motel. First of all, she would never drink out of a bathroom water glass. She would never walk barefoot over the floors. She would never assume the bathroom was sanitized. Beyond that, she would definitely remove all but the sheets from the bed before sleeping. And that would be only after she'd checked the mattress for bedbugs.

Did she feel like a failure because the motel she managed couldn't maintain even the most basic standards of cleanliness? Of course! But she also knew that there was little use trying to change things as long as the owners didn't back her. One could only beat one's head against the wall for so long before one looked up and saw the writing on the wall. Maybe it was time to go.

As Anna walked back to the reception area, she made a managerial decision. Maybe it was partially prompted by the visions of the New York boutique hotel that were dancing in her head, or maybe she had simply had enough of the Value Lodge. But back at her desk, she knew it was time to do something drastic. Even if her efforts aggravated the owners and led to her dismissal, she was going to do it. At least she'd know she went down for a good reason.

She typed out various warning letters — several that sounded familiar — letting the recipients know this would be their final warning. She made it clear that failure to comply with her corrections would result in joblessness (possibly her own too, although she didn't mention that). She also informed the staff involved that these letters would be followed up by a meeting tomorrow morning. She would come to work an hour early, so that Jacob would be here. She might even bring doughnuts just to reassure everyone that she wasn't trying to be mean.

Hopefully they would go home and read their letters carefully and perhaps truly grasp the gravity of their situation. She wanted their full attention. Tomorrow morning, she would spell out to them, in no uncertain terms, that her only goal was to make this Value Lodge a better place for everyone — but particularly for the guests, since that was her job. She would be positive at the meeting, and she would tell them that she hoped they were fully on board with her, but if they were not, she would tell them to start looking for new jobs.

Thinking of new jobs made her check her iPhone to see if Marley had gotten back to her yet. Other than confirming that she'd received the résumé, she had no other news. Really, was it realistic to think that a busy New York real estate mogul, property developer, and hotel owner would drop everything in order to respond to the manager of the Value Lodge in a town the size of Springville? Probably not. Chances were he hadn't even gotten her résumé yet. As Anna set the employees' letters in their message boxes, she wondered just how close Marley's brother Max really was with the Newmans. Just because Max and Elsie rented shop space did not mean they were chummy. It was possible that Marley had overblown this whole thing.

In fact, as Anna walked home, she began to think that was probably what had happened. Marley had always been a somewhat dramatic person. Certainly she had enjoyed telling Anna all about the building restoration and the boutique hotel. What if she'd simply been telling this story for its pure entertainment value? As Anna approached Lou's Café, she considered popping in to ask Marley about this, but remembering it was the dinner hour and seeing that all their tables were filled and customers were waiting at the counter, Anna decided to wait.

Her grandmother's apartment building came into view. It was really a rather inviting complex with its butter-colored stucco walls, ornate iron railings up the staircases and around the balconies, and nicely landscaped grounds that were maintained by the management.

Anna had been alarmed when she'd first learned that her grandma had sold her home — largely to help cover Anna's college expenses. By now, though, she knew that her grandma had gotten quite comfortable in her new lifestyle. If only she could be comfortable with the idea of letting Anna go.

As Anna walked toward the entrance of the first-floor apartment, she was already rehearsing the speech she planned to give her grandma. She would simply be honest. She would confess how unhappy she'd been at the Value Lodge — something Anna had never felt free to do before because her grandmother was such good friends with the owners, Sharon and Rich. Grandma often acted as if Anna were lucky to have employment at all and owed the Morgans a boatload of gratitude for giving her such an important job. Her grandmother had no idea what it was truly like to work at the Value Lodge. But somehow Anna had to tell her the truth, and she had to do it in a way that wouldn't make her grandmother think less of her good friends. That would not be easy.

4

"How about if I take us out to dinner?" Anna asked as she came into the house.

Her grandma frowned from the rocking recliner. "But I've already made us a tamale casserole. It's in the oven right now."

"You could save it for another night."

"But it's nearly done." Grandma looked at her watch, then leaned forward and pushed herself to her feet. "In fact, I should check on it before it gets scorched."

"You could just put it aside to cool," Anna suggested. "Then we could go out. That way you'd have dinner all ready for tomorrow night."

Grandma peered curiously at Anna. "But why do we need to go out for dinner? It's so expensive. It's not a special occasion, is it?"

Anna made a stiff smile. Of course, she was well aware that her grandmother had grown up on a midwest farm where cooking had been secondary to breathing and going out for a meal had been considered wastefully decadent. Apparently old habits really did die hard. "No, it's not a special occasion," Anna conceded. "I just hoped that we could talk."

Grandma brightened. "What better place to talk than right here? That way we don't have a bunch of people interrupting us every five minutes."

Anna nodded. "Yes, you're probably right."

"You go get yourself into some comfy clothes," Grandma said. "I'll set the table."

Instead of protesting like she wanted to, Anna went to the coat closet by the front door. This narrow space served as her clothes closet, and since the front drapes were closed to keep the afternoon sun out, she proceeded to do a quick change right there by the front door. Originally, when they'd set up this "temporary" arrangement — with Anna sleeping on the sofa, keeping her clothes in the narrow closet, and using the tiny powder room for her personal bathroom — Grandma had been on a waiting list for a larger two-bedroom apartment. But because most of the two-bedroom units were on the second level and Grandma had a bad hip, she was still down here. Maybe that was a good thing. It would make it easier for Anna to leave.

Comfortable in some lightweight capri pants and a sleeveless shirt, Anna rejoined Grandma in the stuffy kitchen. The smell of the tamales combined with the overly warm kitchen made Anna feel less than hungry. She glanced longingly out at the tiny patio with the bistro table and chair set that Anna had gotten Grandma for her last birthday. She considered suggesting they eat out there since it was probably about the same temperature in the shade, plus the air was fresher. But she knew her grandma would think that was "too much trouble," especially since she'd already set the table. Plus, those "stiff metal chairs" were hard on her hip. Anna knew the drill.

"So what is it you want to talk to me about?" Grandma asked after she'd said the blessing. "You've aroused my curiosity, Anna."

"Well . . ." Anna took in a deep breath as she laid her paper napkin in her lap. "I ran into my old friend Marley Ferris today. She's back in town to help out with her mom's café for a few days. Did you know that Louise Ferris had back surgery?"

"I hadn't heard that." Grandma handed Anna the salad bowl. "But I haven't been to

Lou's Café in a year or two, maybe more."

Anna filled her in on Marley's career change. "I was so surprised. I thought all she ever wanted to do was teach school, but she sounds like she couldn't be happier."

"She gave up her teaching job?" Grandma looked shocked. "What about all of her education? Seems a waste to go to school all those years to become a teacher and then just toss it aside. To quit teaching after such a short time — and to become a stewardess? What about her retirement? And surely she knows that teachers get their whole summers off. They can travel and —"

"Oh, she travels all the time now. Because she's fluent in so many languages, she gets to be on the international flights. She's been all over the world."

"Sounds pretty risky to me." Grandma dismally shook her head as she shook the salad dressing bottle. "With all the nutcases in the world nowadays . . . terrorist kooks with bombs in their underwear . . . well, you couldn't pay me enough to fly to a foreign country on an airplane. And just imagine — what if you got stuck in some ghastly place with no way out?"

This was not going at all how Anna had hoped. She had planned to use Marley's career change to segue into her own revised plans. "I'm sure it wouldn't be your cup of tea, Grandma." Anna smiled patiently. "But honestly, I've never seen Marley happier."

"Yes, well, I'm glad for her. I suppose one has to sow one's oats. Best to do it while you're young. I'll wager that she'll tire of flying all over the place someday. Then she can return to a more dependable job — like teaching." Grandma nodded as if this settled it.

Anna was rethinking her approach now. Obviously, her plan of getting Grandma on board with Marley's new lifestyle was not working. Time to move to the second part of her strategy. "You know that the reason I was attracted to working at the Value Lodge was to gain some managerial experience," she said carefully.

"Yes." Grandma nodded as she buttered a piece of bread. "And you've got almost two years in. That's impressive."

"Yes, well, I think maybe two years is enough."

"Enough?" Grandma set her knife down. "What do you mean?"

Anna started telling her the truth, starting with the troubles with Mickey and the rest of the staff and how her dreams of making improvements were constantly dashed. "The Value Lodge is just not where I see myself in the future," she finally said.

"Oh." Grandma just stared at her.

"I'm sorry," Anna said contritely. "I know your friends Rich and Sharon were very generous to give me this opportunity, especially straight out of college. I had hoped that I would bring something to the job. Instead, I just feel stuck."

"I see."

"I really appreciate that I was able to earn enough to pay off my student loans," she continued. "I've managed to put aside some nice savings too."

Grandma just nodded.

"I feel like I've hurt your feelings," Anna said sadly. "Like you think I'm not grateful for all you've done for me." She felt tears coming. "But I am. I really am. I don't know where I'd be without you, Grandma. I'll always be thankful for all you've done for me. Please don't feel bad."

Grandma blinked. "Oh no, I don't feel bad, Anna. I was just thinking about all you were saying."

"Oh?"

"I never expected you to stay here in Springville forever, dear girl."

"You didn't?"

"No, of course not."

Anna felt slightly blindsided. "So you

don't mind if I move on?"

"Not if you have a good solid place to go." Grandma reached for another serving of tamales.

"Well, I don't really know for sure what I'll do next, but Marley told me about something that might have potential." She began telling Grandma about the boutique hotel in SoHo, starting out cautiously but gaining enthusiasm the more she talked about it.

Grandma seemed surprised. "New York City? You'd actually want to live there?"

"Yes," Anna declared. "I've always dreamed of working for a specialty hotel in a large city like New York. I realize it's probably a long shot for me, but if it really happened — well, I would be thrilled."

"You honestly think you could be happy in such a big, busy place?"

"I absolutely do. I'll admit that it would be a huge challenge and a major adjustment. But I think it'd be truly rewarding. I could finally use the skills and training I got in college." Anna confessed how she'd dreamed of working for a hotel that appreciated the finer things in life. "With all the amenities and where the guests come first." She sighed. "Instead of boasting the cheapest rates in town, we would practice true hospitality."

Grandma smiled. "When you say it like that, it really does sound appealing."

Anna continued talking about the things she'd love to see practiced in an upscale hotel. "I've even heard of quality hotels that cater to singles, offering a social hour where they meet and greet," she said. "Not anything improper, of course, but just a way for single professionals to mingle while they're visiting from out of town." She went on and on but eventually realized that her grandmother was probably getting overwhelmed. "Sorry," she said quietly. "I guess you can see this is something I feel passionate about."

"I never realized how important this was to you."

For a long moment, they both just sat at the small kitchen table. Anna could hear the kitchen clock ticking and a lawn mower running outside. "So you don't mind if I pursue something like this?" Anna asked hopefully. "I mean, even if the hotel in New York doesn't work out, well, there might be another hotel somewhere else."

Grandma reached over and clasped Anna's hand. "I want you to follow your dreams, Anna. That's all I ever wanted."

"Really?" Anna couldn't hide her surprise.

"You don't want me to stay here with you and keep working at the Value Lodge?"

Grandma laughed, waving her other hand. "Oh, my dear. You know how small this apartment is. Did you really think I expected you to keep sleeping on the sofa forever?"

"No, probably not."

"It was just a stopping place until you were ready for the next stage of your life." Grandma made a little sigh. "Of course, I love having you here. I will miss you. But I never want to stand in the way of your dreams."

Anna got up, went around the table, and wrapped her arms around her grandma's shoulders to hug her. "Thank you," she said happily. "You don't know how much that means to me."

"If you ever need to come home, you know you are always welcome." Grandma slowly stood and Anna could see that her eyes were misty. For that matter, Anna's were too.

"The same will be true for you," Anna declared as she began to clear the table. "If I have a home someday, you will always be welcome. You can live with me or just visit or whatever."

"I've heard it's terribly expensive to live in New York City," Grandma said as Anna took her empty plate. "Do you think you'll make enough to afford your rent?"

"Managerial jobs in good hotels pay pretty well," Anna said as she rinsed the plates. "I'm sure I'll be just fine."

"Maybe they will let you live in the hotel."

"Maybe." Anna said this for Grandma's benefit, not because she thought it was true. "Or maybe I can share an apartment with Marley." Again, she said this for her grandmother. From what she'd heard, Marley's apartment was already overly full.

"Oh, wouldn't that be fun for you two girls." Grandma smiled as she covered the leftovers with foil. "I remember when I was about your age. Actually, I suppose I was quite a bit younger, but I felt very grown-up at the time. My best friend Karla and I were just nineteen when we both got jobs in Indianapolis."

"What?" Anna was shocked. "I've never heard about this."

Grandma chuckled. "Well, it was all rather short-lived. You see, Karla and I had taken business classes in high school, and we got the idea we could make it in the big city. It was the mid-sixties, and a lot of young women were pursuing careers. We both got hired at a big insurance company, and with the help of our parents, we managed to rent ourselves a little apartment right downtown."

"I had no idea." Anna shook her head as she placed a plate in the dishwasher. "I always thought you and Grandpa were high school sweethearts and that you got married right out of high school."

"It's true we were high school sweethearts. But your grandpa got drafted into the army right after graduation. Got sent straight to Vietnam. That's when Karla and I got it into our heads to go out and try our wings. I must admit that it was all rather exciting, for a spell anyway. We only lasted about a year before it all came apart." Grandma frowned as she hung up a dish towel.

"What went wrong?"

"Oh . . . several things. Karla got involved with a fellow — he turned out to be good for nothing, but poor Karla didn't see it. She married him anyway. That marriage didn't last for long."

"What about you?"

Grandma made a sheepish smile. "Even before Karla decided to part ways with me, I was already homesick for my family. I missed the farm and the slower paced lifestyle. I went back home to live with my parents. Stayed there until your grandpa came home from Vietnam. That's when we got married."

"I never knew that." Anna closed the dishwasher door.

Grandma winked. "Well, a girl's got to have a few secrets."

Anna laughed.

Grandma let out a sigh as she wiped off the kitchen table. "Then your mother came along, just a couple years after we got married. I thought our lives were so complete."

Anna cringed inwardly. She really didn't want Grandma to go there unless she really needed to. She knew how painful the memories could be for her — how difficult it was to talk about Anna's mother, both for Grandma and for Anna. As Grandma often said, some stones were better left unturned.

"Your grandpa and I had a lot of happy years," Grandma continued wistfully.

"I know." Anna filled a glass with water, taking a long sip.

"And we had some hard years."

Anna nodded. She was well aware that her mother had made some bad choices in life — she'd gotten pregnant at seventeen, married an addict, and moved away from the protection of her parents, and her sad little life had ended tragically. These were facts Anna could never escape, and some of those early childhood memories remained indelibly imprinted in her mind.

"Your mother lived life on her own terms. In a lot of ways she reminded me of my old friend Karla." Grandma hung the dishrag over the faucet, then turned to peer into Anna's eyes. "I'm so relieved that you are not like your mother, Anna. Not in that regard. I feel certain you will never make the same mistakes that she made."

Anna nodded with a somber expression. "You can count on that."

Grandma hugged Anna now. "I won't be worried about you, Anna. I know you will be okay — even in a big city like New York. You have a good head on your shoulders."

Anna felt tears in her eyes. "If I do have a good head on my shoulders, it's because of you, Grandma. I owe you my gratitude."

Grandma patted her on the back. "And the Good Lord too. Let's give credit where credit is due."

5

As Anna walked to work the following morning, her feelings were mixed. One part of her wanted to skip and sing — in the hopes that she might be getting a job offer from New York before too long. The other part of her was dreading the follow-up meeting she had scheduled with some of her less than motivated staff members. What had she been thinking? Wouldn't it have been easier to just let them continue sliding? Then she could simply make a quiet exit and move on to new and better things — a life beyond the Value Lodge.

"I hear there's going to be a showdown," Jacob said as she came through the lobby.

She grimaced. "Uh, yes, I guess so."

He frowned. "You don't sound very enthusiastic."

She took in a deep breath. "I know there are things that need to be said. I'm just not sure I still want to say them."

He pointed at the box of doughnuts in her hands. "Looks like you came prepared."

She smiled. "I thought I might be able to sweeten them up a little."

"Before you really give it to 'em?" he teased.

She set the pink box on the counter, then went around to put away her purse. "I plan on ending the meeting in time to be back for my shift," she told him as she pinned on her name tag. "But if it runs longer, do you mind?"

"Not at all. I wish I could be a fly on the wall while you're giving 'em what for."

She frowned. "So you think it's a good thing I'm doing this?"

"If I was head manager, I'd do it in a heartbeat."

"But you don't want to be head manager?" She studied him closely, wondering if he regretted not taking this position back when he'd had the chance — and whether he'd jump on it after she left. "You still like being Mr. Mom while Kendra goes to work during the day?"

"It's a good setup. I get time with Maizie during the day, plus I actually get some studying done during the night shift here. No complaints from me."

"Right." Anna picked up her box of

doughnuts, bracing herself as she headed for the staff room.

"Good luck," he called.

She suspected she would need good luck as she headed down the hallway. This would not be easy. And yet, she reminded herself, she would probably emerge a bigger, better person — not to mention manager — for it.

"Hello," she said cheerily as she entered the room where her disgruntled staff members were loitering. Mickey, seated on the table, appeared to be holding court with several of the housekeeping girls. Meanwhile, Shawna was glaring at him from across the room.

"I brought doughnuts." Anna set the box down, opening it up as if it contained the crown jewels. To her relief, this got their attention, and as they were helping themselves, she positioned herself at the head of the table.

"Well, you know why I called this meeting," she began in an official-sounding tone. "It's because as manager, I care about the quality of service and accommodations we offer our valued guests here at the Value Lodge." Okay, she could hear how silly this sounded as it rolled off her tongue. Really, the Value Lodge cared about quality? Since when? "And because I care about quality, I care about you." She made a forced smile. "You see, I was thinking about the name of our motel — the Value Lodge — and I got to thinking that the key word is *value*." She pointed at Shawna. "Do you *value* yourself?"

Shawna shrugged.

"How about you?" Anna pointed to a maid. "And you?" She pointed to another. "Do you all value yourselves? Because I think that if you do value yourself, you will care about how you perform your jobs here at the Value Lodge." She smiled. "I know, I know, you might be thinking that you deserve a better job — something more than just housekeeping. But do you realize that this is the place where lots of people start out? Did you know I once worked in housekeeping too? I used my time cleaning rooms to prepare me for the next step on my career ladder. I took my work seriously and I did the best I could." She waved toward them. "That's all I'm asking of you. Just to do your best."

"And if we don't?" Mickey narrowed his eyes slightly. "You're going to give us the boot?"

She took on a somber expression. "That's my job. As manager, I must do what needs to be done to ensure that our guests receive the quality of service and accommodations they deserve."

"What they *deserve*?" Mickey stood up. "This is the Value Lodge, Anna. You can act like it's all about being valued, but we all know that the Value Lodge means just one thing. It's cheap." He winked at a maid. "We all know that you get what you pay for." He chuckled. "If our guests want to be treated like they're at the Ritz, they should go to the Ritz. Right?" He looked at the others as if he expected their support.

"Right," one of the newer maids echoed. "Like Mickey said, the guests get what they pay for. This place is cheap. Why should they expect more?"

"They don't even leave tips," another maid complained. "I hear that in some places — nicer places than this — the guests leave tips."

"Yeah," Mickey agreed. "If our guests want us to treat them better, they should leave tips."

Anna tried not to be distracted by the ridiculousness of this statement. "The bottom line is that each one of you here was hired to do a specific job. You all know what that job is — right?" She waited, watching as they reluctantly nodded. "It's all spelled out for you. I shouldn't have to play policeman and follow you around and remind you of what you're expected to do, should I?"

A couple of them shook their heads no, but the others just stared blankly at her, and Mickey reached for another doughnut. She looked at the motley crew and wondered if perhaps she really was expecting too much from them. She considered pointing out how the Gonzales sisters were an exemplary illustration of what a good employee should look like. However, she knew this would only make life more miserable for Rita and Consuelo, so she didn't.

"Does anyone have any questions?" she asked in a slightly sharp tone. She knew this meeting had been a complete waste of time, not to mention doughnuts. "Okay, then" — she took in a deep breath — "as of now, you are all on disciplinary probation. If you fail to perform your job as expected, you will be let go." She looked around the table, trying to lock eyes with each of them, which wasn't possible since most of them were either staring blankly or looking at their phones. "Perhaps you know of other job opportunities in Springville," she said in exasperation. "Places where employees get paid *not* to do their jobs. If so, you may want to send them your résumés."

"Yeah, right." Mickey made a sarcastic

laugh. "Maybe that's what you should be doing, Anna. If you're so unhappy with your staff, I mean. Did you ever stop to think that the problem might not be with us?" He pointed at her. "But maybe it's with you?" Naturally this elicited a few giggles.

She looked him in the eyes. "That's a possibility, Mickey. The truth is, I am not cut out to run a motel that is substandard. The reason I've called you all on the carpet today is so that we can make this place better." She looked hopefully at them. "Really, wouldn't it feel nice to work in a motel that had a reputation for quality? A place that people came to not because it was cheap but because it offered great hospitality?"

Again she got the blank stares, or else the heads bent downward with eyes on their phones. Clearly, these people couldn't care less. "Well, thanks for coming," she said glumly. "Keep in mind what I said. I'm not kidding — your jobs could be at serious risk." Without saying another word, she turned and left. She had no doubt that her words had fallen on deaf ears.

"How did it go?" Jacob asked quietly as she returned to the reception area.

"How do you think it went?"

He gave her a sympathetic look. "That bad?"

She shrugged. "I think it's hopeless."

He glanced at the clock, and although it wasn't even time for his shift to end, he looked hopeful. "Mind if I leave a few minutes early?"

"Why not," she said dismally.

He looked slightly offended. "I'll stay if you want."

"No, it's fine." She waved him away. "I'm just discouraged."

He leaned over to peer directly into her eyes. "Anna, this is *the Value Lodge.* I understand your longing to make it better, and I'm sorry to break the news to you, but this might be as good as it gets."

She made a tolerant smile. "Yeah, I know."

"Hang in there." He waved as he headed for the door. "Remember, it's just a job — not your personal identity."

As she watched him leave, she realized she'd forgotten to ask for his updates. But maybe it didn't matter. As she went through the morning mail and her usual routine, she reminded herself that her days at the Value Lodge were numbered. Really, why should she feel down or discouraged? She had bigger, better things to look forward to. Still, she knew she had to follow through with the probationary warnings she'd just delivered. She couldn't just forget about it.

Although, she reassured herself, she didn't have to deal with it today. In all fairness, she should give them at least twenty-four hours before she lowered the boom.

Anna always kept her phone handy while at work, but today she kept an even closer eye on it, hoping to hear something back from Marley. When her lunch hour came, Anna was tempted to run down to Lou's Café in the hopes of having an informal conversation, where Marley would just happen to mention her brother Max. Then Anna would casually inquire about the hotel job. Yet when 1:00 came around, Anna couldn't bring herself to do it. She didn't want to appear anxious or desperate. If this was meant to be, it would be . . . right? Marley would call if she had news.

By the end of her shift, Anna had not heard a word from Marley. She considered stopping by the café on her way home, but knowing it was the dinner hour and that Marley probably had her hands full, Anna decided to be patient. However, if Marley just happened to pop out as Anna walked by, well, perhaps she would broach the subject with her. But Anna passed the café with no sign of Marley. As she continued on home to Grandma's apartment, she began to wonder if she'd made a mistake to put so much hope in what seemed like a true long shot. Really, why would some fancy SoHo boutique hotel want an inexperienced young woman who couldn't even manage the Value Lodge very well?

As she went into the apartment, she remembered that it was her grandmother's bunco night. Fortunately, it was at someone else's house this week. Anna kicked off her shoes and, since the drapes were still shut, proceeded to strip off her work clothes. Although she wasn't really some weird exhibitionist who liked to walk around her in her underwear, moments like this, when she had the apartment to herself, were rare. Since she was hot from walking home in the high temps, she just wanted to cool off.

She placed her phone in the charger and went to the fridge, still in her underwear, to see what looked good for dinner. Then she stood in front of the kitchen sink, eating last night's leftover salad right from the serving bowl. As she rinsed the bowl in the sink, she realized how pathetic her little life had truly become. Really, was this what she had come to?

She went back to peer at her phone, wishing that Marley or someone in New York would call her with good news. After several minutes of just staring at her phone, she knew she was being silly. This simply wasn't going to happen. She pulled on a T-shirt and shorts, picked up the paperback novel that Grandma had recommended to her last night, and settled herself on the sofa to read until she fell asleep.

The next morning, Anna felt more than a little discouraged as she walked to work. She was seriously troubled by three things this morning: One, Marley had not called and was probably not going to call. Two, Anna's life was probably not going to change, ever. Three, she would have to follow through on her probationary warnings or risk looking like a wimp. When she reached the motel parking lot, though, she got mad. It still had not been cleaned up! Honestly, that was the same cigarette package in the same place it had been two days ago. Mickey was clearly not taking her seriously.

As she marched into the foyer, Jacob watched her with interest. "Hey, Anna. You look like you're on a mission."

"I am." She slammed her purse down on the counter. "I'm fed up."

"With what?"

"With the way our staff are not doing their jobs." She told him about the parking lot.

"I've asked him again and again to clean it up, and it's got the exact same trash in it as two days ago."

"Oh." He nodded. "So what're you going to do?"

"I'm going to fire Mickey."

Jacob's brows arched. "Really?"

She looked at the clock. "You don't leave for ten minutes — that gives me just enough time."

"You sure about this?"

"Absolutely." She pointed to her purse. "Lock that up for me, please. I'm going to speak to Mickey right now."

"Anna, do you know what you're do—"

"I refuse to sweep this under the rug again," she declared. "Even though that's how Mickey likes to clean up a mess. I'm finished with him, Jacob." Without another word, she turned away and marched off to hunt down Mickey.

Swinging by the pool, partly because she was curious if he'd sprayed down the decks and arranged the chairs like she'd asked him to do the other day, she was almost relieved to find it undone. One more reason to give the lazy bum his walking papers. She was about to leave when she spotted a small cloud of smoke at the opposite end. Shading her eyes from the morning sunshine, she realized it was Mickey and Shawna, sitting on a table and smoking.

Anna took a deep breath, striding purposefully toward them. She'd never actually fired anyone before and wasn't even sure she knew how to do it properly. Perhaps it would be better to do it in writing. Except that if she worded something wrong, it wouldn't surprise her to have Mickey use something she put in a letter against her.

"Excuse me," she said in a formal tone. "Am I interrupting you?"

"That's okay." Shawna smiled as she extinguished her cigarette. "But good news — Mickey and I are back together again. We ironed things out."

"I'm so happy for you," she said in a chilly tone. "If you don't mind, I need to have a word with Mickey."

"Nothing you can say to me that Shawna can't hear," Mickey said with a defiant look in his eye.

"Okay then." Anna nodded. "Mickey, you are fired." She waited.

"You can't fire me." Mickey stood up and glared at her.

"I'm the manager," she pointed out. "I can fire you."

"On what grounds?" he demanded.

"You are not doing your job." She held up

her fingers and listed the things he had failed to do.

"But I was about to do that," he argued.

"That's what you always say." She frowned. "Or else you lie to me and tell me you have already done it — when you know you haven't."

"You're not being fair," he protested.

"It's not fair for you to pretend you're an employee here, Mickey, when you clearly have no intention of actually working."

"You can't talk to me like that." Mickey turned to Shawna. "You heard her, didn't you? You'll back me in this, won't you?"

Anna pointed at Shawna. "You're already on probation, Shawna. And I just caught you smoking on motel property too."

"Are you firing Shawna too?" Mickey demanded.

Anna shrugged. "Sure. Why not just get it over with?"

"You can't do —"

"I just did," Anna told them. "Please get your things and leave the premises immediately." She turned and walked away, feeling a bit like an evil employer. As she entered the building, she could feel her hands shaking. She hurried back to the reception area, starting to question herself. She felt worried that she had handled it all wrong. Worse than that, she felt worried that she wasn't cut out for management. Because really, if she couldn't handle this kind of stress at the Value Lodge, how could she expect to handle it in New York?

6

Not long after the registration hour ended, the motel owners showed up. "Rich will watch the reception area," Sharon briskly told Anna. "You will come with me."

Anna simply nodded. She had been expecting this. Mickey had obviously gone whining to his aunt, complaining about how Anna had been unfair. Now Sharon was here to force Anna to take him back. She would make excuses and promise that he would do better. Just like she'd done before.

Sharon closed the door to the staff room, then turned to look at Anna. "Mickey told me what happened."

"I'm sure he told you *his* version of what happened."

"Not only his version," Sharon corrected, "but Shawna's as well."

"Oh?"

"Yes, they both claim that you have been too hard on all the staff. They say that you are always complaining about the motel and how cheap it is and how no one works hard enough. It sounds as if you have created a very hostile work environment for everyone. It sounds as if the guests have even mentioned it."

Anna blinked. "You're kidding."

"No, I am not." Sharon firmly shook her head. "I've tried to overlook it in the past when you and Mickey locked horns. But I'm afraid the time has come to let you go, Anna."

"Let *me* go?"

"Yes. I know your grandmother and I are old friends, but I'm sure she'll understand. We gave it a good try. Some people just aren't cut out for management."

"But I —"

"I'll admit that I was taken in by your fancy college degree and your pretty face, but it's been a mistake from the get-go. I can see that now."

"But I never —"

"I didn't come here to argue with you." Sharon held up her hand like a stop sign. "Rich is cutting you a check for two weeks' pay. He said it's in your contract. If I had my way I'd —"

"I can't believe this." Anna was pacing back and forth in the small room. "You are firing *me*? Because I expected employees to care enough to do their best here? Simply because I've tried to make this motel a better place for —"

"Make this a *better* place?" Sharon looked offended. "There is nothing wrong with the Value Lodge, Anna. We serve thousands of happy customers each year. You obviously don't understand how an establishment like this is best operated."

"Obviously not."

"Blame it on your youth and inexperience." Sharon slowly shook her head in a dismal way, as if Anna was beyond help. "For the time being, Rich will return to managing, until we find your replacement. Someone who understands the way a motel like this should be run."

Anna forced a stiff smile. "I wish you good luck with that."

Sharon narrowed her eyes. "I'm sorry I won't be able to offer you a letter of recommendation."

Anna felt a chill run down her spine. "But I've done my job to the best of my ability, and I've never had —"

"You've been fired, Anna. Do you not get it?"

Anna felt angry tears filling her eyes, but she was determined to keep Sharon from witnessing her cry. "You don't have all the facts," Anna told her. "If you did, you wouldn't do this." She turned and walked out of the room. Rushing past one of the maids that she'd just put on probation, she went straight to the reception area, grabbed up her purse and a few belongings, and without saying a word to anyone, she left.

As she hurried home, Anna felt certain she had never been so humiliated in her life. To be falsely accused and treated like she'd been in the wrong, and then to be fired with no recommendation for her next job? It was just too much! With tears of frustration streaming down her cheeks, Anna didn't want to be seen by anyone as she walked down Main Street. She took a side street instead, but as she got closer to her grandmother's apartment complex, she wished she had someplace else to go — a private place where she could have a good cry.

Thankfully, Grandma wasn't home. Anna went straight to her little powder room bathroom, and after closing the door, she sat down on the toilet seat and proceeded to sob. Using toilet paper to blow her nose and wipe her tears, she allowed herself to just cry it all out. This was all so unfair, so wrong. Two years of her life — and for what? Why had it happened like this? What could she have done differently? What would she do next?

Finally, she felt cried out. She tossed a big ball of toilet paper into the wastebasket and splashed cold water on her face. It was time to put on her pragmatic hat. She had to figure this thing out. There must be a way to fight the unjustness of her situation. She imagined going back to the motel and gathering up accounts from other employees — not the disgruntled ones but the ones who liked and respected her. At least she thought they did; she hoped they did. She could present their testimonies to Sharon and Rich, pleading her case. Not to get her job back but simply to garner a recommendation for her future.

Yet she knew it would still come down to her word against Mickey's, and Mickey was family, whereas she was not. Besides, was it really fair to drag the other employees into this? To put their jobs and livelihoods on the spot for her sake? Most of the dependable employees needed their income just to put food on their tables and a roof over their heads. No, she couldn't do that.

Feeling like it was useless, she finally emerged from the powder room and sat down on the sofa, attempting to think. What should she do? Where should she go? Without references from her last two years of work, it seemed unlikely she could get a job — certainly not a good one — in the hospitality industry. But one thing she knew for sure: as much as she loved her grandmother, she did not want to remain here in Springville. Whether she liked the circumstances or not, it was clearly time to move on. The question was, where should she go?

She was just taking off her work clothes when she heard her iPhone ringing in her purse. Wondering if it might possibly be Sharon — perhaps someone had spoken out in Anna's defense — she grabbed it up to see. To her surprise, it was Marley.

"Sorry to call you while you're at work," Marley said quickly. "But Max just got back to me, and it sounds like he's arranged for you to meet with Vincent Newman."

"The owner of the SoHo hotel?" Anna asked eagerly. "Seriously?"

"Yes. Max wants to know if you can get to New York by Saturday morning at ten."

"You're kidding! Mr. Newman wants to meet with me in person?"

"It's the only way he'll hire anyone. He has to see them face-to-face."

"I, uh, I don't know if I can —"

"Anna, if you want a chance at this job, you have to go there and see him in person," Marley insisted.

"I'd love a chance at a job, it's just that —"

"I can probably get you a reduced airfare rate, but I need to do it ASAP," Marley told her. "You can stay in my room, since I'll still be here."

"That's very generous —"

"So tell me you'll do it," Marley said. "I'll arrange for your flight and everything, but you have to want it."

"I do want it. But I —"

"No buts. And sorry I can't talk. Two of our waitresses are out with some kind of bug today and we're short-staffed."

Anna considered offering to lend a hand at the café. After all, she was jobless now.

"You've got to do this, Anna. I know you're miserable at that old fleabag motel. This is your big chance. It's like fate. But to be there in time for the interview, you have to fly out on Friday. Are you in or not?"

"I'd love to go to New York and get the job, but —"

"Great. I'll send you the ticket information as soon as I have time to book it. But now I gotta go."

Before Anna could get in another word,

Marley hung up. Feeling slightly dizzy, not to mention dazed and confused, Anna sank down on the sofa and attempted to sort out her jumbled thoughts. In the end all she could do was sit there and slowly shake her head. What was she getting herself into?

Grandma was barely through the door before Anna began telling her the whole story of getting fired from the Value Lodge. Sparing no details, she unloaded the whole thing, and then she apologized. "I know you're good friends with the Morgans, and I'm really sorry if I've put you in a bad position. But Sharon is determined to believe Mickey over me. He's her nephew, and she's got a giant blind spot where he is concerned."

Grandma waved her hand. "Oh, I'm not that good of friends with Sharon. Rich and your grandpa used to play golf together. But the truth is, I always thought Sharon was a little snooty. As if she's superior to the rest of us just because she owns that silly motel. Trust me, there's nothing Sharon can do to make me feel one way or another, Anna." She patted Anna's cheek. "I'm just sorry you got caught in the crossfire. From what you've told me, that no-good nephew of theirs deserved to be fired. You were just doing your job."

"Thanks, Grandma."

"What difference does it make?" Grandma set her handbag on the bench by the door. "You wanted to get that job in New York anyway."

Anna bit her lip, wondering if she should mention Sharon's statement about not giving her a recommendation. Perhaps this was something that was better left unsaid.

"Maybe it's just a divine intervention." Grandma grinned. "God's way of pointing you in a new and better direction."

Anna told Grandma about her phone call from Marley.

"Well, there you have it. It's like they say, when life shuts a window, God opens a door." She chuckled. "Or something like that."

Just then, Anna's phone rang again. "It's Marley," she told Grandma. "She's helping to arrange things. I need to take this."

Anna never had a chance to tell Marley about getting fired from the Value Lodge or that she would have no recommendation from the Morgans. She convinced herself it was simply because there hadn't been time. Marley had monopolized most of their conversations by telling Anna how to print out her boarding pass, how to get around in New York, what she should wear for her interview, and directions to the apartment Marley shared with the other flight attendants.

Anna told herself that she'd tell Marley the whole truth about her job situation eventually, but for now they were both just too focused on getting Anna set to go. She wanted to believe that was true, but a part of her knew she was keeping her mouth shut simply because she was ashamed. It stung to think she'd been fired. It hurt to think of how unfair it had been. How it might have ruined her chances at succeeding in New York.

Even so, she told herself as Grandma drove her to Indianapolis on Friday morning, even if Vincent Newman was disappointed in her references — or lack of them — she still wanted to do this. She wanted to see New York. She would use her week there to look around and possibly find another job. Even an entry-level job at a chain hotel would be better than being stuck in Springville and the Value Lodge. And as signs for the Indianapolis airport came into view, Anna reminded herself, *This is an adventure!*

"You really don't mind flying?" Grandma looked worried as she pulled up to the passenger drop-off curb.

"It's not my favorite thing," Anna admitted. "But it will be worth it. I know it will."

Grandma leaned over to kiss Anna's cheek. "I'll trust God for your safety. But you call me when you get there, okay?"

Anna kissed her back. "I will."

Grandma let out a sigh. "You're a brave girl, Anna. And a smart girl." She smiled. "I always knew you'd go far."

"Beyond Springville?"

Grandma laughed. "Yes. Beyond Springville."

Anna thanked her again as she gathered her carry-on and purse, and then, waving good-bye, she turned toward the terminal. It felt so surreal being here like this. Just days ago she'd been on her way to the Value Lodge, feeling like her life was stuck on a dead-end street. Now she was on her way to New York City. However, as she took her place at the end of a long security line, she was fully aware that she was probably on a fool's errand. Interviewing for a high-level job with no references? What was she thinking? Still, she decided, it was better than being stuck in Springville, moping around and feeling sorry for herself. At least she would get to see the Big Apple.

7

Anna had been puzzled when Marley told her she'd booked her flight to New Jersey. "I thought I was going to *New York,*" she'd said with confusion.

"Newark is so close that we consider it a New York airport," Marley had explained. "It's a relatively short taxi ride from Newark into the city. It's really your best option. Trust me." Since Anna really had no choice, she had trusted Marley — with everything.

As the plane began its descent into Newark, Anna peered out the little window to discover that it did look like one huge city below them. It was impossible to tell which part was New Jersey and which part was New York. As they got closer, it simply looked like a lot of massive buildings sitting right on top of the water. Oh, she knew New York was made up of islands, but from this vantage point it looked more like floating skyscrapers. Hopefully they weren't about to sink.

Marley had not only booked the ticket and instructed Anna on how and what to pack (to avoid checking a bag) but also emailed her an explicit list of directions. Anna had these readily available on her phone now, a huge comfort as she climbed into the taxi, reading off the address of where she wanted to go. "My friend told me to ask the taxi driver to point out the Statue of Liberty when it comes into sight," she said hopefully. "I'd love to see it."

"No problem," he said with what sounded like a Russian accent. "Your first time in New York?"

"Yes. It's so exciting."

Anna watched everything with interest as the taxi zipped in and out of traffic, and it wasn't long before the driver was telling her to look to her right. "See there," he said. "That is the Statue of Liberty. The beautiful green lady."

Anna spotted it, but too soon it was gone. Still, she felt a thrill to think that she'd actually seen it with her own eyes. Perhaps if she had time, she'd take a trip to view it up close. But, she reminded herself as the taxi went into some sort of tunnel, her primary focus was to find gainful employment. She suspected this tunnel was going beneath the water — not something she felt overly comfortable with. Blocking feelings of claustrophobia, she stared at her phone. She would use this time to memorize the names of Marley's roommates. Tia, Sophie, and Kara. That wasn't too hard. Then, seeing what Marley had written down regarding the taxi expense and how much to tip, Anna extracted the right amount of cash, carefully counting it a second time just to be sure.

"Velcome to New York," the taxi driver announced as the taxi emerged from the tunnel.

Anna felt a rush of excitement as she looked at the tall buildings all around. This was it — she was really here. She watched with wide eyes as the taxi driver zipped down one street, turning on the next, honking if someone was in his way, and after just a few minutes more, stopping. "Here you are." He read off the address she'd given him.

"Which building is it?" she asked, peering up at the row of brick buildings.

"Right there." He pointed directly out the side window as he pushed something on his taxi meter and told her the amount, then hopped out to get her carry-on bag.

"Thank you." She handed him her money, surprised at how close Marley's estimate had been. "That was a nice taxi ride."

"Enjoy your visit." He tipped his head as he handed her the handle of her carry-on.

"I'm sure I will," she said as she began pulling her bag up to the building. Marley had told Anna the security code to get inside and given Anna her own key to get into the apartment until Marley came home on Tuesday.

After a couple tries, Anna got the security code to work, and soon she was nervously riding the elevator up to the fourth floor. Marley had told her the elevator was fairly dependable and that they used it when they had baggage. "But a lot of times we just take the stairs. Good exercise and no chance of getting stuck."

Thankfully, the elevator didn't get stuck, and soon Anna was slipping her key into the tall wooden door of apartment 408. She had no idea if anyone would be in there or not, but Marley had promised to advise her roommates of Anna's arrival and that she would be using Marley's bed. Anna knew it was a two-bedroom apartment and that Marley shared her room with Tia while Sophie and Kara shared the other room, but she wasn't prepared for how small it was once she got inside. Although there was a window, the shades were down, so the small space was dimly lit — and very cramped. Besides a love seat and a pair of wicker chairs, the room was filled with boxes and plastic storage containers. Clearly this was only a stopping place.

"Hello?" Anna said quietly. "Anyone home?"

Marley had warned her that due to their differing schedules, someone was often sleeping in the apartment, even in the middle of the day. She had also told Anna that her room was the door to the right. "It's away from the street, so it's a little quieter."

Anna quietly tried the doorknob. Worried that Tia might be sleeping in there and not wanting to disturb her, she barely cracked it open, cautiously peeking in. But to her relief, both twin beds in the tiny room were empty. Anna set her carry-on next to the bed on the left side of the room, let out a long sigh, and sat down. She had made it!

Before she unpacked or did anything else, Anna called Grandma. "I'm here," she said happily. She told her about seeing the Statue of Liberty and how the neighborhood she'd been dropped off in seemed perfectly charming. She even gave her a description of the tiny apartment. "Looks like I have the whole place to myself."

"You're off to a fine start," Grandma told her. "Good luck with your interview tomorrow. I'm sure you will impress them."

"I hope so." Anna felt some of the wind going out of her sails. How do you impress someone with no references for the past two years?

"You'll be in my prayers," Grandma continued.

"Thanks . . . . I'll need it." As Anna hung up, she thought once again that she'd probably come to New York on a fool's errand. Even so, she would make the most of it!

After settling into the apartment a bit — mostly just unpacking her carry-on bag and hanging and steaming her dark blue interview suit — Anna set out to explore the neighborhood. Marley had given her directions to Elsie Dolce, and Anna intended to "happen" by to pick up a pastry and hopefully get a sneak peek at the Rothsberg hotel. She didn't want to be too obvious, and if she saw anyone who looked like owners or upper management, she would keep a low profile. But she was so curious to see this place, she couldn't help herself. Wearing sunglasses, casual-looking khaki capris, and a T-shirt, she carried a walking map (hoping to look more like a tourist than a spy) as she strolled around the Greenwich and eventually SoHo neighborhoods.

By the time she located Elsie Dolce, Anna was in love with New York City. At least with this section of New York. According to her walking map, she'd only seen a teeny-tiny percentage of the huge city. But she was definitely in love.

As soon as the bell tinkled against the door of Elsie Dolce, Anna could smell an intoxicating mix of aromas: chocolate, cinnamon, and other scents she couldn't even identify. With its black-and-white checkerboard floors, white Carrara marble countertops, and sweet pink walls, the shop was adorable.

"Welcome," a petite blonde wearing a pink chef's apron called out from behind the glass case that was filled with fabulous-looking treats.

Anna looked around in appreciation. "What a delightful shop," she said as she approached the counter.

"Your first time here?"

"My first time in New York."

"Well, I hope you're enjoying yourself."

"I absolutely am," Anna assured her.

"Anything in particular you're looking

for?" The blonde woman held out a silver tray with some bite-sized pieces of chocolate arranged on a paper doily. "Care to sample a lavender truffle?"

"Thanks!" Anna reached for a small piece and slid it into her mouth. "Oh my." She nodded with approval. "That's fabulous."

The woman smiled. "One of my specialties."

Anna blinked. "Are *you* Elsie?"

She laughed. "Yes, I am. The way you say that makes me feel like a celebrity."

Anna grinned. "Well, owning this shop should make you feel like a celebrity. But as it turns out, I sort of know you. Marley is my —"

"Oh, you must be Anna!" Elsie came around from behind the counter, extending her hand. "Max said you were arriving today." She looked Anna up and down. "But he didn't tell me you were such a gorgeous girl."

Anna smiled nervously. "Well, Max probably still remembers me as his kid sister's scrawny little friend who was always in the way. Marley and I used to drive him nuts. We'd sneak his video games when he was gone, and if he caught us he'd threaten to throttle us."

"Yes, well, he's still protective of his

electronic stuff." She laughed. "Have you met the Newmans yet? I just saw Vincent about an hour ago."

"No, my interview isn't until tomorrow." Anna waved down to her casual outfit. "I was going incognito today. You know, playing the tourist. I just wanted to get a sneak peek at the hotel. Marley made it sound pretty grand."

"It is pretty grand. Denise has pulled out all the stops."

Anna nodded. "Yes, even from the outside, it's impressive. I can't wait to see more tomorrow."

"I wish Max were here to see you. He's working at home today." Elsie glanced to the door as another customer entered the shop.

"Tell him hi for me. I was surprised that he actually remembers me."

"Oh, sure he does. And if you're here for a while, maybe we can have you over for a meal."

"That'd be great." Anna moved aside, making room for the woman who was behind her. "I'll just look around a little. There's no way I'm leaving here without something."

As Elsie waited on the woman, boxing up two dozen assorted pastries, Anna decided on what looked like a chocolate éclair. She was just paying for it as well as some more lavender chocolate truffles when several more customers came in.

"It always gets busy this time in the afternoon," Elsie whispered. "People need their three o'clock sugar hit."

Anna nodded, clasping her little pink bag. "Makes sense. Thanks, Elsie. I'll see you around."

"Good luck tomorrow," Elsie called.

Anna thanked her and exited. Trying not to look conspicuous, she slowly walked alongside the hotel, taking it all in. From its restored brickwork to its gleaming glass windows to the big, beautiful mahogany and glass doors leading into a foyer with rich-looking travertine floors, it was all perfection. She wished she could just stand there and stare at it, but she did not want to accidentally run into the owners. One thing she remembered from school was that first impressions are lasting, whether it's the first impression of a hotel building or an employee.

As she hurried on her way back to the apartment, she wondered if the suit she'd picked for the interview was really going to work. Marley had assured her that it was perfect, but Anna had gotten the Ralph

Lauren suit more than two years ago. What if it was dated and she just didn't know it? Marley had suggested adding a scarf, even offering to loan one from her own closet. Perhaps Anna should do some browsing there. Anna considered her shoes. She'd brought the black Nine West pumps, but she'd been wearing them a lot lately. What if they showed it more than she realized? She reminded herself that she'd used Grandma's shoe polishing kit on them only yesterday. They were probably fine. She was just being too hard on herself.

The real problem, she knew, was her lack of references. She could dress impeccably and say all the right things, but without references, what good would it do?

8

The apartment was still uninhabited when Anna returned around 5:00. She'd stopped by a little grocery store that Marley had mentioned and picked up a few things to tide her over. As she put them in the small fridge, she was surprised at how sparse it was. The few things in there, mostly leftovers in take-out cartons, looked a little old. She was tempted to clean the whole fridge out and give it a good scrubbing, but she was concerned that might be stepping over a line. Besides that, putting outdated food cartons in the garbage might result in some bad smells. Best to leave well enough alone.

Still, she decided as she looked around the tiny kitchen, it probably wouldn't hurt anyone's feelings if she did some cleaning in here. It certainly could use it. As she scrubbed the grimy porcelain sink, hoping to get it clean enough to wash the dirty dishes that were piled up, she imagined the weary flight attendants coming and going on their busy ways, worn out from long flights and waiting on demanding passengers. She could understand how it might be easy for them to overlook the general squalor in here.

With the sink gleaming white, she proceeded to wash the dirty dishes. Too bad this apartment had no dishwasher, but as she looked around the small space, she could see there was no room for one. She dried the dishes and found their places in the narrow cupboard, then scrubbed the laminate countertop. Since she was making such progress, she continued her cleaning frenzy by washing the faces of the painted cabinets. By the time she finished, the whole space looked much more inviting and rather sweet. Even better than that, she felt happy that she'd made herself useful.

It was strange having this apartment all to herself, and as she made a little dinner of yogurt, banana, and a bagel, she was curious if any of the flight attendants would be coming home tonight. She was just finishing up when she heard her phone ringing. She ran to get it, pleased to see it was Marley. After she thanked her for all her help and the use of her apartment, she mentioned that no one was home.

"Well, Tia might be out of the country. Possibly for the whole weekend. As for the other two — it's Friday night."

"Oh?"

"At the most, you might see Sophie and Kara pop in to change clothes, but then they'll leave again. Sometimes if they're on a late flight, they just go out straight from the airport. We girls always carry extra clothes and shoes in our bags so we can do a quick change if we want to go have fun."

"That makes sense." Anna told Marley about meeting Elsie and how much she liked the neighborhood. "The hotel is awesome."

"Well, I'm crossing my fingers that you get hired, Anna. It would be so fabulous if you were in New York. And I got to thinking, you could probably sleep on our couch if you wanted — until you found another place. Maybe you and I could share an apartment, just the two of us. That would be a huge improvement."

"That sounds great."

"So knock their socks off tomorrow," Marley told her.

"I'll do my best." Anna felt that familiar feeling of hopelessness washing over her.

"Let me know how it goes."

Anna promised she would, then hung up.

Marley sounded so hopeful and optimistic, but then, she had no idea that Anna was walking into this interview with no real references.

Because it had been a warm day and the apartment had no air conditioning, Anna opened the living room window. Hearing the noise out on the street, she decided to go outside. She wanted to get a feel for what it was like in New York on a Friday night. The way Marley had talked about it made it sound like a holiday. She'd seen a gelato shop near the grocery store, so she decided that a cool treat might be just the ticket for helping her battle the blues.

As she walked down the street, watching people coming and going, she could imagine herself turning into a real New Yorker. Oh, she knew the odds were stacked against her, but it didn't cost anything to entertain a dream. She got a raspberry gelato, found a vacant chair out on the sidewalk, and sat down to slowly eat her treat.

By the time she finished her dessert, she had made a decision. In her interview tomorrow morning, she would simply tell the truth. She would explain that she could provide no references for the past two years — and the reason why. She would do her best to convey her enthusiasm for being hired. She would point out her outstanding school records and even encourage the interviewer to contact the manager at the Pomonte Hotel, where she'd worked in college. Sure, it wasn't managerial experience, but if she'd stuck around she might've been managing by now. They had appreciated Anna's work ethic there.

As she walked back to the apartment, she felt hopeful and energized by the general vibe of the city. The sights, sounds, and smells all seemed strangely familiar to her — almost like déjà vu. Almost like she truly belonged here. Oh, if only it were true.

After a restless night of sleep and being awakened at odd hours by the sounds of people coming and going from the apartment, Anna got up early. To her relief the bed beside hers had not been slept in. Tia probably was out of the country. Anna tiptoed out of the bedroom and through the quiet living room. She suspected, thanks to the pair of carry-on bags by the door, that Sophie and Kara were home. She continued into the kitchen, trying not to feel too disappointed by the messy take-out boxes and dirty dishes now cluttering what she'd cleaned yesterday, and she got a yogurt and an orange from the fridge. After all, this wasn't her place.

She went back to the bedroom to eat her breakfast, and as soon as she finished, she decided to take advantage of the unoccupied bathroom. Marley had mentioned how it could get crazy in there with four women. "Fortunately, we're usually on different schedules, but occasionally we all want a shower at the same time." Anna took a fast shower and decided she would do her hair and makeup in the bedroom, just in case the other girls needed the bathroom. It wasn't ideal, but then again, this wasn't her apartment.

By 9:15 Anna was carefully dressed in her dark blue Ralph Lauren suit with a simple white blouse underneath. She'd dressed it up a little with a pretty blue and green silk scarf, borrowed from Marley's closet. She kept her jewelry minimal with a pair of faux diamond studs and a sleek silver bracelet. With every hair in place, she slipped into her recently polished pumps, picked up her matching black purse, and proceeded out to the street.

She knew it only took thirty minutes to walk to the hotel from here, and that was at a leisurely strolling pace, but she wanted to be there at least fifteen minutes early. A manager was punctual — and, she thought wryly, preemptive and positive. As she walked, she decided to focus on the positive. Really, why shouldn't she be optimistic about her upcoming interview? She had a lot going for her. She was a hard worker, she was dependable, she was efficient, she was a people person, she was creative . . . With each step she mentally listed all the qualities she possessed that made for a great manager. Finally, she told herself as she paused by the tall mahogany and glass doors, she was honest. Hopefully that wouldn't kill her chances this morning.

The door to the lobby was unlocked, but the lobby itself was dark and quiet. Although it looked as if everything was in place, or nearly, the hotel was obviously not open yet.

"Can I help you?" a young man behind the reception desk asked.

"I have an appointment with Mr. Newman," she said politely. "Not until ten o'clock. I'm a few minutes early."

"Right." He pointed to a hallway that started just past the reception desk. "The business offices are that way. Mr. Newman's is at the end. You'll see his name on the door."

"Thank you." She continued on down the dimly lit hallway. She wasn't sure if she should just stand outside his door, waiting until her appointment time, or perhaps go back and wait in the lobby. But seeing the women's restroom, she decided to make a short layover there. It wouldn't hurt to give her hair and makeup one last look. Because she knew in this business — especially in an upscale hotel — appearances mattered.

She smoothed her strawberry blonde hair into place, wondering if it had been a mistake to wear it down. Putting it up did make her look older, but it was too late for that. She knew it was a good cut, and it barely passed her shoulders. It would have to do. She leaned forward to check her teeth and finished by freshening up her lipstick, a warm peachy shade that was both natural looking and attractive.

"This is as good as it gets," she whispered to her reflection. "Now, don't blow it." She glanced at her watch — five minutes till 10:00. "Here we go."

She exited the restroom and continued to the end of the hallway. She knew it was silly to feel this nervous. It was just an interview. Mr. Newman was just a business owner. And she had much to offer.

"Are you Miss Gordon?" a young woman dressed in a dark suit asked.

"Yes." Anna nodded. "I have an interview with Mr. Newman."

"I'm Patricia, Mr. Newman's executive assistant."

Anna shook her hand. "I'm pleased to meet you."

"Mr. Newman can see you now. Go ahead and go on in," Patricia told her.

"Thank you." Anna took a deep breath and pushed open the large wooden door.

"Hello," a dark-haired man called from where he was standing next to a bookcase. "Come in, come in." He walked over to shake her hand, smiling warmly. "You must be Anna Gordon. It's good to meet you. Go ahead and take a chair and we'll get right to it."

She thanked him and sat down, holding her purse in her lap. He seemed friendly enough. Very personable, actually.

"You might be surprised that I'm not having our personnel director conduct this interview," he began as he sat down at his desk. "But, you see, my wife and I are so involved in all this, so invested, that we're still being very hands-on." He smiled. "It's kind of like our baby. You know?"

"Absolutely." She nodded eagerly. "It's a beautiful hotel. I can understand why you'd want to be hands-on. I have great respect for that."

"Good." He picked up what appeared to

be her résumé but then set it down again, looking at her with interest. "Tell me about yourself, Miss Gordon."

Trying not to sound arrogant, she launched into a positive accounting of her skills and abilities. She talked about how much she loved the hospitality industry. How she had excelled in college. How she had enjoyed working at the Pomonte Hotel. "It was nothing compared to the Rothsberg," she said finally. "To be honest, I've never been in a hotel quite this grand. But I would love to work here."

"As a manager?" He studied her carefully, and she wondered if this was a trick question.

"I trained in management," she told him. "I believe I have managerial qualities. And I've been working in management" — she sighed — "for the past two years."

"Uh, yes." He cleared his throat. "I see that." He looked curiously at her. "To be honest, that part was a bit confusing to me. Frankly, if my good friend Max hadn't told me about you, you wouldn't be sitting here right now."

She nodded. "That's understandable." Knowing it was time to lay her cards on the table, she started to tell him about her grandmother, including how she had raised

Anna and sacrificed to help her through college. "My grandfather passed on during my last year of school. I knew my grandmother was lonely and depressed, and I felt I owed it to her to stay with her awhile. Just until she adjusted to her loss. The Value Lodge was in my grandmother's town, so I took the job there to be with her. At the time it seemed a good idea. I could garner managerial experience as well as be there for my grandmother. I had even hoped I might be able to help turn the economy motel into something more." She made a slightly bitter laugh. "I was wrong."

He gave her a sympathetic smile. "Well, it might not have been a great career move, but your motives were honorable." He looked down at her résumé again, his mouth twisting to one side as if he was deep in thought.

"There's one more thing I have to tell you," she said meekly.

"Yes?" He looked up.

"About the Value Lodge," she said slowly. "You won't be able to get references from them for me."

"No references?" He gave her a puzzled look. "After two years of employment?"

"No. I mean yes. I *did* work there. Full time as head manager for nearly two years.

I worked very hard the whole while."

"Then why wouldn't they give references?"

"Because I was fired."

His dark brows arched slightly. "Fired?"

"Yes." She nodded glumly. "You see, the owners employ a nephew. The young man is supposed to be in charge of janitorial, but he is a lazy bum." She grimaced over her careless words. "I'm sorry. But really, that's the truth. He was not motivated to work."

"What did you do about this unmotivated employee?"

"I gave him warnings — both verbally and in writing. I had a meeting to encourage him and some of the other staff. I encouraged them to step up and do their jobs. I even held training sessions. But the morale in that motel, well, it was so low. Honestly, it was like beating my head against the wall."

"I see . . ."

"So I fired the nephew. His girlfriend too. Well, the owners didn't appreciate that. They fired me. Just this week." She looked down at her purse. There, she'd said it. Let the chips fall where they may.

"I can understand how frustrating that must've been for you."

She looked up. "Oh, it was. It really was."

"You say you're looking for a management

position now?"

"Yes. Absolutely. It's what I trained for. I know I can do it. Especially in a hotel where the owners are committed to quality and hospitality." She made a nervous smile. "You can't imagine what a refreshing change that would be for me."

He nodded. "Well, thank you, Miss Gordon. My assistant will be in contact with you." He stood to shake her hand again.

"Thank you." She returned his handshake with a firm grasp. "I really appreciate your time, Mr. Newman."

"And yours." He made a polite smile.

A lump grew in her throat as she looped her purse strap over her shoulder.

"Is this the number you can be reached at?" He pointed to her résumé still laying on his desk. "Even while you're here in New York?"

"Yes." She started to leave, then stopped abruptly, turning to look him in the eyes. "I know you're not going to hire me, Mr. Newman."

He only looked partly surprised, but she could tell by his expression that she was right. He had no intention of hiring her. Who could blame him?

"I understand completely. Just for the record, I think your hotel is going to be an amazingly wonderful success. I wish you the very best with it." She forced a final smile. "In the future, after I get some really good experience under my belt, I hope you'll allow me to apply here again. I would love to work for you . . . someday."

"Absolutely, Miss Gordon. I encourage you to come back and apply . . . whenever you feel you have the references."

She thanked him again and quickly turned and left, feeling precariously close to tears. As she walked down the dimly lit hallway, she told herself she was not going to cry. But when she remembered how hopeful Grandma and Marley had been for her, how they'd asked her to call them as soon as the interview ended, she just couldn't help herself. She saw the door to the women's restroom and hurried inside, hoping to find a quiet refuge where she could hide her tears.

9

Since another woman had just entered the restroom ahead of her, Anna ducked into the first stall. Taking in several slow, deep breaths, she attempted to compose herself. Really, it was not the end of the world. She would get past this in time. Besides, all of New York was out there waiting — why was she cooping herself up like this?

Finally, she was ready to emerge and get on with her life, but a pair of women were chattering in front of the mirror. They sounded like newly hired employees. Not caring to speak to anyone — especially a new employee — Anna remained cloistered in the stall until she heard them leave.

When the coast was clear, Anna stepped out and went over to the sink area to wash her hands. As she did, she noticed that the stone countertop had been carelessly splashed with water and that some splats of liquid soap had slopped onto one of the gorgeous glass vessel sinks. Anna automatically reached for some paper towels and began to mop it up. Cleaning and drying and even polishing the elegant surfaces, she worked at it until it all glistened like a showroom.

"What are you doing?"

Anna turned to see a woman dressed in blue jeans and a gray T-shirt leaning against a bathroom stall door and watching with what seemed amusement. Anna gave the vessel sink one last swipe. "Just cleaning."

"In your business suit?"

Anna frowned down at her good suit. A lot of good it had done.

The woman frowned. "Are you on staff here?"

"No . . ." Anna gave one last buff to the gleaming stone surface, nodding with approval. "It's just such a beautiful restroom." She made a slightly apologetic smile. "Seems a shame to leave it looking messy."

"But it wasn't *your* mess."

"I know." Anna tossed the used paper towels into the trash.

"Yet you cleaned it up?"

Anna shrugged, ready to change the subject or at least get out of here. "Do you work here?"

"I do." The woman finished washing her hands and, following Anna's example, used her paper towel to wipe up her own drips.

"Well, you're lucky to be employed here." Anna adjusted her purse. "It seems a lovely place to work." She turned to leave.

"What about you?" the woman asked.

"Me?" Anna turned back to the woman.

"Yes. If you're not on staff here, what are you doing at the Rothsberg?" She tossed her paper towel in the trash, then, with her head tipped to one side, shoved her hands into her jeans pockets and waited. Anna wondered what this woman had been hired for — if it was housekeeping, they might be sorry. She seemed too nosy and chatty.

"I just interviewed for a job. I was on my way out."

"Oh? So maybe you *will* be working here then?"

"No." Anna sighed.

"You mean the interview wasn't so hot?"

"I guess it was okay. But I, well, I'm just not what Mr. Newman is looking for at this point in time. That's all."

The woman's expression grew even more curious. "Did you interview for the managerial position — the day manager?"

Anna was surprised. "Yes, as a matter of fact."

"But you say you *weren't* what Mr. Newman was looking for?"

Anna simply nodded. Who was this woman anyway?

"What about applying for a different position?"

"What do you mean?"

"Well, I understand it's probably disappointing not to land the day manager job. But did you ever consider applying for a different position? There are still a number of management jobs."

Anna was confused. How could this woman — especially as a maid — know so much about the hotel's personnel needs?

"Forgive me." The woman stuck out her hand with an apologetic smile. "I'm Denise Newman."

Anna blinked with realization as the two shook hands. "I'm Anna Gordon," she said meekly. "Pleasure to meet you, Mrs. Newman. I, uh, I just met your husband."

"Do you have a minute?" Mrs. Newman asked as she pushed open the door.

"Sure. Of course. What can I do for you?" Anna followed her out of the restroom.

"Let's talk in my office." Mrs. Newman led Anna back down the dim hallway and into an office that was a few doors away from her husband's. "Have a seat, Miss Gordon. Let's talk business."

Anna sat down, wondering where this was

leading. On one hand, it seemed likely that Mrs. Newman might be about to offer her a job — possibly as a maid since she'd just caught Anna cleaning the women's restroom. Actually, Anna might even accept such a job simply for the opportunity to work here. But what would happen when Mrs. Newman discovered Anna had been fired and had no references? For all Anna knew, she would change her mind and rescind her offer. Best to go carefully — not get her hopes up.

"I know that you're a friend of Max and Marley. I saw your résumé, and I'm the one who talked Vincent into interviewing you. I've been worried that he's getting us overly loaded up with male managers. I told him we need some good women too."

Anna just nodded. "That makes sense."

Mrs. Newman leaned forward with an intense gaze. "So, tell me, Miss Gordon, what went wrong in the interview? What made my husband send you away?"

Anna took in another deep breath and explained the whole situation, trying not to go into too much detail but talking so fast that when she finally paused, she was practically breathless. "It was stupid of me to think I could get hired without any references from the Value Lodge," she said slowly. “Stupid for me to waste money on a trip to New York. But Marley had already sent you guys my résumé, and she was so eager to help me. My grandmother was all on board too. I just thought, why not?” She held up her hands in a helpless gesture. “Because the truth is, I know I’m a good employee. I know I have a lot to give. I was top of my class. The hotel I worked for in college gave a wonderful recommendation. I even think that in time, I could get an honest recommendation from the Value Lodge too. Once Mickey’s aunt and uncle see what his work ethic is really like and how he influences the other employees . . . well, they might see things differently.”

“Might even give you your job back?”

“I wouldn’t take it.” Anna firmly shook her head. “I’d rather flip burgers at a greasy spoon.”

“What about working here?”

Anna frowned. “But what about my references? Rather, my lack of them?”

“I saw your references in the ladies’ room.”

“But I —”

“Look, I’m co-owner of this hotel. Both my husband and I are overseeing the hiring. And right now I have a position to fill.” She peered at Anna. “Although you might not want it."

"Are you kidding?" Anna felt a rush of hope. "I'll gladly take any job you offer me, Mrs. Newman. Even if it's just housekeeping."

She smiled. "As a matter of fact it is housekeeping."

Anna tried not to regret her hasty offer. Instead, she just nodded. "Fine. I'll take it. I really do know how to do housekeeping. I was a maid at the Pomonte during college. I'm actually quite good at it." She frowned with realization. "Although I'm not sure I could afford to live in New York on housekeeping wages. But you know what — I'd make it work somehow. Even if I had to use my savings to get by. It would be worth it, just for a chance to work here." She nodded. "If you have a job in housekeeping, I'll take it."

Mrs. Newman looked amused. "Well, the job is in housekeeping, but it's not a housekeeping job. I need someone to manage housekeeping. Do you think you'd be up for that?"

Anna blinked. "Absolutely. Yes."

"It's not the same as being a day manager."

"It's a very important job," Anna assured her. "Housekeeping is the closest interface with the guests. A housekeeping staff can make or break a hotel."

"That's right. And I want you to make it."

"Are you serious?" Anna was afraid to get her hopes up. "Even without references, you'll give me this job?"

"I've always been a pretty good judge of character. I believe you'll do an excellent job, Miss Gordon."

"Please, call me Anna. I mean, if you'd like. And I will do an excellent job. I promise I will."

"Unlike your last employers, we will back you in your management. Your staff will be your responsibility. I'm sure you know that can be its own can of worms."

"I know that housekeeping jobs bring in all sorts." Anna remembered the careless women in the restroom, splashing the counters. Chances were they would be working under her. "I also know that good leadership makes a difference."

"That's what I like to hear." Mrs. Newman picked up her phone. "I'm going to send you to personnel to deal with the paperwork." She paused. "I forgot to ask, when can you start?"

"Whenever you like."

"Monday?"

Anna nodded eagerly.

"We have only a few weeks before our grand opening. I've already hired about half of the housekeeping staff. You'll be responsible for hiring the rest."

"Great."

"Virginia?" Mrs. Newman said into the phone. "I'm sending Anna Gordon your way. I've just hired her as head manager of housekeeping. Will you get her set up, then send her back to me?" She thanked her and then hung up. "Okay, Anna, Virginia's office is two doors that way. Says Personnel on the front."

Anna thanked her as she stood. "I won't let you down," she promised.

"I know you won't."

As Anna walked to the personnel office, she felt like the condemned man who'd just been pardoned from the gallows. Oh, she knew that was being overly dramatic, but it's how she felt. Like she'd been in the depths of despair and suddenly lifted to the heights of hope. Sure, there might've been a time in her life — three years ago to be exact — when she'd have turned her nose up at the offer of a management job in housekeeping. But not anymore. And not in a hotel as swanky as this. She would do this job to the best of her ability. She would prove to Mrs. Newman — and her husband too — that even without references, she was worth taking a risk on. She'd meant what she'd said: she wouldn't let them down.

10

After filling out some paperwork and being measured for a uniform, Anna returned to Mrs. Newman's office, tapping quietly on the partially opened door.

"Come in, Anna." Mrs. Newman waved from where she was talking on the phone. "I need them here by today," she was firmly telling someone on the other end. "If the shipment's not here by 6:00, I will stop payment and be in contact with my attorney. Do you understand me?" She waited with a furrowed brow. "Thank you very much. I thought you would. Good-bye." She hung up and rolled her eyes. "When someone promises something, I expect them to deliver."

Anna nodded. "That seems reasonable enough."

"How about if I give you a two-bit tour?"

"I'd love a tour. Unless you're too busy."

"I'm on my way to meet a designer in the

penthouse right now. She doesn't expect me until 11:30. I'll give you a quick tour on my way up."

Anna could hear the pride in Mrs. Newman's voice as she led the way through the luxurious lobby, describing where certain pieces came from and how some of the original grandeur had been restored. "As you can see, most of the furnishings are in place." She pointed to an area where several leather club chairs and a soft-looking, enormous, olive green velvet sofa were arranged around an ornate fireplace. "A huge antique cocktail table with a white marble top will go right there."

"*White marble* and cocktails?" Anna glanced at Mrs. Newman. "Hopefully no red wine will be involved?"

"The stone comes with a stain-resistant finish." Mrs. Newman gave Anna a knowing look. "But I like how you're thinking." She pointed out several other spots where various antique accent pieces were missing. "That was the vendor I was just talking to. He was supposed to have had them here last week. He assured me they are on their way right now. Hopefully he won't let me down. Or I'll make him pay."

"I love the old-world style you've gone with," Anna said as they rounded a corner.

"So classic and refined and elegant. It fits the building."

"In the beginning, when we first bought the building, Vincent tried to talk me into going modern. So many were doing it. You know the look — minimalist, sleek furnishings, lots of metal and glass. A lot of the finest SoHo hotels have gone that route. Trump, for example. But I wanted to be different. I envisioned ours to be more like a small version of the Plaza or the St. Regis." She laughed. "Oh, I wouldn't go around repeating that."

"It makes sense, though," Anna agreed. "This does feel like an intimate version of one of those old fine hotels."

"Thank you." Mrs. Newman smiled. "I do like modern, but it can be so cold and impersonal. Besides that, it will go in and out of fashion. And I am convinced there are lots of people who like the grander things in life, the type who appreciate this old-world elegance and style. Let's face it, some guests want all the bells and whistles. They like feeling pampered. Why not give that to them?" She paused to point out the area dedicated to a coffee shop. "Don't tell anyone, but we gave the contract to Starbucks last month. Vincent said it was simpler than the private vendor that was bidding for

it. However, we've asked Starbucks to wait until our grand opening to reveal their name."

"I'm sure guests will appreciate a familiar coffee. You know how people can be about their morning joe."

She nodded. "You're right." She took Anna over to what appeared to be a lounge area. "This bar came from Italy. It was shipped here in five pieces."

Anna slowly shook her head as she took in the ornately carved woodwork. "It's massive," she said. "I can't believe it was only five pieces."

"Five enormous pieces." Mrs. Newman slid her hand over the smooth bar counter. "But well worth the effort and expense, don't you think?"

"It's beautiful."

"It will be a real moneymaker too." Mrs. Newman pointed to a tall set of double doors nearby. Although glass windows were set into the heavy wood frames, they were covered with paper, making it impossible to see inside. "This is the restaurant. Chef Henri is in charge and he is absolutely fabulous. We're so lucky to get him. The plan is to open it simultaneously with the hotel. He's been equipping the place for several months. He's in there training his staff right now."

"That's ambitious — I mean, opening both the hotel and restaurant at the same time. But it does make sense."

"Actually, it's not as ambitious as it sounds. We've leased the restaurant to Chez Henri for the first three years. So for now, it's separate from the hotel, which means less stress in our lives. But Chez Henri will fulfill our room service, and that's huge. We plan to take the restaurant back someday. That's why we gave Henri such a short lease, although I know he already hopes to extend it. We'll see." Mrs. Newman led Anna to another set of doors. "And this, as you can see, is the courtyard."

Anna stepped out to the tiled outdoor space and looked around in wonder at large potted trees, overflowing flower planters, an Italian-looking water fountain, iron dining sets with marble-topped tables, and even a gas fire pit in the center. "It's absolutely beautiful."

"It is, isn't it? The landscapers were just here last week." She pointed to the strands of lights strung around the tree branches and the perimeter of the courtyard. "You should see it all lit up at night, with candles on the tables and the fire burning."

"I'll bet it's magical."

"Oh, it is." She pointed to the wall of windows that went into the restaurant. "Those are folding glass doors so that the whole restaurant opens up to this on a warm day."

"That's brilliant."

Mrs. Newman smiled. "My idea."

"I love it." Anna kept studying everything. "What a great place for a wedding."

"Yes, but it would have to be a small, intimate wedding. The restaurant only seats about fifty — less if we needed a dance floor, but I've planned for that too."

Anna looked at Mrs. Newman with admiration. "The Rothsberg is going to be a huge success. I can feel it."

Mrs. Newman beamed. "I believe you're right, Anna. Vincent and I have invested everything in this venture. It has to be a success."

Next she showed Anna the small but well-furnished conference room. "It's only big enough for a dozen or so," she said. "But it's not as if we're a conference facility. We'll use this for our staff meetings, but it's mostly for the guests' convenience." Next they went down a long hallway, which Mrs. Newman explained led to the housekeeping section. She pointed to a plain wooden door. "This will be your office." She opened it up, flipping a light switch. "It's not terribly impressive, but you can personalize it if you like."

Anna peered into the small windowless room with a midsized desk, several chairs, and some shelves and storage units. "It's perfectly fine."

Next they visited the staff lunchroom and the maids' locker room. Both were serviceable and nice but nothing like the splendor that was to be found in the rest of the hotel. Of course, that was to be expected. Mrs. Newman pointed out the various housekeeping storage areas and finally the laundry.

"This is impressive," Anna said as she surveyed the large, efficient-looking machines. "I'm glad the linens are done onsite. That's always a plus."

"Yes. We think one of the secrets of success in a small boutique hotel is to maintain as much in-house control as possible."

"It's the best way to maintain a high level of quality. No middlemen to deal with."

"That's right. The buck stops here. Consequently, it saves us a few bucks too." Mrs. Newman glanced at her watch. "I don't have time to show you a guest room right now, but maybe you'd like a sneak peek at the penthouse since I'm going up."

"I'd love to see it."

After they boarded the service elevator, Mrs. Newman slid in a key card, giving them access to the top floor.

Anna studied the elevator buttons and the legend alongside of them. "There's a pool in the basement?"

"Yes. It's nearly finished."

"That's a nice amenity for guests."

"Yes. We sacrificed our on-site parking, but we're leasing some space a few blocks away. Guests expect valet parking anyway — they don't have to know their cars aren't in the basement." Mrs. Newman was checking her iPhone as she talked. "The spa facilities will be down in the basement too. Like the restaurant, we're leasing the spa space. But only for two years. In time, we hope to run it ourselves."

The elevator doors opened into a light, bright space. Anna looked up as they emerged. "Is that a skylight?"

"Yes. That was Vincent's idea. Expensive, but a nice touch."

"It's lovely." Anna looked around the generous space. She knew that it was simply a foyer for the penthouse, but with its beautiful jewel-toned carpet, several carefully chosen antiques, some large potted plants, and a pair of inviting armchairs upholstered in smoky blue velveteen, it was very inviting. "Is there just one penthouse suite?"

"Actually, there are two." Mrs. Newman pointed toward the hallway that ran between the two sets of elevators. "Vincent and I are using the other penthouse for now. It's been a real time-saver being right here. We thought it was just temporary, but we've gotten pretty used to it. Right now, the plan is to stay here until this place is running like clockwork. I'd consider staying longer, but Vincent won't hear of it. Lost revenues." She slipped a key card into the slot next to an oversized and ornately carved door. "Now for the pièce de résistance."

"I can't wait." Anna felt almost like a kid at Christmas as the huge door opened.

"It's still a work in progress. But you'll get the gist of it." As Mrs. Newman went inside, she called out, "I'm here, Valerie. Come to see your emergency."

"I'm in the kitchen," a voice called back.

"Feel free to explore," Mrs. Newman told Anna. "Might as well see the lay of the land before it's occupied. Especially the penthouse. I want you to know this hotel inside and out, Anna. Well, mostly inside. But you know what I mean." She slipped her phone into her pocket. "Excuse me while I meet with Valerie."

Anna had never seen such a luxurious suite in her life. Not in person, anyway. She might've seen something similar to this in a magazine or on a hotel website. Then again, maybe not. The view from up here was fabulous too. She could only imagine what this space would go for — possibly as much as ten grand for one night. As ridiculous as that seemed, she knew there were suites that went for more in this city. For instance, one very posh New York hotel had a Presidential Suite that was in the $35,000 range. Crazy.

Anna walked around, carefully examining each piece of furniture. As she looked, she noted which parts of this room might be problematic in regard to housekeeping. She knew that these expensive suites attracted a very different sort of clientele. On one hand, these guests expected elegant perfection fit for royalty — on the other hand, they could totally trash a place like this in just one wild night.

At some point before the hotel opened, she would need to come back up here to make a careful list and take some photos. Then she'd need to see what kind of backup plan they had for replacing the items that might not survive a rock star's rampage. This beautiful white couch, for instance.

Was there a way it could be slipcovered in an emergency? She hoped it had been treated for stain resistance. The area carpet was gorgeous in pale tones of blue and beige hopefully they had a spare similar carpet stored somewhere in case this one needed to go out for cleaning. She would have to check on that. Did this discourage her? Not at all. These were just the kinds of challenges she welcomed — situations that required some thinking and planning on her part.

She decided to explore the second floor first. An elegant staircase led up to a comfortable "home theater" with enough seating for eight people. Beyond this room she found a seating nook with two easy chairs and a wall of bookshelves. Connecting to this, she discovered a small but very adequate bedroom, complete with its own bath. It was probably considered a guest room and would be used only rarely.

She went back downstairs to check out the master bedroom, discovering that there were two, separated by the luxurious living area. Since one of the rooms had a superior view of the river, she suspected it was the true master suite. Even without the bed linens and with some pieces of furniture missing, she could imagine how grand this room would look. With an elegant yet peaceful color scheme of pale blue, ivory, and gold, it was truly going to be fit for royalty.

The bathroom was enormous and equally elegant with a perfect palette of white marble floors and wainscot, silver fixtures, black tile accents, and pale blue walls rising up to a very high ceiling with wide crown molding. A couple of well-placed massive antiques and a pale blue velvet fainting lounge added to the old-world elegance, yet its oversized jet tub promised spa-like relaxation. All it needed was an attractive towel shelf, maybe an antique, stocked with thick white towels and scrumptious toiletries and placed close enough that the pampered bather could easily reach it from the tub.

Anna was just about to exit the luxurious bathroom when she heard the sound of strained voices in the main room. They weren't actually loud, but the tones suggested a disagreement of some kind. She didn't want to walk in on them — that would be embarrassing for everyone. Yet she didn't like the idea of being stuck here, almost as if she were eavesdropping. What could she do?

"Since when do I need *your* permission," Mrs. Newman was saying. "I thought we were partners."

"We *are* partners," the male voice responded. Anna knew it must be Mr. Newman. "Partners are supposed to communicate with each other, Denise."

"You didn't communicate with me when you decided *not* to hire her. Why should I communicate with you when I decided *to* hire her?"

Anna gasped. Were they arguing about her?

"Perhaps there was a reason I *didn't* hire her."

"Such as?"

"This isn't the time or place," he said more quietly, almost as if aware she was behind the partially open door. She stepped back even farther, holding her breath and hoping they were finished and that they'd get back to whatever they were doing up here.

"I disagree, Vincent. There's no time like the present. Are you saying you don't trust me? You don't think I'm a good judge of character?"

He chuckled. "Yes, dear, I think you're a marvelous judge of character. You picked me, didn't you?"

"Then why are you questioning me about this?"

"You left me out of the loop, Denise. And

to be perfectly frank, it just doesn't feel like you thought it through very carefully."

"You mean like how you carefully *thought through* the young man you just hired — without consulting me?"

"He comes with fantastic references, Denise. And you already met him last week. As I recall, you were fairly impressed. Remember?"

"But you didn't even ask me if I approved."

"Well, I guess we're even then."

"Okay then. I don't want to hear another word about it."

"Still friends?" he asked quietly.

There was a short quiet spell, and Anna hoped that perhaps they were hugging — making up. She hated to think that she'd been something they'd fight over. Even more than that, she hated to think that Mr. Newman was opposed to her working for them. She would prove to him that his wife hadn't made a mistake. She would prove that despite her unimpressive references, she was worth taking a risk on. She would show them she was a keeper. Even if she had to work night and day, seven days a week, she would do what it took to surpass their expectations.

Suddenly Mrs. Newman started to giggle.

"What's so funny?" her husband asked in a slightly indignant tone.

"I was just thinking, maybe I do approve of your choice for our head manager after all. Now that I think about it, that young fellow was very easy on the eyes. Dreamy, in fact."

"Oh, brother." Mr. Newman made an irritated groan. "Try not to drool all over that new Persian carpet, okay?"

"I'm just saying . . ."

"I've got to go, Denise. Our new manager is already on his way over here. I promised to meet with him to go over some things."

"Tell him hello for me," Mrs. Newman called out in a good-natured, teasing tone.

Anna remained behind the door, listening as Mr. Newman made his exit and then as Mrs. Newman started to joke with another woman — probably the designer, Valerie — about the hot manager her husband had just hired. Satisfied that they wouldn't know she'd heard their whole conversation, Anna eventually meandered out of the bathroom. She checked out the second master bedroom, seeing that although it wasn't completely furnished yet, it was nearly as nice as the first master. Then she went out to where Mrs. Newman and the designer were intently discussing something in the kitchen.

"The penthouse is beautiful," Anna said as she joined them. "This kitchen is fabulous too."

Mrs. Newman introduced her to the designer. "Well, it will be even more fabulous when this is fixed." She pointed to the pale granite that topped the large island. "See this crack?"

Anna leaned forward to peer at the gleaming surface, observing that it was marred by a fine line. "Oh, yeah. That's too bad."

"The challenge is that we can't get this exact same granite," Valerie said sadly. "To match the other counters." She waved her hand behind her.

"Does it have to match?" Anna asked. "I mean, you often see something different on an island."

"That's the obvious solution," Mrs. Newman said a bit irately. "One we'd like to avoid."

Valerie slid a pair of very similar-looking granite samples in front of Anna. "These are the options."

"Valerie likes one of them, and I like the other." Mrs. Newman turned to Anna. "Let's pretend you're the tiebreaker, Anna. Which one do you prefer?"

Feeling like she was taking a test, Anna

studied the two pieces of stone. One was cream colored with veins of gold. The other was cream colored with shiny metallic flecks, also of gold color. She mentally compared these with the dark walnut kitchen cabinets. "I like this one." She pointed to the piece with the gold veins.

"Aha!" Mrs. Newman picked up that piece. "That is why I hired you, Anna. You agree with me." She handed it to Valerie. "This is our choice."

Feeling almost like she'd won the lottery, Anna beamed at her new boss. "I think it might even be prettier than the original granite." She pointed to the existing countertop. "More classic and timeless looking."

Mrs. Newman patted Anna on the back. "Feel free to keep looking around the hotel, Anna. Get a feel for the place. I'll expect to see you here Monday morning at 9:00." She pointed to Anna's suit. "Eventually you'll be in uniform, but it's okay to dress casually for a few days. Think comfort. And walking shoes. We have a lot of ground to cover next week."

"Sounds great." Anna smiled brightly. "Thanks again for giving me the chance to prove myself to you."

"I have high expectations," Mrs. Newman said in a no-nonsense tone.

"I won't let you down." Anna told them both good-bye and, feeling a mixture of excitement and nerves, let herself out of the penthouse suite. Because she suspected there were surveillance cameras running in the hallway, she controlled herself from doing a Snoopy happy dance as she waited for the service elevator.

Remembering Mrs. Newman's invitation to look around, Anna decided to check out some of the guests' floors on her way down. She stopped on the ninth floor, but seeing no one around and all the doors closed, she went on down to the next and then the next. Finally, on the fifth floor, she discovered signs of life. Seeing some of the guest room doors open, she decided to sneak a peek.

The first one had workers doing some installations. Seeing a housekeeping cart in front of another open door, Anna decided to investigate. She poked her head into the room to spy a pair of women making up the king-sized bed. Suspecting they were some of the maids that had already been hired, Anna approached to introduce herself.

"Can we help you?" a short, stout, gray-haired woman said in a slightly abrupt tone.

"Are you lost?" the other one asked.

"No, I'm just looking around. Are you maids?"

The short woman rolled her eyes as she fluffed a pillow. "Well, we ain't doing this for the exercise."

"I'm sorry," Anna said. "My name is Anna Gordon, and I've just been hired as head of housekeeping."

Both the woman sort of came to attention, as if they were being called on the carpet. "I'm Velma Martellini," the older one said. "This is Cindy Snider."

Anna shook their hands. "Pleased to meet you both."

"What can we do for you, Ms. Gordon?" Velma asked respectfully.

"I just wanted to see a room," Anna explained. "I don't mean to interrupt your work. I saw the door open and thought I'd check it out. I was just meeting with Mrs. Newman and she encouraged me to look around. I don't officially start work until Monday."

"Feel free to look," Velma told her.

"The rooms are real pretty," Cindy said as she smoothed a white sheet. "I never saw linens this nice before. Really first class all the way."

Anna walked around, checking out all the details of the well-appointed room. She examined the layers of curtains on the big window, the pair of comfy-looking easy chairs and ottoman, the small dining table and matching chairs, the lovely reproduction pieces of old-world style furnishings here and there, the rich-looking paintings, the luxurious linens. The room was perfection. She went into the bathroom, admiring the lavish use of travertine going halfway up the walls. Instead of a tub, there was a roomy walk-in shower with a pair of showerheads. Everything was clean and new and fresh looking. It would fall upon her shoulders to ensure that it remained this way — all sixty rooms plus the penthouse suites. Was she really up to the task? She had promised not to let Mrs. Newman down — and she intended to keep that promise.

"Excuse me," she said as she exited the bathroom. "Have you been instructed on how to clean the travertine in the shower yet?"

Velma frowned. "No. Does it need cleaning? No one's even used it yet."

"I mean for the future." Anna smiled. "I know some of these surfaces require special products. I was just curious if you'd been informed about it."

"No one told us how to clean it," Cindy told her. "I guess you'll have to do that."

Anna smiled. "Yes, of course. You keep up

the good work. I'll see you on Monday. Don't worry, we'll have meetings and classes and things. I want all my maids to fully understand what's expected."

"A lot of maids don't speak English," Velma told her.

"Yes, I expect that. I'm sure we can figure things out." Anna headed for the door. "See you next week."

As Anna rode the service elevator down to the housekeeping area, she felt relieved to see how different these New York maids were from the ones she'd left behind at the Value Lodge. Oh, she knew that could all change overnight — especially if the housekeeping staff was mismanaged. But she intended to do her best to keep her relationships with them professional and positive and productive. Another kind of three *P*s. She should probably make note of this. Perhaps she should carry a notepad with her. As she went to her new office, she remembered the iPad she'd purchased to use on the job at the Value Lodge. Her plan had been to install handy apps on it to make notes and all sorts of useful things. Of course, it hadn't taken her long to realize she had little need for such efficiency there. Thankfully, she'd brought the device with her to New York. Once she charged it up, she'd start putting it to use.

11

Anna was just leaving her new office when she heard the sounds of male voices coming her way. Thinking it was some of the maintenance guys and looking forward to getting to know all the employees on a friendly first-name basis, she waited in the hallway. To her surprise, it was Mr. Newman and a tall man in a dark suit.

"Miss Gordon," Mr. Newman said cheerfully when he got closer. "I hear that my wife has placed you on staff. Congratulations, and welcome to the team." He reached out to shake her hand. "Now may I introduce you to our new head manager, Sean O'Neil."

Anna felt her eyes growing wide as she stared at the young man by Mr. Newman's side. "Actually, I believe we've already met," she confessed.

"Really?" Sean tilted his head to one side. "When was that?"

"Oh, that's right." Mr. Newman nodded. "You're both friends of Max Ferris. I almost forgot about that. Small world, isn't it?"

"Actually, I'm friends with Max's sister Marley," Anna corrected. "But I remember Sean from growing up in Springville — back when he and Max were friends."

"You're Anna Gordon," Sean exclaimed as he grasped her hand, firmly shaking it. "Yes, I do remember you. My apologies." He tipped his head with what felt like approval. "But you must admit that you've changed some, Anna. Grown up a lot since the last time I saw you."

She made a shy smile. "So have you — I mean, changed some. Although as I recall, you were always tall." The truth was, he looked surprisingly similar to how she remembered him. He was still incredibly handsome — just more refined and polished in his stylish charcoal suit, crisp white shirt, and burgundy tie. Sean O'Neil, with his wavy brown hair and sparkling blue eyes, still had the kind of looks that would make some girls weak in the knees. Obviously, he had caught Mrs. Newman's eye.

"Well, it's great to see you again. I'm glad you'll be on my team." Sean beamed at her, giving her the feeling that he really meant it.

Anna braced herself as she took in a quick, steadying breath. "It's good to see you again too, Sean. Congratulations on the job." She was trying hard to act natural, as if it didn't sting a little that this good-looking small-town boy had actually beat her out of the job of head manager. Or had she beat herself out of it by having no references? Really, she should simply be thankful she even had a job.

"Thank you, Anna. I interviewed with Mr. Newman earlier this week. I was eagerly waiting to hear back from him."

"I had to finish interviewing the other candidates," Mr. Newman clarified.

"I was so relieved to get the phone call this morning." Sean grinned at his new boss, then looked back at Anna. "Since I'm staying nearby, I rushed right in to fill out the paperwork." He laughed as he nudged Mr. Newman with an elbow. "I guess I was afraid you might change your mind."

Mr. Newman chuckled. "No worries there, Sean. I talked to your previous boss on Thursday — by the way, he begged me *not* to hire you."

"Not to hire him?" Anna felt confused.

"That's right." Mr. Newman winked at Sean. "Mr. Donnell even asked me to send you packing back to Ireland."

"Ireland?" Anna asked.

"I managed a boutique hotel in Dublin," Sean explained to her. "A little bigger than the Rothsberg, but not nearly as nice. It was actually pretty run-down when I went to work there four years ago."

"Your previous boss told me that you played a big part in rescuing that hotel." Mr. Newman patted Sean on the back. "I expect great things from you, son."

"And I expect great things from the Rothsberg. I can't wait to get to work." He turned back to Anna. "I don't officially start until Monday. How about you?"

His enthusiasm was contagious. "Same here. It is exciting, isn't it?"

He nodded. "Here we are, two small-town kids who grew up together, working for this outstanding New York hotel." Sean turned back to Mr. Newman. "Go figure."

"Max is the one who told me about Anna," Mr. Newman explained.

"Our buddy Max should get a headhunter's fee," Sean teased.

"Well, Max and I have become good friends. I'd told him how I hoped to get some applicants from beyond the New York pool."

"Did you get a managerial job too?" Sean asked Anna.

"That's right." Although she was grateful that Mr. Newman hadn't told Sean that she'd interviewed for the job that he had just snagged, she wasn't that eager to admit she'd been hired as head of housekeeping. Still, she reminded herself, it was better than nothing, and it was a start. "Mrs. Newman hired me as head of housekeeping," she confessed. "My degree is in business management and hospitality, but I don't have nearly as much experience as you. I'm still building my résumé."

"Excellent," he said. "It'll be great experience for you. As head manager, I can assure you there's no position more important to me than the head of housekeeping. It makes my job easier to know the maids are being managed efficiently."

Anna knew he meant this as a compliment, but a small part of her felt slightly offended. As absurd as it was, she couldn't help feeling he was looking down on her. "Well, it's good to know that the hotel will be in such capable hands, Sean." She made a polite smile. "I look forward to working with you." She excused herself and ducked back into her office as they continued on the tour Mr. Newman was conducting.

Okay, she had absolutely no reason to return to her office, but it was a place to make a quick retreat. After waiting about ten minutes to be sure they'd continued merrily on their way, she finally slipped out. Seeing no one around, she hurried toward the employees' exit that Mrs. Newman had shown her earlier.

Anna had no idea why it galled her that Sean had been hired as the head manager, but it did. Truly, he had far more experience. Plus he had come with high praises after turning around a boutique hotel in Dublin, Ireland. Oh, if only she had something like that to her credit. Besides his stellar professional references, Sean seemed incredibly sure of himself. Not an arrogant, obnoxious sort of sureness either. In his defense, he had an easy kind of confidence — a charming, likeable quality. An especially good quality in a hotel manager. Obviously, he was the best man for the job. Even so, it irked her. And then it irked her that it irked her.

As she walked back to the apartment, she analyzed her antagonistic feelings toward Sean O'Neil. Why was she so aggravated at the handsome young man? What had he done to deserve such resentment? By the time she was putting in the security code to the apartment building, she thought she knew the answer. It was simply because he was the kind of guy that everything came to so easily. Sean had always been attractive and athletic and admired. As Anna unlocked the door to the apartment, she wryly considered those three *A*s. Sean could've been the president of his own triple-A club.

Sean O'Neil had lived a charmed life. Although his family wasn't wealthy, they did own a successful tire business in Springville, and from what Anna could tell, they lived comfortably. The O'Neils had always been well liked and respected. As had Sean. Anna felt fairly sure that about half the girls in her high school had been secretly crushing on Sean O'Neil. Certainly she and Marley had, but being three years younger, they'd never really had a chance.

Anna kicked off her shoes and sat down on the love seat, pondering whether or not it was long enough to sleep comfortably on. But instead of testing out the love seat, Anna continued obsessing over Sean. She was still ruminating over how some people — like Sean O'Neil — just seem to be born under a lucky star. From what Anna had observed back in high school, whatever Sean had wanted had come his way, whether it was sports or girls or even the car he drove. Sean had been the golden boy. So why was it surprising that he could waltz in and take the job that Anna had so desperately longed for? Oh, that's right, he had references. From Dublin, Ireland, no less, where he'd turned a hotel around. That had probably come easily to him as well. How silly was it for her to be this jealous?

"Hello there." A tall, blonde woman dressed in a short, silky pink robe emerged from the bathroom. "You must be Marley's friend. Emma?"

"Anna." She smiled. "I got in yesterday afternoon. No one was here, so I've kind of just made myself at home. Hope you don't mind."

"Not at all. I'm Sophie." She sat down on the love seat, picking up a fashion magazine from the cluttered coffee table and casually flipping through it. "Kara and I share the other bedroom. She's already left for work. I don't have a flight until tomorrow night. So I'm just vegging out today."

"I just interviewed for a job at the Rothsberg hotel," Anna told her.

Sophie looked over the top of her magazine. "How'd that go?"

"I got the job," Anna said brightly. Of course, even as she said this, she realized that she hadn't gotten *the* job. Just *a* job. A job managing maids.

"Congratulations!" Sophie gave her a

thumbs-up. "It looks like it's going to be a pretty swanky hotel. What'll you be doing there?"

Anna explained about being head of housekeeping. "It's a managerial position," she told her. "It will look good on my résumé. Maybe someday I'll get a higher-level management job, but for now, I'm happy just to have a job."

"Yeah. You were lucky to get it on the same day you applied. That doesn't always happen. Not in this city."

"That reminds me, I promised to call Marley with the news." Anna extracted her phone from her purse and headed to the bedroom for privacy. First she called her grandmother. "Your prayers worked," she cheerfully announced.

"You got the job!" Grandma exclaimed.

"Yes, well, it wasn't exactly the job I was interviewing for —"

"But it's in management?"

"Yes. Absolutely."

"Oh, honey, I'm so happy for you. To think our little Anna is going to work for a fancy hotel in New York City. Oh, I can't wait to tell my friends. They'll be so impressed. Especially after they've heard about you being let go from the Value Lodge." Grandma laughed. "Next time I run into Sharon or Rich, I'll just casually let it drop that you're working for a fancy-schmancy New York hotel. That'll get their goat."

Anna described the penthouse suite in detail to her grandmother. By the time she finished, Grandma was even more impressed than she'd been earlier. "I'll send you photos," Anna promised. "Maybe after I've been here awhile, you can come out and visit and stay in one of the rooms."

"Imagine me staying in some swanky New York hotel." She chuckled. "When do you start work?"

"I promised to go in on Monday."

"You go to work on Monday? But aren't you coming home on Tuesday?"

"I might have to change my flight. It sounds like they're going to be super busy the next couple weeks. They plan to open in late June."

"Goodness, that's just around the corner."

"I know."

"What about your clothes and things? Do you need anything?"

Anna considered this. "I'm not sure. I'll have a uniform for work, but I still might want a few things."

"Well, you just make me a list and I'll send them to you."

"Thanks."

"Where will you stay?"

Anna looked around the tiny bedroom. "I'm not sure. Marley said I could sleep on their couch for a while."

"Well, that's something you're used to doing. But I do hope you find better accommodations eventually. Maybe they'll let you stay at the hotel."

"I doubt that. But don't worry. Something will work out. I'm just so happy to have a job. I still have the rest of today and all of tomorrow to see a bit of the city too."

"You'll have your days off to explore too," Grandma pointed out.

"That's right." Despite her earlier reservations, Anna's joy returned to her. "I'll become a real New Yorker."

They talked awhile longer, then Anna said she should call Marley with the good news. "I really owe her a big thank-you for telling me about the job and everything."

They said good-bye and Anna called Marley. "I don't want to disturb you at work," she said quickly. "But I promised you I'd call."

"That's okay. I'm due for a break. What's up?"

Anna shared her news, and Marley let out a little whoop of joy. "This is going to be fabulous, Anna. You and me in New York together. I can't wait to get back there."

"How's your mom?"

"Much better. She's actually here at the café today. I told her that I might even see if I can move my flight to tomorrow evening. Flying standby on a Sunday night is usually pretty doable. I wouldn't mind getting home with a couple of vacation days still left."

"You're not going to believe who I ran into today."

"You mean besides the Newmans?"

"Yes. Besides them."

"Let's see . . . My brother? Elsie?"

"No. Although I did meet Elsie yesterday. She's sweet."

"Who then?"

"Do you remember Sean O'Neil?"

"Are you kidding? Of course I remember him. For years I imagined myself walking down the aisle with him. Sometimes I still entertain that daydream." She laughed. "Last I heard, Max said he was living in Ireland. Dublin, I think. In fact, I'd been hoping to be on a flight that got laid over there — I was going to look him up."

"Well, he's not in Ireland anymore."

"Tell me!" she exclaimed. "Where is he?"

"He's going to be working at the Rothsberg."

"No way!"

Anna held the phone away from her ear as Marley let out a happy squeal. "Seriously, our Sean O'Neil? The guy I used to practice writing 'Mrs. Sean O'Neil' for?"

"That's the one."

"Max never even told me. The dirty rat."

"Maybe he didn't know. Sean just got hired today. Like me."

"So you're going to be working with Sean?"

"Well, we're both managers." Anna hadn't told Marley yet that she was in charge of housekeeping. Not that she was hiding this . . . but there was no hurry.

"Maybe you can put in a good word for me, Anna. I mean, if Sean's single. Is he single?"

Anna frowned. "I honestly don't know. For some reason I just assumed that he was. I mean, I didn't look for a ring or anything. Who knows? He could be with someone. I mean, he's the same age as Max, so it's possible he's married too."

"No, no. He can't be. He's got to be single," Marley insisted. "Tell me he's single. Please."

Anna laughed. "Well, just because I tell you he is doesn't mean that he is."

"Is he still as good-looking as in high

school? Or has he gone bald and gotten a beer belly from drinking all that Irish Guinness?"

"He still has his hair and his waistline."

"Oh, good."

"I actually think he might've gotten better looking."

"Oh, Anna, you're killing me. Now I can't wait to get home."

"Hey, is there any way you could check a suitcase for me when you come?"

"Sure, why not?"

"I'm supposed to start work on Monday, so I probably need to change my return flight too. Do you think that'll be a problem?"

"No. I mean, they might charge you a little, but I'll handle it for you while I'm at the airport tomorrow. We'll just leave it open-ended."

"I told Grandma I'd give her a list of things I might need. She offered to mail them, but —"

"Tell her I'll pick them up tomorrow. Probably in the afternoon."

Anna thanked her. "It'll save her from having to take it to the post office."

"No problem. They might even let me check it for free."

"Great. Already I'm wishing I'd packed a

few more pieces of clothing."

"Well, my closet is next to the bed. Like I told you, feel free to use whatever you need."

"Thanks. I'll let Grandma know you're coming."

"This is so exciting, Anna. We're going to have such fun in New York together."

"I hope your offer to sleep on your couch is still good."

"Totally. And as often as the girls are in the air, you can probably have a bed a lot of the time."

"Thanks, Marley. I owe you."

"Well, you can pay me back by finding out everything you can about Sean. First of all, find out if he's single. If he is, I'll see if I can get Elsie to throw a dinner party soon. Maybe next weekend. Naturally Max will want to invite Sean. And us too. Maybe the Newmans can come, just to make it bigger and more festive."

"Sounds fun." But as Anna listened to Marley making plans for Sean's future, she started feeling uneasy. Oh, she knew Marley was kidding about scheduling her wedding date and how some of the best venues were booked years in advance. But not that long ago, Marley had told Anna they could get an apartment together eventually. Anna had been looking forward to it. What if Marley really did catch Sean's eye and they did get engaged — and married?

Anna was experiencing another disturbing emotion. She didn't even quite get what it was at first. But by the time she dropped her phone back in her purse, she knew it was jealousy. Plain old green-eyed envy. And that was perfectly ridiculous. She had no right to feel jealous. For one thing, Sean and Marley weren't even a couple. Besides that, it wasn't as if she'd had any real interest in Sean. Well, other than admiring him from afar. Like Mrs. Newman said, he was awfully nice to look at.

All these things aside, Anna knew that Sean had never shown any serious interest in her. She was surprised that he'd even remembered her name. Today when he'd seemed so enthused and attentive, she knew that he was just being polite. Professionally polite. Nothing more to it. There was absolutely no reason for her to feel jealous of Marley's "big plans" for Sean O'Neil.

Besides all that — and probably more importantly — Anna and Sean were co-workers now. And everyone knew that co-workers were not supposed to get involved with each other. She grimaced to remember Mickey and Shawna at the Value Lodge —

what a disaster their on-again, off-again relationship had been. No, it seemed perfectly clear, if anyone should go after Sean — if he really was single — it made sense that it would be Marley. Really, wouldn't that be advantageous for everyone — Marley snagging her big brother's old best buddy? How handy!

12

Anna changed into comfortable clothes and, armed with a walking map, set out to see some sights in Lower Manhattan. She wasn't sure about exploring by herself, but once she got outside and walking around, she felt perfectly safe. Anna suspected that the sunny Saturday afternoon had lured a lot of people out of doors today. It felt good to be out among them. She started her walking tour by exploring the Greenwich Village neighborhood surrounding the apartment. She took her time, pausing to study the various forms of amazing architecture and taking numerous photos with her phone.

Eventually she looped back around, going, she hoped, toward the SoHo district. She was curious as to whether she could find the Rothsberg without using her map. Eventually she got confused and feared she was lost. Oh, she knew she could grab a taxi if necessary. Instead, she asked for directions and to her delight discovered that she was actually fairly close, although she had been turned around. Perhaps she needed to walk with a compass in hand.

When she finally got back into familiar territory, spotting the Rothsberg from a short distance, she noticed a charming little Italian café. Tired and hungry, she decided to take a break. "May I have a table outside?" she asked the hostess.

"How many in your party?"

"Just me," she said apologetically.

Although the café was busy, Anna was soon seated at a tiny bistro table down on the edge of the dining area. That was fine with her. She mostly wanted a chance to sit down and catch her breath. She'd been hoofing it over the pavement for close to four hours and was ready for a break. Even though the waitress seemed to have no interest in coming to take her order, Anna didn't care. It felt so good to be here in New York, sitting outside like this, watching the people going on their way, enjoying themselves and this gorgeous day — it was all good. Life was good. New York was going to be her new home, and she even had a job. Who cared if it wasn't her dream job? It was a great job in a great hotel. Far better than where she'd been just days ago.

She felt amazed to think how little time had passed since she'd been stuck at the Value Lodge. That all seemed like another lifetime to her now. Well, she decided, it actually was another lifetime, because she was a totally different person now. A person with a future and with all of New York stretched out before her like a big, fat, happy promise. She felt a tiny bit silly sitting there with a big smile on her face, but she couldn't help herself. Everything felt so right. So perfect.

"Anna?"

She looked up to see a man in jeans and a T-shirt, a Yankees ball cap, and aviator sunglasses peering down at her. Squinting into the bright light behind him, she tried to determine who he was. When he grinned, it hit her. "Sean?"

"Yeah." He nodded as he flipped up his shades. "Sorry to sneak up on you like this."

"I didn't recognize you." She made a nervous smile.

He laughed, pointing to his hat. "Playing the tourist this afternoon."

"Yes." She nodded. "So am I. I mean, I was. I'm taking a break now."

"Sounds like a great idea." He pointed to her empty table. "Just finishing up?"

"Actually I haven't even been waited on yet." She shrugged. "Not that I mind. I'm just enjoying the ambiance."

He nodded, studying her with interest. "Meeting someone?"

"No."

He seemed pleased with that. "Want any company?"

She blinked. "Uh, yeah, sure. Why not?"

Just like that, he pulled out the chair next to her and sat down. "I'm starving," he said as she handed him her menu. "I've been sightseeing all afternoon. Mostly on foot."

"Me too," she confessed. "I actually got a little lost. At least I thought I was lost. I was really just a few blocks from here." She laughed. "I think I might need a compass."

"That's not a bad idea." He handed her back the menu.

As they waited for the waitress, they compared notes on what they'd seen. When Sean discovered her interest in architecture, he told her she had to get to West Tenth Street. "There's this row of great townhouses that were built in the mid-1800s. Designed by James Renwick Jr. and really worth seeing."

She pulled out her map, and he pointed out where they were. "It's a bit of a walk from here. Especially if you've already had a long day."

They paused as a waiter came to take their drink orders, promising that their waitress would take their food orders soon. After he left, Sean told Anna about visiting the site of the Triangle Shirtwaist Factory fire. "I'm still feeling slightly haunted by the photo images of the victims." He slowly shook his head. "Really gruesome."

"That factory fire sounds familiar, but I don't really recall the details."

"The fire happened in 1911. On a Saturday afternoon. Not so unlike today. It was one of the deadliest industrial disasters in the history of New York City. One hundred forty-six garment workers — mostly young women — died in that fire."

"How tragic."

"And unnecessary. Exits were locked. The owners claimed it was because of problems with theft." He scowled. "But even the stairwells were blocked. The workers never had a chance to escape. Many plunged to their deaths out of the windows, if you can imagine."

"That's horrible."

"I know. It's a good reminder to me as a hotel manager of how important it is to take the city's fire and safety codes seriously."

"Yeah . . . absolutely." She hated to

imagine what it would be like if there were a fire at the Rothsberg. "Surely the Newmans have done everything right."

"I have no doubt about that. I'm sure they've passed all their inspections too. Just the same, I think I'll check it out for myself. Just part of the job, you know."

"Of course." She nodded solemnly.

His serious expression warmed up as their drinks were set down. "Sorry to sound so gloomy," he said quietly. "I didn't mean to bring you down, Anna. I guess it was just weighing on me. My apologies."

"It's okay. It's actually rather interesting to hear about it." She didn't want to admit this, but she was impressed that Sean had immediately applied his fire safety concerns to the hotel. No doubt, he really was the best man for the job.

"The upside of the Triangle Shirtwaist Factory tragedy is that the laws changed afterward. Public sympathy put serious pressure on the city, and conditions for workers slowly improved. Plus the garment workers came together to form a union."

"Well, that's something." As she studied him, she realized there was a lot more to this guy than what met the eye. He wasn't just a pretty face.

Their conversation paused as the waitress

finally arrived to take their orders. By then Anna had completely forgotten what she'd wanted. She apologized as she grabbed up the menu again, quickly scanning it while Sean placed his order.

"Oh, that's right." She pointed to what she'd decided on earlier. "I'll have the pesto linguini with scallops."

The waitress grinned at Sean like they were sharing a private joke. "You're both having the same thing then?"

Anna handed her the menu. "Yeah, I guess so."

"You want the house dressing on your salad too?"

Anna nodded. "Thank you."

"Thank *you.*" The waitress winked. "For making it easy."

Anna knew it was silly to feel embarrassed by this. "That was really what I was planning on having," she explained to Sean. "I was so focused on the menu that I didn't even hear you ordering it."

"Hey, I think it's pretty cool that we like the same thing." He lifted his drink glass like a toast. "Here's to fellow employees with similar tastes."

She clinked her glass against his and smiled. Sean was so different than she'd imagined him before — back in high school.

As a young teen she'd always thought of him as removed and superior and unattainable, almost like a rock star. But seeing him like this, well, he was so warm and easygoing, so friendly and approachable, that she felt taken slightly off guard.

They continued talking about the sights to be seen in New York. Since Sean had been there a few days longer than Anna, he had lots of suggestions. "But I don't want to try and see everything at once," he finally said. "I want to spread it out. Some things, like the Museum of Modern Art, will take some time."

"Yes, I'm really looking forward to that myself."

"Well, if we ever have the same day off, maybe we can see it together."

She wasn't sure how to react to this, so she simply nodded, then pretended to be distracted by a pair of young parents who were wheeling a stroller past them. Inside was a fussing infant, and the man was tugging a reluctant toddler, plus they had a small dog on a leash. "Looks like they have their hands full," she commented.

Sean nodded with a furrowed brow. "That reminds me. I want to ask Vincent about something." He pulled out his iPhone and made a note. He looked back at her. "I'd be interested in your opinion too, Anna."

In an instant, her mind spun in several directions. She was impressed with how he was so focused on the Rothsberg, and she was flattered that he cared about her opinion, but more than these and more disturbing, she was curious as to why he was already calling Mr. Newman by his first name.

"I've noticed there are a lot of young families around and about the city." He peered at her. "Have you noticed that too?"

She considered this. "Now that you mention it."

"I think of SoHo as kind of a young, hip neighborhood. People who come to visit here are too."

She just nodded, wondering what he was getting at.

"But the Rothsberg has this traditional old-world elegance, you know?"

"Yes. Absolutely."

"I was trying to figure out, where do noisy children and perhaps even dogs fit into that picture?"

"Good question." She frowned to imagine unsupervised children and dogs racing about the lobby. "Do they?"

"Well, they're part of our culture. Do you

know how many American households have pets?"

She shook her head.

"Last time I checked, it was more than half."

"Wow. That's significant."

He looked at her. "Do you have a pet?"

She sadly shook her head, remembering a mutt she'd found on the street when she was about ten. She'd named him Bingo and brought him home. "I wanted a dog once, but I lived with my grandparents and my grandfather had allergies, so I never did get to have one."

"Too bad. We always had pets in our house. Even when I was in college, I adopted a homeless cat. My parents kept him while I was in Ireland. Someday, if I get a place where I can have pets, I'll bring him here."

She tried to imagine Sean with a cat. "What does he look like?"

He slowly smiled. "He's a great big tiger-striped cat. Everyone who knows him agrees that he's got the laid-back personality of a dog, though. His name is Burt."

"Sounds sweet."

"Anyway, here's what I'm thinking in regard to the Rothsberg, Anna." Suddenly he was leaning toward her, outlining a plan where the hotel would have an entire floor dedicated to children and pets. He explained how the staff would cater to their young and furry guests, making their visits as pleasant as possible, and all without interrupting the serenity of the other guests. But all Anna could really think about was how it sounded when Sean had said her name. "What do you think?" He waited for her response.

"It's a really great idea," she conceded. "Brilliant, in fact."

He beamed at her. "Really? You think so?"

"Absolutely."

"Cool." He nodded eagerly. "If we do this, I'll need housekeeping to back me on it, because it might require extra work on the staff's part. We would add an extra security deposit to cover damages or cleaning expenses."

Their food arrived, and as they ate their pasta, the conversation continued. It was relaxed and interesting and amazingly fun. As they were finishing up, Anna remembered her promise to Marley — to determine if Sean was single. Everything about him, including his conversation and lack of a ring, seemed to suggest he was not in a relationship. Even so, she was determined to find out.

"This has been so much fun," she said as

a waiter was clearing their table. "So unexpected."

"Thank you for letting me crash in on you."

"Yes, you crashed my party of one." She laughed. "The truth is, I always find it a little uncomfortable eating by myself at a restaurant."

"Not me," he said. "I like watching people. Sometimes I pretend to be reading, but I'm really secretly studying the folks around me. I think it helps me in managing hotels."

"Interesting." Anna could see how this actually would be a smart practice, perhaps even something she should try. "Do you eat by yourself a lot?"

He chuckled. "Well, I'm not exactly a hermit. I like eating with people too."

"You know, I would've thought someone like you would've been snatched up by now." She felt her cheeks warming. "I mean, I know your buddy Max just got married."

Sean's countenance seemed to fall now.

"I'm sorry," she said quickly. "I don't know why I suddenly got so nosy." She laid her napkin on the table. "It's none of my business." She almost added that the only reason she asked was because of Marley's interest, but she knew that wasn't the smartest thing to admit.

"It's okay." He set his napkin on the table too. "The truth is, I was in a relationship . . . in Ireland . . . but it just didn't work out how I'd planned."

"Oh." She felt terrible now. Like she'd just ripped off a bandage, exposing a wound that had yet to heal. "I'm sorry."

"Really, it's okay." He waved his hand. "It's because of . . . her . . . that I'm here in New York. I always wanted to live here." He paused as the waitress returned, setting their bill in the center of the table. "And here I am." Without missing a beat, Sean picked up the leather-covered folder and flipped it open.

"Here." Anna handed him her debit card. "Since we had the same thing, they can easily split it in half."

He pushed her card away. "No, Anna. I crashed in on you, and you were good enough to listen to me prattling on about my ideas for the hotel. This is my treat." He studied the bill, then slid in his own card.

Anna continued to protest, but he wouldn't back down, insisting that the waitress take only his card. "Thank you," he said cheerfully to the waitress. "Don't let us waste any more of your time on our little disagreement."

"All right." Anna slipped her card back

into the pocket of her mini-purse. "Next time is my treat."

He grinned at her. "You got it."

Of course, now she registered what she'd just done — insinuate that they would do this again. Did he think she was asking him out? "Well, thank you," she said primly. "It was a delicious meal."

"It was." He chuckled. "Thanks for recommending this place."

She couldn't help but laugh.

The waitress returned quickly. Seeing the café now had a waiting line of customers, Anna realized she was eager to reseat this table. Sean quickly signed the receipt, adding a tip, and they both stood.

"I really enjoyed this," Anna told him as they moved over to the edge of the sidewalk. "The truth is, I was just starting to feel a little bit lonely."

"I know." He looked up and down the sidewalk. "Which way are you walking?"

She pointed to the right.

"Mind if I stroll with you a ways?"

"Not at all." She felt slightly giddy now, incredulous that Sean O'Neil was actually walking her home. Back in high school she probably would've passed out over the prospects. But as quickly as the light-headed feeling came over her, she shoved it down, burying it deep. They were simply co-workers — kids who'd grown up in the same town together. "It's nice that you have Max here," Anna said as they walked.

"Yes, but I've been trying not to take too much of his time. After all, they're still kind of like newlyweds, you know?"

"I guess, but I'm sure Max likes having you here." She told him about Marley and how she was working as a flight attendant and sharing an apartment with three other girls. "It's pretty tight. Marley said she might consider getting an apartment with me after I've worked here awhile. In the meantime, I might be sleeping on their couch."

"That's what I'm doing right now," Sean confessed. "Max introduced me to a buddy of his. He's got a tiny apartment over on Worth Street."

"Amazing what people will sacrifice just to live and work in this city," Anna said with wonder. "But I believe it will be worth it in time." She shook her head. "What am I saying? It's already worth it. I couldn't be happier."

"Really?" He slowed down his steps, peering curiously at her. "Not even if you'd been offered the head manager's job?"

She grimaced. "Did Mr. Newman tell you

about that?"

"Just in passing."

"Oh." She felt her earlier gloominess returning.

"I think you were wise to take the job you were offered, Anna. I really do. I think you're going to end up with some great references from this. I mean, if you should ever decide to move on."

She nodded. "You're probably right."

"If I owned a hotel, I would be very impressed if an applicant for the manager's position had worked in housekeeping."

"Really?" She felt hopeful.

"Absolutely. The worst kind of manager is the one with no understanding of the folks who keep the machinery oiled and working — maids and janitors and maintenance men."

She nodded. "I agree."

"I have a feeling the Rothsberg will be as good for you as you are for it."

She felt brighter now. "I hope so." She pointed to the building ahead. "That's where I live, at least for now."

He looked up at it, then pointed to his left. "I live about a mile that way."

"So we're almost neighbors."

"Small world, isn't it?"

She reached into her mini-purse, fishing

out Marley's apartment key and trying to think of something sensible to say. "Thanks again for dinner," she murmured, instantly regretting that she'd made it sound like it was a date when she knew it wasn't. "It was fun bumping into you like that," she said brightly. "Serendipitous."

"How about tomorrow?" he asked.

"Tomorrow?" She felt somewhat confused as she paused at the foot of the stairs to her building. Had she missed something? "Uh, tomorrow's Sunday, isn't it? I mean, we don't report to work until Monday, right?"

"Yeah. I was just thinking about how we were both sightseeing today. Are you going to keep playing tourist tomorrow?" He shrugged. "In that case, maybe we should do it together."

She felt her hopes rising. "Yeah," she said eagerly. "I'd love that."

"Great." He politely tipped his head toward the tall brunette woman approaching. She seemed to be studying them as she smiled, then turned to go up the stairs and up to the front door of the building. "One of your roommates?"

Anna studied the woman's back as she entered the security code. "The uniform looks like she's a flight attendant," she admitted. "But I haven't met her. Not yet anyway. I suppose she could be Kara."

He chuckled. "That must be interesting — rooming with flight attendants."

"Yeah . . . and I have a feeling it'll get even more interesting," she agreed.

"Anyway, back to tomorrow," he said. "Since the hotel's about midway between your place and my place, we could just meet up there." He paused to exchange cell phone numbers with her. "In case something comes up."

"What time should we meet?" she asked.

"Well . . ." His brow creased. "Are you a morning person?"

She wondered if this was a trick question. If she told the truth, would she sound like a total nerd? "Actually, I am," she confessed.

"Cool. So is 9:00 too early?"

"Not at all."

"Great. See you then — hotel at 9:00."

She almost added, "It's a date," but thankfully stopped herself. It was *not* a date. It was simply a pair of co-workers eager to explore the Big Apple together during a free day. She wouldn't be surprised if they talked business while they were sightseeing. After all, hadn't they done that over their early dinner? No, it was definitely *not* a date. And she'd better not forget that!

13

Anna was still feeling inexplicably happy as she entered the apartment. What a great day it had been, and so unexpectedly. Once inside, she saw the same pretty brunette she'd observed on the sidewalk earlier. A quick intro confirmed that it was indeed Kara, just back from a flight.

"So who was that with you?" Kara asked with eager curiosity.

"That was Sean O'Neil," Anna informed her. "I would've introduced you outside — I mean, if I'd realized you were one of the roommates."

"Where did you meet him?" Kara peeled off her uniform jacket, tossing it onto a nearby chair as Sophie came into the room. She still had on the same pink silky bathrobe, as if she really was taking her day off seriously.

"Anna has already met a guy?" Sophie

asked with keen interest. "You work fast, girl."

"Not just *any* guy," Kara told Sophie. "Trust me, this one's a real looker. For a second I thought she was talking to Ryan Reynolds."

"You're joking." Sophie's eyes grew wide. "He's *that* good looking?"

Kara nodded firmly as she unzipped her skirt. "Seriously, Anna, where did you meet this handsome dude?"

"And does he have a brother?" Sophie added teasingly.

Anna laughed. "Well, if I could get a word in edgewise, I'd tell you." She paused to discover they were both waiting. "You see, I've known Sean since childhood. We grew up in the same town, went to the same high school, and —"

"And he came here looking for you?" Sophie said dreamily.

"Is he trying to talk you into going back home with him?" Kara asked. "Didn't you just get here?"

"No, no, it's nothing like that." Anna chuckled. "You see, Sean got hired at the Rothsberg hotel. Same as me. We both start work on Monday."

"Wow, that's a co-inc-y-dink." Sophie winked. "Hometown boy working at the same place as you?"

"And you're already dating?" Kara was standing there in her bra and slip, picking up her discarded uniform pieces as if this was her usual routine. "Nice work."

"We're not dating," Anna clarified.

"That's good," Sophie told her. "Always risky to date co-workers."

"Well, unless they're pilots," Kara added with a mischievous twinkle in her eye.

Sophie shook a stern finger at Kara. "No, Kara. Like I've told you a million times, that's a mistake. Pilots never see flight attendants as serious marriage material. To them, we're just a temporary amusement. Leave the pilots alone and you'll be much better off."

Ignoring her, Kara turned back to Anna now. "If you're not dating this dreamy Sean guy . . . are you saying he's available?"

Anna shrugged. "He's not married or with anyone, if that's what you mean."

"Ah-ha." Kara removed a few hairpins, letting her hair down with a shake. "What's Sean's job at the hotel?"

"Head manager."

"Nice." Kara made an approving nod. "That works for me."

Anna felt uncomfortable discussing Sean like this — like he wasn't a person, just an object. "I think Sean's going to be really busy with his job at first," she told them. "There's so much going on at the hotel these next few weeks — getting it all set up and ready to open. I'd be surprised if he had much time for a social life. I know I don't expect to have one."

"What's your job there?" Sophie asked.

"Head of housekeeping," Anna told her.

"Oh." Kara's brow creased as if this was disappointing. "Does that mean you're in charge of the maids?"

"Certainly, that's part of it." Anna stood straighter. "I prefer to think that I'm in charge of the guests' comfort — at least when it comes to their rooms. And really, when you're staying at a hotel, what's more important than your room?"

Sophie nodded. "Yeah, that's a very good point."

"I don't know," Kara added as she headed for her bedroom. "I like a hotel with lots of amenities *outside* of my room."

"The Rothsberg has those too," Anna assured her. "Restaurant, pool, spa, coffee shop, workout room. Everything is beautiful too. But even if you have all those amenities, what good is it if your room's totally uncomfortable?"

"I agree," Sophie told her. "What I want

most, when I'm laid over in a city, is a really comfy bed with great linens and a good down pillow, and quality toiletries too. Oh yeah, and HBO and room service." She laughed. "I could've done with some room service today. I'm starving."

"Speaking of food," Kara called from her bedroom. "You still going out with me tonight, Soph?"

"You bet. I've been looking forward to it all day."

"How about you, Anna?" Kara stuck her head out through the doorway. "Want to come out for a taste of New York nightlife?"

"Oh, I don't know." Anna was uncertain. On one hand, it sounded fun. On the other hand, she suspected these flight attendants were serious party girls. Something she was not.

"I'm sure we can squeeze another in," Sophie told her. "We've got reservations at Atera."

"What's that?" Anna asked as she sat down on the love seat.

"It's a dining experience," Sophie explained.

"That's right," Kara said as she emerged from her room in a terry bathrobe. "Dinner literally lasts three hours."

"Three hours?" Anna blinked. "The

restaurant people don't mind?"

"They expect it to last that long," Kara explained as she opened the bathroom door. "It's supposed to be an all night sort of thing."

"The food is killer," Sophie said. "It's all American cuisine, but done with real flair. Fabulous service too. I think you'd like it, Anna."

Anna glanced at her watch, surprised to see that it was nearly 7:00 and neither Sophie or Kara looked the least bit ready to go anywhere. "What time is your reservation?"

"Nine, but we'll leave here around 8:30. I better get a move on." Kara ducked into the bathroom.

"If your reservation's at 9:00," Anna said to Sophie, "and you stay for three hours, it'll be midnight by the time you're done."

"Or later." Sophie nodded eagerly. "The night will just be starting up by then."

Anna wondered if she'd been living with her grandmother for too long.

"Come on," Sophie urged. "I know we can fit you in. The more the merrier."

"Thanks so much for asking," Anna told her. "But I have an early morning appointment. I think I'd better pass."

"An early morning appointment on

Sunday?" Sophie frowned. "With who?"

Anna made a shy smile. "Actually, it's with Sean."

"Aka Mr. Ryan Reynolds?" Sophie's eyes lit up.

"His name really is Sean O'Neil," Anna clarified. "I promised to meet him at 9:00. We're going to do some sightseeing together."

Sophie gave her a suspicious sideways glance. "I thought you said you two were just friends?"

"Oh, we are." Anna nodded. "Friends can go sightseeing, can't they?"

Sophie's smile returned. "Sure, they can. I don't blame you for passing on tonight. If I had to get up that early, I'd say forget it too. Guess I should start getting ready."

"It's been a jam-packed day already," Anna said more to herself than to Sophie. "I think I'll make an early night of it."

As Kara and Sophie got ready for their big night, taking turns dashing back and forth from the bedroom to the bathroom, Anna kicked off her shoes and curled up on the love seat. Absently flipping through the various magazines on the cluttered coffee table, she tried to imagine what it would feel like to be those two or even the missing Tia and Marley. They all seemed like such happy-go-lucky, carefree New Yorkers. Yet the idea of eating dinner at 9:00 until midnight and then going out on the town after that — well, Anna didn't get it. She couldn't admit as much to her "roommates," but compared to them, she felt like an old lady. Or maybe she was just tired.

She was relieved when they finally made their grand exit, dressed to the nines. They told her to have a nice evening, though it was obvious from their expressions they were certain she'd made a big mistake by staying in. After they were gone, Anna straightened up the little living room a bit. Then she went outside and sat on the top of the steps in front of the apartment building. It was warm and balmy out, and people were still moving up and down the street. Clearly, in the minds of most New Yorkers, the night was young.

Anna watched the passersby with curious interest, almost as if she was a scientific observer, trying to determine what made New Yorkers tick. There was no denying that there was a distinct feeling of energy in the air. Just sitting out here on the sun-warmed stone steps made her want to change her mind about going out tonight. However, it was too late, and with the sky growing dusky and the shadows growing longer, she was reluctant to venture out alone. Maybe she would go out with her roommates the next time they asked. If they asked.

Back in the apartment, Anna decided to call her grandmother and fill her in on her day. She even told her about Sean O'Neil and their plans to do some sightseeing tomorrow.

"Oh, those O'Neils are such nice folks," Grandma said. "I don't really know too much about Sean, but Robert O'Neil is the salt of the earth." She began a story about how Sean's dad had come to her rescue more than thirty years ago. "I got a flat tire a few miles out of town, and my spare was flat too. Well, that was before cellular phones, and the country road was pretty quiet. Straight out of the blue, Robert O'Neil happens along. He stops and offers to fix my tire. Even though he was on his way to some meeting and wearing his good suit, he got down on his knees and put his own spare tire on my car, right there on the side of the road." She paused for a breath. "I hadn't even purchased my tires at O'Neil's, but that good man never charged me for a thing. Just asked me to return the tire when I got around to replacing mine. Well, I became an O'Neil customer that same day. Your grandpa did too."

Anna smiled, thinking that sometimes small towns were nice.

"You be good to that Sean O'Neil," Grandma said. "And you have fun tomorrow, Anna. Take lots of pictures for me."

Anna promised to do that.

"I've got your things all packed up for you," Grandma told her. "They fit just fine in your big red suitcase. I've got it sitting by the door for Marley to pick up tomorrow. Right handy she could do that for you, Anna. Makes me think that the good Lord is really looking out for you." She sighed. "A comfort to me when I think of you out there in New York City."

"It's really a lovely place," Anna told her. They talked awhile longer, but Anna could tell that Grandma was tired. She apologized for keeping her up past her bedtime, and they both said good night. Although it was only 10:00 and probably far too early by most New Yorkers' standards, Anna went to bed with no regrets.

The next morning, Anna woke early as usual. She was a little surprised to notice that the bed across from hers was filled now. Tia must've gotten home late last night. As Anna tiptoed to the bathroom, she felt pretty sure that everyone in the apartment was fast asleep. She suspected they would

sleep like this for a couple more hours, but she didn't mind having the place to herself. She took her time showering and even did some primping.

Even though her "carry-on" wardrobe was limited, she wanted to look good for her sightseeing day. To spruce up her khaki pants and simple white shirt, she added a red and blue scarf she borrowed from Marley. She even put on a pair of small gold hoop earrings and a bangle bracelet. As she was giving her hair a final check, she reprimanded herself. "This is not a date," she whispered into the bathroom mirror. "Not a date — you hear?"

The streets of the city were pretty quiet now. Oh, there were a few folks meandering about. Some even looked like they were on their way to church. Anna wondered if she'd try going to a New York church sometime. That would certainly make her grandma happy.

Before long she was at the hotel, and there was Sean, standing outside of Elsie Dolce eating something gooey.

"That looks good," she said as she joined him.

"I almost got you one too," he said as he wiped his mouth with a napkin. "But I wasn't sure if you were into sweets. So many girls aren't these days."

"Well, I'd probably be better off if I wasn't." She looked longingly into the shop. "Unfortunately, I happen to like sweets. In moderation, of course."

"Let me get you —"

"No," she insisted. "You keep working on that, and I'll go pick something out."

"Then maybe we can find some good coffee to wash it down."

"Sounds perfect." Anna went inside and, feeling a little silly, asked the girl working the counter if she remembered what Sean had just gotten. "It looked yummy."

"Oh, yeah — that was a chocolate cannoli," the girl told her. "Elsie just made those yesterday. A little messy, but dee-lish."

Soon Anna was out on the sidewalk enjoying her own cannoli. After they cleaned off their sticky fingers, Sean led the way to the nearest coffee shop, and with coffees in hand, they headed for the subway.

"I've put together a plan for us," he explained as they went down the stairs. "I hope you don't mind."

"Not at all. I wasn't even sure where I'd start."

"Well, I know it's a little touristy cliché," he said apologetically, "but ever since I spent time in Ireland, I've been dying to see

Ellis Island and the Statue of Liberty. You haven't seen either of them yet, have you?"

"I saw Lady Liberty from a distance," she told him.

"But not up close?"

"No. And I'd love to."

"Great." He led her to a vending machine. "You can get your subway pass here. I suggest you get this one." He pointed to a spot on the machine. "It's the best value if you think you'll ever be using the subway again."

"Well, it's all Greek to me," she said as she retrieved her debit card and slid it through the slot. "I do plan to use the subway."

"I don't like to sound paranoid," he said, "but I always give these machines a good look to make sure there's no monkey business."

"Monkey business?" She retrieved her subway card. "What do you mean?"

"Identity theft." He pointed to the slot where she'd inserted her debit card. "If you ever see a black plastic piece stuck on around here, be suspicious." He explained how criminals would adhere a camouflaged camera in place to photograph victims' cards as well as PIN numbers. "They design the device to look like it belongs there. Most people don't even notice it."

"Wow, thanks for pointing that out to me."

"Emily — that's my ex." He gave her a crooked smile as they got in line. "She used to accuse me of being an overly vigilant, über-protective, type A personality." He made a sheepish shrug. "I suppose in some ways she was right."

"Well, I appreciate your help," she assured him. "The truth is, I feel like a fish out of water in this big city. I'd really like to fit in better, but I think it's going to take some time."

The train came rushing toward them. "Just follow my lead," he said quickly, but instead of going ahead of her, he gently directed her from behind. Before she knew it they were on the train, the doors whooshed closed, and the train took off.

Anna gave him a nervous but grateful smile. As the train sped through the underground tunnel, she felt split in two. Half of her was falling for this guy — falling hard. The rest of her, the sensible half, was holding back. They were co-workers and if she wanted to maintain and protect her job at the Rothsberg — a position she desperately needed — she had to keep a sensible professional distance. That was just what she intended to do.

14

How was it possible that one's entire life direction could change in the course of a single day? Never mind that it was a beautiful, magical sort of day. The kind of blue-skies-and-sunshine day where the very air smelled fresh and good and where noisy children were charming, old people were photogenic, and everything around her looked shiny and bright and new. It was the kind of incredibly wonderful day that only comes once in a lifetime. Oh, she knew that sounded like exaggeration, but deep inside she knew it was true. There were moments, like when they both were silently awestruck by the majestic Lady Liberty, when Anna felt like she was starring in her own film — with Sean playing the romantic lead. It was that good!

Even so, she still could not afford to allow this amazing day to derail her life and her plans. She had to remember what was at stake — and where she had been stuck for the last two years. Did she really want to go back to that? No, she could not give in to the magic of this day. Yet how could she stop it?

Despite her resolve, Anna had felt herself helplessly slipping even as they waited to board the ferry that would take them to visit Ellis Island. All because Sean had knelt down to help a young boy tie his shoe. The boy's parents were distracted by their other two younger children, and this young fellow had been on the verge of tears, trying to get his shoe tied like his mom had kept insisting must be done before it was time to board the boat. Anna had suppressed the urge to grab her phone and take a photo of this sweet scene as Sean consoled the boy and helped him with his laces. Instead, she took a mental picture. That way it would be only for her.

They boarded the ferry, and soon she and Sean were standing together alongside the boat's railing, gazing out over the bright blue water toward the tall green statue. Anna tried to keep her countenance serene, but a battle was waging inside of her. She had no idea how she would keep these overwhelming feelings suppressed throughout the day. Especially since it was still morning!

She wondered if it was useless. Perhaps the best thing would be to just give in. Let the chips fall where they may. Because everything about Sean was so appealing, so unexpected, so perfect. It wasn't just his looks. Even if he was unattractive — and the truth was, she wished that he was a little less gorgeous — she knew she'd still be falling for him. She loved that Sean was so in the moment, so involved and interested in everything around him, and at the same time so involved and interested in her. She could tell that to the casual observer, she and Sean looked like a real couple. And she liked that. At the same time, she was vexed at herself for liking it.

"Ellis Island suffered a lot of damage during Hurricane Sandy." Sean pointed to the island up ahead. "The whole island was submerged and the basements flooded. A lot of the old photos and documents were damaged."

"Oh dear." Anna shook her head. "Was there any way to save them?"

"Yes. They're with conservationists in Maryland. They're being restored, and as the various exhibit areas are repaired and reopened, they'll bring all the artifacts back."

"That's good to know. There's so much history packed into this place."

"Anyway, a lot of the exhibits have opened back up," he explained. "I'm not sure if the elevator is working yet, though. I heard someone say that as a result of Sandy, they had been running the island tours in a way that was very similar to how it was when our ancestors came. Kind of bare bones."

"Oh, I like that." Anna nodded.

"Yeah. So do I."

Sean told her about how his great-great-grandparents came to America from Ireland in the early 1900s. "Growing up, I never thought anything of their migration. It was living in Ireland the past few years that made me curious about them."

"Why is that?"

"I was curious as to why they left. I mean, I realize Ireland has had more than its share of problems. English oppression. Religious bickering. The economy. But being there and seeing everything, well, I wondered why my grandparents gave up on it. Ireland is such a beautiful place." He turned to look at her. "Have you ever been there?"

"No, but I'd love to see it someday. When I was in college, learning hotel management, Ireland was on my short list of places that interested me."

"Well, you should go then. It's a truly magical land. At one point I considered making a permanent home there myself."

"With Emily?" Even as she said this, she wished she hadn't.

He simply nodded. "I know now that wasn't meant to be."

"Still, you didn't remain in Ireland," she pointed out. "Maybe you're more like your grandparents than you realize."

He turned to grin at her. "Maybe I am."

"I realize that visiting Ellis Island is different for everyone," she said quietly. "I've even heard it described as a spiritual experience. I want you to know that if you need to do some exploring on your own, I totally understand."

He peered into her eyes, and she couldn't help but notice that his were the same color as the deep blue water behind him. "Thank you for offering that, Anna. That's very thoughtful. If I get really wrapped up in something, which might happen, I encourage you to keep on moving. I've got your phone number, so we can always reconnect later."

"Yes. That's a good plan." She felt a mixture of relief and angst. On one hand, she would be glad to put some space between them. It would give her a chance to compose herself and deal with these feelings. On the other hand, was he tired of her already? She watched with wonder as the large building came into sight. "It looks like a palace," she said quietly.

"I was thinking the same thing," Sean responded. "It must've been a welcome sight to the immigrants."

Anna studied the architecture of the building as the ferry slipped up to the dock. It appeared to be constructed of red bricks with lots of white trim. What gave it the palace look was the four towers, one on each corner. They were topped with green domes, probably copper that had turned verdigris. But the general appearance was quite regal.

As they disembarked with the others, a quiet hush came over the passengers, as if they were all imagining what it must've been like for immigrants in this moment — how they would have felt after a long hard ocean voyage. Anna honestly didn't know if any of her ancestors had passed through here. She was aware that some of her family's roots in America were very old, as in pre–Ellis Island old. But it was likely that some of her family members, particularly on her father's side, which was mostly a blank slate to her, would have come through Ellis Island.

Anna had overheard someone saying that

since they were here early in the day, it wouldn't be as busy as it would get later. Even so, it was fairly crowded. Something about the crowd of people made this feel important. Like they'd all been on this journey together. As they approached the impressive building, Anna tried to imagine her own unknown ancestors. Where had they come from? How had they felt? What were their dreams? She glanced around at others in the group and could tell they were experiencing similar thoughts. An elderly couple both had tears in their eyes. When she looked up at Sean, she could tell this was moving him as well.

For that reason, she decided to give him space right from the start. Giving him a little finger-wave, she pretended to be interested in a plaque of historical information, allowing him to go ahead without her. She read the words on the plaque, trying to absorb the enormity of what it said. Twelve million immigrants had entered America through the golden door of Ellis Island, and today, the descendants of those immigrants accounted for almost half of the American people. Surely that number must include her.

Feeling even more certain that she was a descendant of some dearly departed immigrant, Anna proceeded into the building. As soon as she was inside, she was awestruck by the beautiful architecture. With its high domed ceilings and massive arched windows, the museum felt like a cathedral, as if something deeply spiritual had transpired here. To her surprise, she felt tears fill her eyes as she followed the group inside. She took her time at the American Flag of Faces, watching as visitors pulled up names of ancestors. She wasn't the only one to shed a tear. Such history — it was moving and amazing.

She continued on through the various exhibits, feeling more and more like she was part of this even if she couldn't name names, she belonged here. By now she'd lost track of Sean, but she was glad for this separation. All the feelings and conflicts she'd experienced earlier were unsettling, almost uncomfortable. She needed a break. Even if it was a slightly emotional one.

Anna went from exhibit to exhibit, pausing often to take in the incredible architecture of the building — the giant arched windows, the way the light reflected from the tiled ceiling — it was really amazing. She paused to study an interesting display of old pieces of luggage, baskets, and trunks, the containers used by immigrants to transport their meager belongings to their new home. More than a few times, Anna lost herself just staring into the faces of immigrants come to life in the enlarged black-and-white photographs.

She wasn't sure how much time had passed, but she eventually found herself on the second floor, staring at a life-sized statue. It was a bronze of a young Irish woman named Annie Moore, the first immigrant to pass through Ellis Island in 1892. What captivated Anna was the look of wonder, hope, fear, expectation . . . and a trace of sadness, probably for what she'd left behind. She knew it was silly to compare herself to that brave young woman of time gone by, but she really felt she could relate. Anna remembered her own feelings upon arriving in New York just two days ago — wonder, hope, fear, expectation, and yes, a trace of sadness for what she'd left behind. Truly, Anna from Springville and Annie from Ireland were not so very different.

"Here you are," Sean said as he joined her. "I just tried to call your cell, but it seems to be off."

She turned to him, feeling slightly dazed, as if she'd just been dragged back into the present. "Sorry. I think I lost track of the time."

"Who's this?" Sean looked at the bronze.

"One of your ancestors, perhaps," she teased. "Meet Annie Moore from Ireland. Annie, meet Sean O'Neil, a descendant of Ireland."

Sean pretended to shake the statue's hand. "You're a comely lass, Annie," he said in a perfect Irish accent. " 'Tis pleased to make your acquaintance, I am."

"I was just thinking that Annie and I had some things in common," Anna admitted.

"Your names, for instance?"

She nodded. "Plus being newcomers to New York. Embarking on a new life. Feeling uncertain but hopeful."

He smiled as he slipped a hand around her shoulders, giving her a friendly squeeze. "Welcome to the new world, Anna."

She liked the feel of his arm around her . . . and yet she knew she shouldn't. "What time has it gotten to be?" She looked at her watch as if the time really mattered.

"I'm not sure what the clocks say, but my stomach is saying it's lunchtime. If we skedaddle we can probably catch the next ferry. I think it leaves in about twenty minutes, but I hear there could be a line by now."

They hurried down the stairs and outside to where there was a line waiting to get onto the next ferry. As they joined the end of it, Sean explained his plan for the remainder of the day. "I figured since this was our big day to act like tourists, we should just go for it. That is, if you're game."

She nodded. "I'm game."

"Cool." He pulled out his iPhone. "Not everyone would be into this."

"What?"

"A hop-on, hop-off double-decker tour of the city."

"A what?"

Sean laughed. "Vincent actually told me about it. He said it was the quickest way to see the New York sights. He even offered to reimburse me for it. Part of my training as manager."

"Really?"

Sean explained how the double-decker bus's runs were between ten and thirty minutes and how you could get on and off as you liked, creating your own personal tour as you went. "You still game?"

"Absolutely!"

"We'll get our passes as soon as we get off the ferry. But before we start hopping around, we have to get some lunch."

"Sounds good to me."

As they boarded the ferry, Anna noticed that the clear blue sky from this morning was clouding up. But the air, even out here on the water, was still very warm. Warm and muggy. "Do you think it's going to rain?" she asked Sean.

"I heard they were predicting thundershowers for Monday. I thought today was supposed to be clear." He frowned up at the sky. "But you never know."

It was nearly 2:00 and pushing ninety degrees when Anna and Sean, armed with hot dogs, chips, and large sodas, climbed to the top of a double-decker bus, finding a pair of vacant seats in the back.

"This is great," Anna said as she sat down. "What a vantage point."

"This bus takes the Downtown Loop," Sean told her. "I picked it since it was closer to where we live. Help us to familiarize ourselves with our neighborhood. But we won't have time to stop and see everything."

"How long would that take?" Anna sipped her soda.

"Probably until tomorrow — but the busses stop at night." He took a big bite of his hot dog. "If we stayed on the bus, no hopping on and off, it would take a couple hours to see everything."

"I wonder if we can do both. I mean, I'd

like to see everything listed here." She held up the pamphlet Sean had given her. "But maybe we just pick the ones we most want to hop out and see." They decided to hop out for the Empire State Building, Radio City Music Hall, and St. Patrick's Cathedral. The rest of the places they would see from the bus. Anna peered up at the sky. It was even cloudier now. She wondered if those thundershowers were really going to hold off until tomorrow.

The Empire State Building was even more grand than she remembered it from two of her favorite movies — *Sleepless in Seattle* and its inspiration, *An Affair to Remember.* While they were standing on the observation deck, it was clear that the clouds were coming in.

"I think the weatherman got it wrong," Sean told her as they headed back to the elevator. "Hopefully it will hold off until we've seen everything."

Radio City Music Hall was fun to see from the outside. The art deco theater was such a New York icon. But Anna felt disappointed that due to a matinee, they couldn't take a peek inside. "Maybe we'll come back someday," Sean said as they hopped onto the next double-decker bus.

"I hope so." Anna nodded eagerly. Okay,

the truth was she hoped that they'd come here together, but there was no way she was saying that. She was still determined to maintain a safe distance between them. For the sake of her job and her future, she had to keep this friendship on a business level.

Next they hopped off for St. Patrick's Cathedral. In the changing light — with sun shining directly on the front of the building and dark clouds gathered behind it — the gothic structure looked truly ethereal. Lots of tourists were taking photos, and Anna was among them. But it wasn't until they went inside that she saw the true beauty of this amazing landmark. The enormous arches looked interwoven as they soared into the intricate ceilings. The carved columns, the sculptures, the jewel-toned stained glass windows . . . it was the grandest thing she'd seen since coming to New York. Amazing.

"Nothing like this back in Springville," she whispered to Sean, making him smile.

To her surprise, he went down a row of seats, sat down, and bowed his head. Feeling unsure of herself, she decided to follow his lead, and finding a seat a few rows behind him, she sat down too. Instead of bowing her head, she just looked up at the ceiling, marveling that the cornerstone had been set before the Civil War. As she considered the lives that had passed through here, she realized that many of them were the same people who had passed through Ellis Island. People who were long gone now. For some reason, she found this very moving and humbling.

Anna bowed her head too. After taking a few calming breaths, she expressed a sincere prayer of gratitude. She felt exceedingly thankful that God had brought her to this big, busy place — New York City. She was thankful for her friendship with Sean. She felt thankful for her job managing maids. After expressing thanks, she asked God to continue directing her path and to strengthen her as she started this new job. Finally, she asked God to bless her grandmother. As she softly said "Amen," it occurred to her that she had actually made it to church on a Sunday. Wouldn't Grandma be pleased about that!

15

As Anna opened her eyes, once again looking up at the majestic columns and arches, she realized that Sean was no longer seated up in front of her. She glanced around the cathedral but didn't spy him anywhere. Feeling a bit displaced, she stood and walked around. Certainly he wouldn't have left her behind. It appeared as if they were getting ready for a service, and she wondered if Sean had gone outside.

When she found him, he was in the vestibule, admiring a sculpture. "I thought I lost you," she whispered from behind.

He turned around, gazing at her with what seemed like an intimate expression — as if they were more than just friends. "No worries, Anna. I wouldn't let that happen."

A warm rush ran through her, and for a brief moment, she wondered what he would do if she kissed him. Of course, she would never in a million years do that. Would she?

Why was she even allowing her mind to go there in the first place?

"I don't think I've ever seen anything as beautiful as St. Patrick's," she confided. "It's kind of mind-blowing."

He nodded. "I felt the same way. It's incredible."

"I think they're getting ready for mass or something now."

"Yes, that's what I heard."

She turned to give the interior of the cathedral one last look, trying to soak in all the beauty and splendor — as well as trying to subdue her raging emotions. Why was she reacting so strongly to every single thing today? Was it just New York? Or was it Sean? Or was it something more?

"Ready?" he put his hand on the small of her back, guiding her toward the entrance. "I think the next bus will be rolling along any minute. We can catch it."

"Yes," she said eagerly. "Let's go."

They had barely reached the street before they spotted the double-decker rolling toward them. Sean stepped out, holding up his hand to flag the driver, and soon they were back on top of the bus. Only this time, it wasn't nearly as crowded, and no one was talking on the PA system, telling them about what they were seeing. Not that Anna cared.

She'd gotten a little tired of that earlier.

As the bus took off, Anna noticed a light flashing overhead. She assumed it was a sign on one of the buildings or a tourist's camera, but not long after the flash came a loud clap of thunder that made Anna jump. "Thunderstorm?" she asked Sean.

"Looks that way." He nodded. "Want to go down under?"

"No." Anna firmly shook her head. "I love thunderstorms."

He laughed. "Well, of course you do. I should've known that."

"Why?" she asked him.

He just shrugged, but the twinkle in his eye suggested there was more to this. But before she could question him, another flash of lightning split the sky, and this time the boom came just a couple seconds afterward. "That sounds closer," she told him.

"Cool, huh?"

"Yeah." Anna watched as the other passengers who'd been on top scurried down to the lower level.

"Scaredy-cats," Sean said in a good-humored way. All of a sudden it started to rain. Not just a light drizzle either. The sky opened up and buckets of water came pouring down. Before they could get below to shelter, they were both drenched — and laughing like crazy people. Anna had never had so much fun in her life!

Still dripping wet but in good spirits, Anna and Sean were surprised when the bus driver pulled over and announced that this was the last stop on the tour. "Everybody out. And you all have a great evening!"

"What?" Anna looked at Sean. "I thought the bus tour went into the evening."

"So did I." Sean called out to the driver, asking him why the tour was over.

"Because it's the end of the line." The driver waited for them.

"But it's just a little past five." Sean frowned out at the pouring rain.

"That's right. Quitting time."

"Well, thanks for the ride," Anna said, leaping out into the rainstorm. Sean followed and, grabbing her hand, pulled her under an awning for cover.

"I'm sorry," he told Anna. "I didn't expect to get stranded like this in a thunderstorm."

"Stranded?" Anna looked around at the city streets where other people were dashing here and there for cover, calling for taxis, and waiting under awnings. "We seem to be in good company."

Sean beamed at her. "You're a good sport." He stepped out in the rain and began trying to wave down a taxi.

Unfortunately, they seemed to be occupied. But he didn't give up, and after about twenty minutes, he finally got one to pull over. He waved victoriously at Anna, they both piled into the back, and Sean instructed the driver to take them to Anna's apartment in Greenwich Village.

"Well, this is an exciting way to end our day," she told him.

"This wasn't how I planned it," he said with disappointment.

"Apparently no one planned on a thunderstorm today. Not even the weatherman." Anna was starting to shiver from her wet clothes but tried to hide it because she didn't want to make Sean feel any worse. "You're soaked to the skin," she pointed out. "You should have the driver take you home first."

"No," he insisted. "You first."

"Thanks," she murmured.

"I wanted to finish off our day with dinner in Little Italy." He sighed. "I thought we could walk there."

"Oh." Anna peered out the fogged up window. "It's still coming down cats and dogs out there."

"I know." He brightened. "But we could take a taxi. Maybe I could even arrange for this one to come back for us. That is, if you're game. Are you?"

"Sure," she said with enthusiasm. "I'd love to see Little Italy."

"Great." He pulled out his phone. "Hopefully this still works. I'll see if I can make a reservation somewhere."

She waited as he made several attempts. Even though it was Sunday and pouring rain, the restaurants seemed to be pretty busy. "Do you think you could be ready by 6:30?" he asked with a doubtful expression. "I know that's early. And it doesn't give you much time to change."

She glanced at her watch, quickly calculating. "I think so."

"Really?" He looked surprised.

She laughed. "I'm kind of a low-maintenance girl."

He grinned. "I like that."

She just hoped that she'd be able to get a turn in the shared bathroom. She really wanted a quick hot shower to warm her up. However, she had no idea what she would wear. She remembered how Marley had offered the use of her closet. Anna wasn't one to borrow clothes, but her only other option would be to wear her Ralph Lauren suit, and that seemed a little much.

"Here you go," Sean announced as the taxi stopped. The windows were so foggy it was impossible to see out.

"I'll be back around 6:30. Our reservation is 6:45."

"I'll be ready," she called as she hopped out, dashing up the steps through the steady rain.

Anna felt chilled to the bone as she went into the apartment. Yet she felt surprisingly warm too. Maybe she was just generally conflicted about everything.

"What happened to you?" a woman dressed in warm-ups asked. "Take a dip in the river?" She laughed. "I'm Tia, by the way. You must be Anna."

"Yes." Anna shivered as she shook Tia's hand. "I got caught in the rainstorm. Is the bathroom available? I'd love a shower."

"You're in luck. Kara and Sophie left for JFK just a few minutes ago." Tia reached for the TV remote. "And I don't work until Tuesday."

"Fantastic!" Anna dashed for the bathroom, stripping off her soggy clothes. Even though their shower pressure wasn't the greatest, she'd never enjoyed a hot shower more. But she knew time was limited — and she wanted to look her best. Okay, she knew that went against everything she'd been telling herself, off and on, all day. This was not a date, this was not a date. But there was no reason she couldn't dress like it was a date. After all, this was New York, and Marley had said she could borrow some clothes. Fortunately, they were about the same size.

Wrapped in a towel and with another one around her head, Anna streaked through the living room. "Someone's in a hurry," Tia said absently.

"Yeah, I'm going out again."

"A date?" Tia's brows arched with interest.

"More like a business dinner," Anna said as she went into the bedroom.

"Well, you're lucky," Tia called. "The rain has stopped."

"Great!" Anna was going through Marley's closet now, trying to find something comfortable yet sophisticated. If her own clothes were here, she would probably wear her white linen sheath dress, but Marley didn't seem to have anything like that. Perhaps she had a little black dress. Didn't every woman in New York own a little black dress? Then — bingo — Anna pulled out a sleeveless black dress, holding it up to her. Hopefully it would fit okay.

Before long, she was standing before the door mirror, appraising her quickie makeover and not feeling disappointed. The dress fit perfectly, and her own black pumps went nicely with it. Worried that it might be cool out after the rainstorm, she borrowed one of Marley's oversized silk scarves to use as a shawl. Since her hair was still damp, she'd pinned it into a French twist. She put on her hoop earrings and bracelet bangles, and she felt like she was ready for her first night out in New York.

"You clean up well," Tia commented as Anna emerged.

"Thanks. I think I'll go out to wait for the taxi."

"I hear Marley's coming home tonight. I assume that means you'll be sleeping here." She patted the love seat.

"Yes." Anna nodded. "That's fine."

"Although Kara and Sophie won't be back until tomorrow. They probably won't mind if you borrow a bed."

"The love seat is fine," Anna assured her. "I wouldn't want to borrow a bed without permission."

"Looks like you borrowed Marley's Hermes."

"What?" Anna was confused.

"The scarf. Marley got it in Paris. It's Hermes."

"Oh." Anna was unsure. "She said I had borrowing privileges. But is this something special? Should I —"

"No, no. Just don't lose it."

Anna saw the taxi down below. "Okay. I have to go. The taxi's here."

"Have fun."

Anna was tempted to remove the scarf, but the taxi was honking. As she hurried out, she was determined to take special care of this scarf. It figured she'd pick something Marley had gotten in Paris. Hopefully it wouldn't rain again. If it even looked like rain, Anna would remove the scarf, carefully fold it, and keep it in her purse. But the sky was clear and the air was fresh.

"Good evening," Sean said as he met her at the top of the stairs. He looked her up and down. "Wow, you look lovely. Nice work."

She smiled as she took in his dark pants and pale blue shirt. "You clean up pretty good yourself."

"I've heard this restaurant is really special," he told her as he opened the taxi door for her.

As the taxi drove, Sean told her a bit about Little Italy. "A lot of those immigrants that passed through Ellis Island — the Italian ones — wound up on Mulberry Street."

"Mulberry Street? Like the children's book."

He nodded. "Little Italy on Mulberry Street. Later it was shortened to Little Italy. They say that ten thousand Italian immigrants lived here in 1910, and it's a small area. Back then it was one of the poorest neighborhoods in New York. As the immigrants got their feet under them and their finances improved, they started leaving the city for places like Brooklyn, Staten Island, Long Island. Oh, not all the Italians left. But as they moved on, this area began to fill up with Chinese immigrants." He pointed down a street. "In fact, Chinatown is right down there."

"I'd like to see that sometime."

"So would I. We'll have to check it out. Anyway, a lot of the Italian-Americans had started restaurants in those early years. This place was crawling with restaurants. There's still around fifty or so. Most of the Italians don't live here anymore, but it's still called Little Italy. The real estate here, just like Greenwich and SoHo, has really soared in value in recent years. So now you've got some of New York's poorest living just down the street from New York's wealthiest. It's really a mixed bag."

"Here you are," the taxi driver announced.

"Let me help with —"

"No." Sean put his hand on hers over her

purse. "This is mine."

Anna tried not to feel like this was a date as they got out of the taxi. Yet part of her wanted it to be a date. "Sean," she said as they were going in. "Let's agree to go Dutch tonight, okay? You paid for our bus trip and —"

"And here I thought you were an old-fashioned girl." He looked wounded.

"I just feel like I should —"

"I *want* to do this, Anna." He looked into her eyes. "This is the best time I've had since arriving in New York." He pushed open the door. "In fact, it's the best time I've had in ages." He lowered his voice. "Just let me have this, okay?"

Feeling both elated and worried, she nodded. "Okay."

He beamed at her as they got in line. "Besides, this is our last day of freedom, remember? School starts tomorrow."

She laughed. "It does feel like that, doesn't it?"

After a bit, they were seated at a small round table, complete with a red-and-white checked tablecloth and a candle in a wax-covered bottle. "I love this," she said as the hostess handed them their menus. "It's perfect."

"Oh, good." Sean opened his menu. "I

was worried when we got here that it might be too rustic for your taste. I've heard the food is killer, though."

"I love everything about it," she said. "And I'm ravenous."

"That hot dog didn't stay with you?" he teased.

"Oh, in some ways it did."

Sean laughed, then got more serious, looking at her intently. "I'm really impressed with what a good sport you've been today. Then the way you pulled yourself together — so quickly — now you look like a million bucks."

She felt her cheeks grow warm. "Thanks. It must be the scarf. I borrowed it from Marley, and one of the roommates informed me as I was leaving that it's pretty special."

"Well, you make it look special."

Anna felt slightly light-headed now. Perhaps it was just hunger, or perhaps it was something much more. How could this *not* be a date? Why was she being so stubborn about it? Really, she finally thought, what did it matter? Why not simply do as she'd been doing most of the day — enjoy the moment?

The waiter came to their table now to tell them the specials and ask for their drink order. "Can I get us a bottle of wine?" Sean asked her.

"Oh, I don't know . . . I'm really not much of a drinker."

"How about just a glass for the lady?" the waiter suggested. "A nice cabernet, perhaps?"

"I wouldn't even know where to start."

"Perhaps a pinot noir," Sean recommended.

"I don't even know what that is," she confessed.

Sean looked at the wine menu, pointing to a spot. "We'll both have this pinot noir from Oregon."

"Excellent choice."

Anna felt a rush of excited nerves. This was all so amazing — out with Sean O'Neil, eating in a charming Italian restaurant in Little Italy, after a fabulous Sunday in New York. Really? Was it just one week ago that her dead-end life had been so pathetic and boring? And now this. She looked around the restaurant, so unlike anything back in Springville. It felt like a dream, or like she was watching someone else's life or reading one of her grandmother's cheesy romance novels. How was it possible this was happening to her?

16

"What're you thinking about?" Sean asked as he sipped his ice water.

"Oh . . ." Anna made an embarrassed smile. "Nothing much."

"You seemed deep in thought." He waited.

"The truth is, I was about to pinch myself."

He laughed. "Well, don't do that. Might leave a bruise."

"I was just thinking about how I was working in Springville just one week ago. Now I'm here in New York. It's just so unbelievable. It's true what they say — you never know what's around the next corner."

"You were actually *working* in Springville? I guess I didn't know that."

She grimaced, wishing she'd left that cat in the bag.

"Tell me, what were you doing in our old stomping grounds?"

"It's kind of humiliating," she confessed.

"But if you promise not to laugh — or feel too sorry for me — I'll tell you."

"I promise." He leaned forward with genuine interest. She told him the whole pathetic tale, clear to the part of sleeping on her grandmother's couch and using the coat closet for her clothes.

"Pretty sad, eh?" She took a sip of ice water.

"It's obvious you love your grandmother a lot, Anna. Nothing sad about that. I think it's sweet."

The waiter set their wineglasses down now. After the waiter left, Sean lifted his for a toast. "Here's to old friends . . . reunited."

"To old friends," she echoed as they clicked glasses. She wanted to add "old friends who never really knew each other," but why spoil the moment? Besides, in some ways it really did seem like they were old friends. Like perhaps they really had known each other somehow. She took a cautious sip of the wine and was surprised that it tasted better than expected.

"Okay?" He watched her.

She took another sip, letting it roll around her tongue. "Yes. I actually think I like it."

He grinned, holding his glass for a second toast. "Here's to old friends who like the same things."

She nodded as their glasses made a pleasant ding. "Speaking of old friends," she began, "my grandma told me a sweet story about how your dad helped her out one day." Because Sean seemed interested, she told him Grandma's roadside tale.

"Sounds like something Dad would do," Sean admitted.

"It must've been nice growing up in Springville with a dad like that . . . a family like that."

Sean got a curious look now. "Did you always live with your grandmother? Or just after college?"

Maybe it was the wine, or maybe it was Sean's empathetic eyes, but Anna's usual reluctance to talk about her family life dissolved and she opened up, spilling out her sad little story. Sure, a part of her was shouting inside, *Shut up — don't let him know or you'll scare him away!* But another part of her just didn't care. If her family history was too much for him, she might as well find out now and cut her losses before she was in too deep. Or was she in too deep already?

Whatever the case, the cork was off and she was telling him how her mother got pregnant when she was seventeen, how she was caught up in the wrong crowd, and how her parents married at such a young age. Was it embarrassing? Yes. But on she went, telling him all the dirt, including how both her parents got caught up in drugs and alcohol and how they couldn't seem to escape it. "Besides their addiction problems, or because of them, they were totally clueless about how to be a family. Even as a young child, I could see that. I tried to make up for them, I tried to hold things together . . . but it was impossible." She took a sip of water.

"I had a roommate in college who grew up in a family like that. Pretty sad."

"Sometimes I feel guilty for blaming my parents. I mean, my mom's not even around to defend herself. She might've grown up in time. But the fact was, they were too young to have children. And they were too selfish . . . and too addicted." She sighed. "My dad left Mom and me when I was in first grade. I've never heard from him since then. I wouldn't be surprised if he was in prison . . . or dead. My mom died a couple years after my dad left. I think it was an accidental overdose."

Feeling tears coming, but wanting to hold them off, she paused to take a sip of water, steadying herself with a couple of deep breaths. Then she looked up to see how

Sean, the golden boy, was taking the more gruesome chapters of her life. His face was creased with concern, but he was still attentive. "I'm sorry you had such a lousy childhood, Anna. What happened after your mother died? Is that when you went to live with your grandmother?"

She nodded. "I was nine when my mom died, but I only made it to school about half the time because I'd been taking care of her. That's when my grandparents took me in. They lived in this totally normal neighborhood in Springville. In a totally normal ranch house with three bedrooms. I went to a totally normal school and made some totally normal friends." She grinned. "It was great. I felt like I'd won the kid lottery."

"Is that when you and Marley became friends?"

"Marley and I became friends in middle school."

"Yeah. I remember seeing you hanging around with her."

"Seriously? You remember me from that long ago?"

"Hey, I might've been a little full of myself back then, but I wasn't blind. Marley had her little gang of girlfriends — some who were pretty obnoxious, but I remember you as always being kind of quiet and nice."

"Really?" She was shocked. "I always thought I must've been invisible to someone like you."

As they talked and ate and drank, they reminisced about things that had happened in Springville, retelling community events they each remembered from their own perspective. By the time they were finished with dinner and exiting the restaurant, it really did feel like they were old friends. Anna suppressed the urge to grab his hand.

"It's so nice out," Sean said as they stood on the sidewalk. "We could walk home. I mean, if you feel up to it."

"I'd love to walk," she said happily.

"It's about a mile." He pointed at her shoes. "Are you okay in those?"

She held out a foot and nodded. "These pumps have walked me back and forth to the Value Lodge — for many a mile. I think they can go one more."

"Your feet okay too?"

"You bet."

He laughed as he linked his arm in hers. "Then we're off."

"Off to see the Wizard," she said merrily. He joined her in singing a few lines, but neither of them could remember all the words, so they ad-libbed and wound up laughing like goofballs. Anna wasn't sure if her giddiness was a result of the wonderful day they'd shared, or perhaps partly due to the wine, but the walk home was entirely enjoyable. It felt like it ended too soon.

"Here you are, my lady," Sean looked down at her as they stood at the top of her steps. "Thank you for a grand evening."

"Thank *you*!" She paused to look into his eyes, which now looked dark . . . dark and romantic, making her feel less silly. "I honestly think this was the best day of my entire life. Thanks for making it great, Sean." Okay, was that too much? But his expression seemed to match how she felt. In a moment he was leaning down toward her, and even though she knew she should say good night and nip this before it budded, she leaned in toward him. The next thing she knew, they were kissing. Really kissing. She felt like fireworks were going off in her head, and she didn't want him to stop.

"Sorry," he said a bit breathlessly as he stepped back. "I didn't mean to do that, Anna."

"No," she said, fumbling for the door handle behind her and using it to steady herself. "I didn't either. Sorry."

"Must've been the wine," he said apologetically.

"Yes," she agreed. "The wine." She forced a goofy smile. "Thank you for a wonderful night, Sean. I'll probably see you at work tomorrow. Unless we're both über-busy." She made a nervous smile.

"Yes." He nodded. "Good night, Anna."

As she turned to enter the security code, she heard his footsteps scurrying down the steps and away. Entering the building, she could not help but feel as if she'd blown it. She wasn't exactly sure how. Perhaps it was in allowing the kiss. Or perhaps she'd actually initiated it. She didn't even know.

She quietly let herself into the apartment but was barely inside when Marley lunged toward her, giving her a big hug. "It's so good to see you!"

"You too," Anna told her.

Marley held Anna at arm's length, checking her out. "Wow, don't you look chic."

Anna grimaced. "Because of you. I hope you don't mind that I took advantage of your generous offer."

Marley fingered the silk scarf, gently slipping it off Anna's shoulders. "Tia told me that Hermes went out with you tonight." Marley examined the scarf carefully.

"I'm sorry," Anna said contritely. "I had no idea it was special. It was so pretty. Tia told me right as I was leaving. But I put it in my purse during dinner."

"It's okay." Marley put the scarf over her own shoulder. "Hermes seems to be in good condition." She pointed to the red suitcase by the door. "Now you have your own threads."

Anna felt bad about the scarf but thankful that nothing had happened to it. "I'll go take off your dress —"

"Don't worry about that old thing. I don't wear it anymore. Last time I had it on, it was too tight anyway." She studied Anna. "Seems to fit you just fine. Why don't you keep it?"

"Really?" Anna looked down at the simple dress. "Thanks. I do like it."

"So, Tia says you were out at a business dinner. With the Newmans?"

Anna slipped off her shoes and started to unpin her hair. "No, not the Newmans."

"Who then?"

"Actually it was with Sean O'Neil."

Marley's brow creased. "You were on a date with Sean O'Neil?"

"Not a date." Anna wondered if it was possible for anyone to see the top steps from the front window. Curious, she walked over to take a peek.

"You went out to dinner with Sean, but it was not a date?" Marley came over to see what Anna was looking at.

"Well, we'd spent the day sightseeing together," Anna began. "Since we're going to be working at the Rothsberg, it's important for us — especially Sean — to know a little about New York. You know, in case guests ask for advice."

"Right . . ." Marley sounded suspicious.

"Anyway, we got soaked by a thundershower around five, and we'd meant to get a bite to eat then. So we went home and changed clothes first." Anna turned to smile at her friend. Okay, she knew that wasn't exactly how it had gone down, but it wasn't really a lie either.

"Apparently that means Sean is single, right?" Marley frowned. "Or did his wife or girlfriend go along too?"

"He's single." Anna sat down in a chair and for a moment considered telling Marley about Sean's ex in Ireland, simply as a distraction technique. But not wanting to betray a confidence, she started to talk about seeing Ellis Island instead. She went on and on about how amazing it was and how she wanted to go back there again after the damaged exhibits were repaired. "Did you know the island was completely submerged by Sandy?"

"I think I heard that," Tia said. "But there

was so much going on that it was hard to keep track."

"You lived in New York during Sandy?" Anna asked.

"Yes. It was crazy." Tia groaned. "It's painful even to remember what a mess it was."

"I was here too," Marley chimed in. "I'd just moved in. It was pretty freaky."

Both of them began sharing their memories from the brutal storm and the chaos it brought to the East Coast. Anna felt like maybe she'd dodged a bullet in regard to Sean. Because the truth was, she'd almost forgotten about Marley's interest in him. But really, was it Anna's fault that she and Sean had hit it off so quickly? It wasn't as if she'd gone after him. It all seemed fairly serendipitous. Besides, it was a free world, wasn't it? And Marley would have her chance with him. It certainly wouldn't hurt that Max and Sean were still good friends.

As Tia and Marley argued about the date of the hurricane, Anna went over to her suitcase and picked it up. "I think I'll slip into something more comfy. I'll get my stuff out of your room too."

They hardly noticed as she slipped into their bedroom and quickly changed into a pair of sweats that Grandma had packed for her. Then she gathered her other clothes, put them back in her carry-on, and brought both bags out into the living room. Not wanting to add more clutter to the already cluttered space, she parked her bags near the door.

"Getting ready to go somewhere?" Tia teased.

"No. Just trying to keep my things out of everyone's way. And trying to figure out where I should sleep tonight."

"Just use Kara and Sophie's room tonight. They won't be back until tomorrow night anyway."

"You sure they won't mind?"

"Nah." Tia waved her hand. "It's not like you're a real slob."

"Thanks." Anna smiled gratefully. "Then if you guys will excuse me, I'm going to call it a night. It's been a long day, and I start the new job tomorrow."

As Anna got ready for bed, she knew it would take some finely tuned organizational skills to keep her act together in this tiny apartment with four other women and one bath. The living situation here made sharing a house with her grandmother look like a day at the beach. It seemed her best solution would be to organize her two bags in such a way that finding things would be easy. If that was even possible. Perhaps, if Mrs. Newman had no objections, she could store some of her clothes and personal things in her office and just keep a minimum of things here — kind of like camping.

By the time she got into bed, she had a plan of sorts. It wouldn't be easy, but hopefully it would be temporary. Maybe she and Marley would find a place of their own to share in time. Of course, thinking about sharing an apartment with Marley reminded Anna of the friction she'd felt when Marley had started to question her about having dinner with Sean. It wouldn't be pleasant rooming with a girl who had her eye on the same guy. Not that Anna really had her eye on Sean. Really, today might've just been a great big fluke. It was possible that she'd made it into something it wasn't. And that kiss at the door — well, she could blame it on the wine.

However, as she rolled over, trying to force herself to sleep, all she could think about was Sean O'Neil. Everything about him seemed so perfect. Not just because he was a gentleman, or because he had an appreciation for things like architecture, history, and good food. But because he seemed to get her. And she felt like she got him. It was like they fit together — they thought alike and enjoyed the same kinds of things. Neither of them was faking it either. She could tell. Anna had had boyfriends before. Never anything terribly serious. And never anything that felt like this. Never anyone like Sean O'Neil.

He honestly seemed perfect. Oh, she knew that was impossible, and she really didn't want to be with someone who was perfect anyway. But he did seem perfect — perfect for her. She remembered what Grandma liked to say, something Anna had heard off and on throughout her life: "If it seems too good to be true, it probably isn't true." But somehow, she just didn't believe that adage could possibly apply to Sean.

17

On Monday morning, Anna felt a sense of excitement and adventure as she walked to work. Admittedly, this had as much to do with Sean as it did with her new job. Perhaps it was also partially thanks to Sean that Anna had reached the place where she was perfectly happy with the idea of overseeing the housekeeping staff. Just hearing his perspective of how vital housekeeping was to management and how it would be such great experience for her painted her position in a whole new light.

Even though Mrs. Newman had said to dress casually, Anna had dressed carefully. First of all, she wanted to be perceived as a professional. Besides that, she just wanted to look nice . . . probably because of Sean. For that reason she'd passed on jeans and a T-shirt, like she'd seen the maids wearing. Instead, she went with a pair of dark blue cotton trousers and a white lace-trimmed tank with a light blue denim shirt over it, along with her comfy Cole Hann loafers. She'd pulled her hair back into a sleek ponytail and tied a blue bandana around it. She looked casual but neat. At least she hoped she did.

As she went into the hotel, she felt a little nervous. As much as she wanted to see Sean, she also didn't. In some ways it was similar to how she'd felt in high school when she'd had a crush on Stefan Rollins during her junior year. Every day she went to school hoping that he'd notice her, which he never did. That just irritated her — not that Stefan hadn't noticed her, but that she was feeling just like that times ten about Sean. *Time to grow up,* she told herself as she headed for her office. *Focus on your job.*

Already she'd started making a to-do list on her iPad. She was also listing questions she had for Mrs. Newman. Hopefully she'd get to meet with her today. Anna's office looked just the same as it had on Saturday, with the addition of a new laptop on top of her desk. But today she felt so much happier to see this space. Her very own office! Perhaps it was related to sharing an apartment with the four flight attendants, but she felt so glad to have a place of her own. For a moment she imagined sneaking in a cot and attempting to sleep in here. But that probably would not do.

"Anna — you're here."

She turned to see Mrs. Newman standing in the doorway. "Good morning," Anna said cheerfully.

"Good morning to you. Glad to see you're already on the job. All bright-eyed and bushy-tailed too."

Anna chuckled. "Yes, I'm one of those early bird types."

"In our business, that's a good thing." She came into Anna's office. "Getting all settled in?"

"Working on it." Anna set her iPad down on the laptop carton. "I'm so pleased to see this laptop."

"Yes. Our computer technician already set them up for the management staff, so that one should be ready to go. In the future, when you're not on the job, we ask that you keep it locked up, unless you take it home with you." She pointed to a storage unit with locking cabinets and the keys already in the locks. "Anyway, I just came by to tell you I want to meet with you at 11:00. Okay?"

"Great. Where do we meet?"

"My office."

"I'll be there."

"I think Vincent also wants to have a management meeting at the end of the day today. I'll let you know when I hear for sure."

After Mrs. Newman left, Anna continued organizing her office, using colorful Post-its to mark file drawers, planning where she'd keep various necessary information, from personnel files to professional cleaning resources. Before long the office looked like a Post-it patchwork quilt. The truth was, she didn't know exactly what she would need, but she planned to be ready for anything.

Time flew by until it was nearly 11:00 and Anna was on her way to Mrs. Newman's office. As she strolled through the lobby, she wondered if she would run into Sean — and if she did, what she would say — but she didn't see a trace of him. She felt a mixture of relief and disappointment as she turned down the hallway to the executive offices.

"There you are," Mrs. Newman said from her desk. "Right on time too."

Anna grinned. "I didn't want to be early and have to stand outside your door. You might think I was stalking you."

Mrs. Newman laughed. "Take a seat. I wanted to go over some things with you."

She was shuffling through some papers and files on her desk.

Anna sat down and opened her iPad, ready to take notes if necessary. Ever efficient. "I just have to say, I'm so excited to be part of this," Anna said as Mrs. Newman continued to organize her desk. "It feels like we're all embarking on a great adventure."

"That's exactly what my husband keeps saying." Mrs. Newman seemed to have found what she was looking for. "Here it is." She handed a paper to Anna. "This, importantly, is your housekeeping budget."

Anna glanced down the lengthy list.

"As you can see, I've attempted to break it down for you. However, I want you to go over it carefully — make sure that it's all right. I really don't want to go much over the figure I've budgeted, but at the same time I absolutely refuse to skimp on quality."

"I understand completely."

Mrs. Newman pushed a thick folder toward Anna. "These are the rest of the maid applications. I've been handling the interviews so far. Virginia's been so busy with other applicants. I've only hired four maids. I'd like you to take over from here. Okay?"

"No problem." Anna set the file on the

chair next to her.

"Great. I've marked the ones that I've already done a first interview with, and I made notes on some of the applications that I'd planned to call back. I know they'll be eager to hear from you. We really need at least half of the maids to be fairly fluent in English. That's all I've hired so far. But we probably need a couple more. I never want to see a shift without at least one English-speaking maid, but I'm fine having half without English skills. I honestly think they're the hardest workers. But they must have a green card." She eyed Anna. "Right?"

"Absolutely. And I have to agree with you. Two of my most dependable maids back in Springville were immigrants from Guatemala — they were sisters and they were excellent. I could always count on them."

Mrs. Newman's brows arched. "Think those girls would want to come here?"

"Oh, I don't know." Anna frowned. "I assume they want to be with their family, you know. And would be more comfortable in a small town. I'm afraid New York would feel like another planet to them."

"Yes, that's probably true." Mrs. Newman put on her reading glasses, looking at the stack of papers in front of her. "I want to go over some suppliers with you first of all. I've been dealing with them, but I want you to take over." She started listing companies they'd been working with and what she liked about them and what she didn't. "If you research some companies you think are better — and less costly — you can make some changes. The truth is, I've had to throw things together rather quickly."

"I can imagine."

"You'll need to hire an assistant. Someone to step in for you when you have time off."

"Yes, of course." She wrote that down.

"Vincent had been nagging at me to hire a head of housekeeping for weeks. I just kept putting it off." She shoved the pile of papers toward Anna and continued going over other miscellaneous things related to housekeeping, explaining what needed to be done to the guest rooms in detail. "I meant to write that all down, but there just hasn't been time."

"I understand." Anna continued taking fast and furious notes. She hoped she was getting it all.

"I'm sure I'm overwhelming you," Mrs. Newman finally said. "If you have questions, feel free to ask." She held up her own iPad. "I prefer email." She slid another paper toward Anna. "Here's the info on getting your hotel email address. First initial, last name, at the Rothsberg dot com. Simple, eh?"

"Yes. Simple is good."

"This list is the landline phone numbers for everyone in the hotel." She slid some stapled pages toward Anna.

Like a magnet, Anna's eyes went straight to the manager's phone number as she set the paper on the chair.

"I know you have a million things to do, but I want you to put together a little employee manual for the maids." She slid what looked like an employee manual from another hotel toward Anna. "A friend sneaked this out for me. Use it as a guideline, but keep it simple."

"Okay."

"From what I hear, the biggest concerns with maids are stealing, laziness, and substance abuse."

"Yes, well, I think those kinds of maids are in the minority. Unfortunately, they give the others a bad name."

"I'm sure you're right. My other big concern — and something I want you to speak to your staff about directly *and often* — is that hotel romances are strictly forbidden. I've heard too many horror stories about maids having affairs with other employees. Your maids need to know from the get-go that a hotel romance will be grounds for immediate firing. It's in their contract and in the employees' manual. No exceptions. No warnings. No mercy." She eyed Anna. *"Right?"*

Anna felt her throat getting dry. "Yes. Right. Of course. Absolutely."

"I hate being so hard-nosed about this. I realize that some maids come from impoverished backgrounds, and I understand how some poor girl might see another hotel employee as her ticket out of her circumstances. But that is exactly why we have to be very clear on this — right from the start."

"Yes, of course." Anna cleared her throat, trying to block out the amazing kiss she and Sean had shared just last night. Did that mean they could both be fired?

"You must also make it clear to your staff that even flirting will not be tolerated at the Rothsberg."

"That might be difficult to monitor."

"Not for me." Mrs. Newman made a sly smile. "I have a very good eye for this sort of thing. I used to have a management job at Lord and Taylor. I could sniff out an employee romance even before the offenders figured it out." She laughed.

"I assume this rule applies to all hotel employees, not only the maids, so I'm sure everyone will be clear on this policy."

"Absolutely. It was even in the contract you signed. Although I'm not so worried about upper management." She twisted her mouth to one side. "When I say hotel romances are forbidden for the maids, I don't mean just limited to employees. If a maid is caught with a guest, it means immediate dismissal. No questions asked."

"Of course." Anna nodded eagerly. "That's to be expected."

"Just make sure your maids understand."

"I will do my best."

Mrs. Newman went over a few more things, and although Anna took fastidious notes, she was having a hard time focusing. When the meeting ended at a little past noon, her head was swimming.

"Remember, Anna, just email me if you have any questions." Mrs. Newman stood.

Anna nodded as she gathered her pile of files and paperwork. "I'll do that."

"According to my math, we need a total of twelve maids, but you can figure it out for yourself. I've hired four, but I want the rest hired by tomorrow. I know that will keep you busy today, but make that your first priority."

"I'll do that."

"And don't put off hiring that assistant."

"I won't." Anna happily underlined her previous note on this.

"You should have a meeting ASAP with the maids I've already hired. They know what's expected of them for right now, but I want them reporting to you from here on out. Without close supervision and direction, they assume they're on a break."

"I'll schedule a meeting for tomorrow afternoon," Anna assured her. "I'll go post it on the bulletin board straight away."

Mrs. Newman shook Anna's hand. "I knew you'd be good at this job, Anna. I knew I could count on you when I caught you wiping down sinks in the restroom." She smiled. "It was like fate."

"Thank you," Anna told her, "for giving me this chance to prove myself."

As Anna left Mrs. Newman's office, she felt a shadow of gloom hovering over her. Was it really possible she had jeopardized her job yesterday, just by spending time with Sean? Did he know about this policy yet? Surely he did. If not, someone should tell him. But not her — she had no intention of having a personal conversation with him after hearing Mrs. Newman's warning. From now on everything between her and

Sean O'Neil would be strictly business. Naturally, he would understand. If he was smart — and she knew that he was — he would even be grateful.

As she went into her office, she felt fully deflated, and as she shut the door, she felt a lump in her throat. Really, this was going to be the end of what had seemed to be budding between her and Sean?

She set her stacks of files on the desk and took in a deep breath. *Put on your big girl pants,* she told herself. *You're an adult, not a schoolgirl. You must provide for yourself and build your references.* She knew that her future was at stake right now. She needed to take it seriously. Everything that had happened yesterday — everything she had felt and hoped for — she would now have to bury deep down. Too bad she hadn't listened to that inner voice that had warned her to be careful, to keep the relationship casual, and to remember they were coworkers. But she was only human, and yesterday had been so amazing . . . so magical . . . so perfect. Yet she knew from experience that what seemed wonderful one day could blow up in your face the next. For that reason, she was determined to go cautiously.

18

As Anna plunged into a to-do list that was longer than her arm, she reminded herself that hard work would be a great distraction for the state of her heart. With all she had to accomplish this week, she would have little time to mope around over her shattered love life . . . or Sean. Instead, she rolled up her sleeves and dug in. First on her list was to post an announcement for tomorrow's meeting with the maids. Hoping that she'd get the rest of the maids hired by the end of the day, she decided to schedule the meeting for tomorrow afternoon. If the new hires could attend the meeting, it would be both an introductory meeting and a training session.

After Anna posted an announcement for the meeting on the lunchroom bulletin board, she started looking over the maid applications. Before she began calling, she went over the math herself, using the formula she'd learned in college. But instead of planning for a 75 percent occupancy of the sixty rooms, she pushed it up to 100 percent. Maybe that was optimistic, but she would rather be overstaffed — especially at the beginning — than understaffed and scrambling. It would also compensate for things like sick days, vacation times, and cleaning of the public areas. As it turned out, Mrs. Newman's calculations pretty much matched Anna's. That was reassuring.

One by one, she began to check on the references of the maids who had already interviewed. Satisfied that their referrals were solid, she started to call the applicants who seemed like the best candidates. Some calls went straight to voice mail, but a few were answered. Mrs. Newman was right: these women seemed to have been eagerly waiting to hear back, and every one of them gladly agreed to come in for a final interview with Anna. Two of them were able to come by later in the day. The others agreed to come by tomorrow morning. It seemed that the prospect of working for this new boutique hotel was highly motivating.

By midafternoon, Anna realized that she was hungry. She knew that as a manager, it was up to her to schedule her lunch hour and breaks. She also knew that in hotel management, one didn't always get one's breaks. Since she hadn't brought a lunch, she decided to duck out to a nearby deli. She'd get something to bring back here, allowing her to continue working.

Although she knew no one would mind if she exited through the main lobby, she was reluctant to cross paths with Sean. Not because she didn't want to see him but because she did. Right now she felt like the best cure for her — in getting over him — would be time and space. And perhaps a lobotomy.

It felt good to be outside and invigorating to stroll along the sidewalk. She was still marveling at how different everything here was from Springville. As she passed the little restaurant she and Sean had serendipitously met at on Saturday afternoon, she felt another wave of sadness. Once again, she chided herself for not listening to that cautionary inner voice. She'd known better than to get involved with a co-worker, and yet she'd naively agreed to go sightseeing with him the very next day. Thankfully, Mrs. Newman was unaware of this — and that was exactly how Anna intended to keep it. What was done was done, but it didn't need to continue.

With a brown paper bag containing her

bagel sandwich and an apple, Anna headed back to the hotel. Realizing she'd forgotten to bring her employee pass key for the side entrance, she was forced to enter through the front doors. She was tempted to duck her head down and sprint for her office, but deciding that was childish, she held her head high and strolled into the lobby like she owned the place. Hopefully Sean wouldn't be in the reception area but would be off attending to something or other.

She was halfway through when Sean came rounding a corner. "Good afternoon, Miss Gordon," he said crisply.

She made a startled smile. "Good afternoon to you too, Mr. O'Neil."

"Getting all settled in?" he asked.

"Yes." She nodded. "I'm up to my eyeballs in work." She held up her brown bag. "Eating lunch at my desk."

"I hear you," he said. "Have a good day." Then he went on his way, just as if Sunday had never happened.

As Anna continued to her office, she felt a tinge of relief. At least Sean seemed to be aware of the importance of maintaining a safe and courteous distance. Yet she felt slightly hurt too. He was so formal and cool, as if he didn't even know her. Okay, she knew that was crazy. Of course, he had to act like that. If he'd handled it any differently, people might get suspicious, and she would be worried about her job security. Obviously, he was acting like that for her sake — and for his. So why did she feel so irked?

While she ate her lunch, Anna continued to work. She wondered if all she needed to get done was even possible for a single human being. Then she remembered that Mrs. Newman had recommended she hire an assistant, so she called Virginia in personnel. "Do you have any applicants for clerical assistants?" she asked. "Someone who would be good for a position in housekeeping?"

"I certainly do."

"Could you gather a few applications for me to look over? I'd like to hire someone ASAP."

"Give me half an hour and I'll have some ready for you."

Anna thanked her and went back to working on the schedule that she was putting together for the maids. Well aware of the busiest hours, between checkout and check-in, as well as the peak days of the week, Friday through Sunday, she made the schedule accordingly — first on paper and then converted into a pdf file on her computer. Her plan was to make it accessible to all of housekeeping electronically, for those with smartphones, as well as on paper for those without, plus she would post it in the lunchroom.

At four o'clock her first interviewee showed up. Anna suspected from the accent over the phone that Gina was Eastern European, and she quickly discovered that the shy girl was Ukrainian. Although Gina's English skills left something to be desired, she seemed friendly and eager, and her appearance was neat and her manners good. "I'd like to offer you a job," Anna said at the end of the interview.

Gina's dark eyes lit up. "Yes?"

Anna nodded. "Yes."

"Thank you — thank you so much," Gina told her. "I vork hard. I promise."

Anna asked if she could make tomorrow's meeting, and Gina eagerly agreed. Anna told Gina where to go to fill out the employment paperwork, and they shook hands. "Welcome to the Rothsberg."

"Thank you!" Gina's eyes were moist with tears. "Thank you much."

The next applicant was already waiting outside Anna's door, five minutes early. "Come in," Anna told the middle-aged Hispanic woman. "You're Carlotta Garcia, right?"

"Si." She nervously twisted the handle of her purse. "I Carlotta."

Anna knew from talking to Carlotta on the phone that she spoke very little English. Fortunately, Anna spoke a fair amount of Spanish, so she interviewed her in both Spanish and English. She was already impressed with Carlotta's job references and felt certain she would be a great addition to the housekeeping team. As she wound up the relatively short interview, she asked Carlotta if she was interested in learning more English.

"Si — si." She nodded eagerly.

"Great." Anna nodded. "I'd like to offer you a job."

"Gracias!" Carlotta's eyes lit up. "When I start?"

"Mañana?"

"*Si — si.* Mañana!" She continued speaking in rapid Spanish as if Anna were fluent enough to keep up.

Anna told her what time to come to work, then sent her to personnel. So far so good. The rest of the interviews were scheduled for tomorrow morning. She'd lined up more applicants than jobs, just in case someone didn't seem right. She hoped to solidify her housekeeping staff by the time she finished her last interview. In the event they were all worth hiring, she would keep the extra names on file, because everyone in the hotel business knew that housekeeping always had a high turnover.

By midday Tuesday, Anna had hired all the maids and was feeling quite pleased about it. She'd also scheduled interviews with what she felt were the top three candidates to be her assistant, and she planned to fill that position ASAP. The work was still piled up around her, and she knew she needed help.

The housekeeping meeting was scheduled for 3:00 in the maids' lunchroom. Just to get off on the right foot, Anna splurged on a selection of cookies from a nearby bakery. Not from Elsie Dolce — that would be more than just a splurge. She even made a fresh pot of coffee, then did a quick cleanup of the kitchen, wiping down the sticky table and countertops and making a note to herself to be sure that spots like this didn't get neglected. She'd already included, she hoped, every square inch of the hotel for housekeeping, but had somehow neglected this lunchroom. She made another mental note for the other staff lunchroom back behind the reception area.

Anna realized that at some point in time, she'd need to meet with Sean to discuss how housekeeping and janitorial would divide the extra cleaning tasks around the hotel. She knew that janitorial would be responsible for things like the hotel's exterior, large cleaning projects, and places like the spa, pool, lounge, and restaurant. She also knew that cleaning responsibilities varied by hotels, but it was the head manager's job to draw these lines. Her job was to follow his direction.

Velma and Cindy, the two maids Anna had met on Saturday, were the first ones to come to the meeting. "What's this?" Velma said, eyeing the plateful of cookies.

"Help yourselves," Anna told them. "First come, first served."

"Oatmeal raisin," Cindy exclaimed. "My fave."

As the other women trickled into the room, Anna warmly greeted them and invited everyone to fill out and wear the sticky name tags she'd set out on the table. "We all need to get to know each other," she said cheerfully.

After a few minutes, she did a quick head count, then glanced up at the wall clock. Two maids were late. "Everyone help yourselves to cookies, and there's fresh coffee," she said as she separated the handouts she'd made. "Feel free to introduce yourself to anyone you don't know."

She decided to allow the maids ten minutes to get their treats and find a chair, hoping that the two MIA maids would show up soon. But it was 3:15 when the tardy maids finally sauntered into the lunchroom like they thought they were elegantly late.

"Oh, did you already start?" a tall blonde asked. Anna recognized her, as well as the other one, from that day she'd been crying in the bathroom. These were the two who'd left a mess on the countertops — a mess that had helped to get her this job. Maybe she should be grateful. She knew that their names were Justine and Bianca, but she wasn't sure which was which.

"The meeting was supposed to begin at 3:00," Anna informed them. "But we've been having some social time and a little snack." She glanced at the cookie plate, happy to see that only one broken cookie remained. "Next time, I'll expect you to be prompt." She smiled and stuck out her hand. "I'm Miss Gordon," she told the blonde.

"I'm Bianca Norton." Bianca nodded to her friend. "This is Justine. Mrs. Newman hired us last week. We've been helping to clean and outfit guest rooms."

"Yes," Anna told her. "I know about that."

She shook Justine's hand, then asked them to fill out name tags and take a seat. "Sorry, it seems there's only one cookie left." She made an apologetic smile as she picked up the agenda she'd written out for this meeting. She started by welcoming them all to the Rothsberg team. She spoke a bit about quality and excellence, explaining that although she knew they all knew how to clean a room, she would go over some quality training at a later date. She told them about what they'd be doing for this week and the next, explaining how the rooms were still being set up and that their job was to clean up after the last of the workers and to eventually prepare the rooms to be ready for guests.

"We will open in just over three weeks. The last week of June. It won't be a grand opening and the hotel won't be full. But it will give us a chance to get the kinks out." She looked at the non-English-speaking maids, knowing that they were probably feeling slightly lost but also knowing that they would probably work twice as hard as maids like Bianca and Justine to catch up.

Next she explained about the uniforms, handing out a form for them to fill out with their sizes and heights. This was followed by a list of locker numbers, which they filled in with their names as well. She gave them the hotel extensions list as well as her own cell phone number, which she explained was only for emergencies. Finally, she handed out the schedules she'd finished making last night. The first schedule was for the period before the hotel opened and only included day work. The second schedule was for the last week of June and the full month of July. Naturally, it was 24-7.

"I realize that not everyone will be pleased with their hours. That's just normal. Not everyone can work the day shift because we need a couple of maids on hand during the other hours. But, as with most hotels, you are allowed to trade shifts with other maids — as long as it gets entered into my main schedule at least twenty-four hours in advance."

She went over some other things, including some warnings about how to avoid repetitive motion injuries or RMIs. "For that reason, I plan to pair maids together. As you can see on your schedule, anyone working the day shift is paired with another maid. The reason for this is twofold. One is to help the maids lacking in English skills to become more fluent. The other reason is to prevent RMIs. I want the maid teams to take turns at tasks so that the possibility of injury is lessened." She smiled. "Not only that, but it's been proven that a team of two can clean two rooms faster than two women working solo on two rooms. It's simply more efficient."

Bianca raised her hand.

"Yes?"

"I'd like to be paired with Justine."

Justine nodded eagerly. "Yeah. We always work together."

Anna gave them a placating smile. "Yes, I'm sure that would be enjoyable for both of you. But it just doesn't align with my paradigm."

They both looked confused.

"My paradigm is my plan for making housekeeping as efficient as possible in this hotel." She smiled at the others. "After all, that's my job. I feel it's in everyone's best interest to partner like this."

"But you said we could trade shifts," Justine interjected.

"That's right. But I still want you to be paired with a non-English-speaking maid, and from what I can see, you're both quite fluent." Maybe too fluent.

Both Justine and Bianca looked disappointed, and Anna felt fairly sure that these two were going to be a pain. She wondered why Mrs. Newman had hired them. Perhaps she'd take a peek at their applications to see what they had to offer.

"Okay, unless anyone has more questions, I think that's all I have." She smiled at her team of maids. "We'll have staff meetings regularly once the hotel opens. Probably on Wednesday mornings. In the meantime, I'll do some training in time management and injury prevention. I want to do all I can to equip you to be the finest maids in New York. I believe you women have the kind of excellence that matches the quality of the Rothsberg. That is exactly why you are here. I hope that you will exceed my expectations."

Several of the women nodded, and several started to clap — then others started clapping, even the ones that didn't speak much English. Everyone was clapping except Bianca and Justine.

"Thank you," Anna said. "I look forward to working with you." She gathered her papers and exited to her office, but to her surprise she was being followed by Bianca and Justine. "Did you have a question?" she asked.

"We want to talk to you," Bianca told her.

"Certainly." Anna smiled. "Come into my office."

Soon they were seated and Anna waited

for them to begin.

"When Mrs. Newman hired me, she said that I might be considered for management," Bianca told her.

"Management?" Anna tried not to act shocked.

"Yeah. She said that because of my experience, I might get a supervisory position over the maids. Not during the really busy times, you know, but on the days when the head — I mean, you — won't be here. You know?"

"No, I didn't know. Mrs. Newman never mentioned this."

"Yeah, well, she mentioned it to me." Bianca sat up straighter in her chair. "That's why I took the job in the first place — why I gave up my job at the Marriott. That's why I encouraged Justine to leave her job and come on board too."

"That's right." Justine nodded eagerly. "Bianca was supposed to be in charge, and I was supposed to be working with her. Now you've split us up. That doesn't seem fair."

"We're not sure we want to work here if that's your para— whatever it was you called it." Bianca locked eyes with Anna.

"I'm sorry to hear that." Anna felt guilty for speaking falsely, but she knew she couldn't say the truth. "I wish you both the best in —"

"Wait," Bianca said quickly. "I didn't say we were quitting."

"It sounded like you said that." Anna frowned.

"I just said we're thinking about it." Bianca looked mad. "Maybe we should talk to Mrs. Newman."

"You're welcome to talk to her," Anna said crisply.

"Okay." Bianca stood. "That's what we'll do. Come on," she said to Justine. "Let's go."

As Anna watched them leave, she couldn't help but think these two had suffered some kind of arrested development — like they were both stuck in middle school. Even so, she reached for the phone, hitting the extension for Mrs. Newman's number. Hopefully she would be in her office.

"Yes?" Mrs. Newman answered in a brisk voice, as if she was busy.

"Sorry to bother you." Anna quickly explained about Bianca and Justine. "I think they're on their way to your office right now, to complain."

Mrs. Newman let out an irritated sigh. "Anna, I expect you to deal with these situations *without* my assistance."

"I know. But Bianca insisted you'd hired her with a promise of a mid-management position. Honestly, I wouldn't like to see her in that position and I —"

"Then *deal* with it."

"Okay." Anna bristled. "I will. Sorry to bother you."

Without saying another word, Mrs. Newman hung up. Anna took in a deep breath. The first rule of management was not to let difficult situations get the best of you. Instead, you had to get the best out of them. Feeling fairly certain that Mrs. Newman would refuse to see Bianca and Justine, Anna decided not to give it another thought. She would deal with these two rogue maids later. Perhaps she'd give the Gonzales girls a call before the end of the week. Maybe they'd like the opportunity to come to New York after all.

19

The first two weeks at the hotel passed in a fast blur for Anna. So much to be done and, it seemed, not enough time to do it. As a result, she was averaging twelve hours a day. At least she'd hired a temporary assistant, an energetic young woman named Krista. She'd started work at the end of the first week, and Anna knew that she'd eventually be helpful, but it seemed to take a lot of extra time just to get her up and running. Anna knew that Krista hoped to make this a full-time position, but Anna had her doubts. Still, if the chatty girl could prove herself invaluable, Anna might rethink that. In the meantime, Anna still had a mountain of her own work to do.

The upside was that by the time Anna got back to the crowded apartment each night, she was so tired that she didn't even mind sleeping on the love seat. Since the other roommates hadn't been on any overnight flights this week, it was her only option.

"This has got to be hard on you," Marley told Anna on a Thursday morning.

"What's that?" Anna quickly folded the blankets she'd used last night, stashing them back behind the love seat. She'd slept later than planned and needed to make up for lost time.

"Sleeping there." Marley frowned. "It's too short for you."

Anna made a tired smile. "Yes, but I sleep on my side, curled up."

"I'm going to start asking around for available apartments."

"Really?" Anna brightened. "That would be awesome."

"Problem is . . ." Marley frowned. "I'm not sure I have enough in my savings for the deposit it's going to take."

"Maybe I could cover your half," Anna offered as she pulled on the clothes she'd laid out last night — her khaki pants and a white shirt. "For now."

"Great. If you can do that, I'll pull out the stops in finding us a place," Marley promised.

As Anna made quick work of her hair and makeup, worried that she might be late for work, they discussed a budget. By the time they agreed on some numbers, Anna knew it was time to go. "Sorry," she told Marley as she headed for the door. "Thanks for looking into this. Good luck."

Anna jog-walked to the hotel. She knew there was a management meeting first thing and didn't want to be the last one to arrive. Nor did she want to be the first one. Most of all, she wanted to avoid any time alone with Sean. So far she'd managed to avoid him almost completely. When their paths did cross, they both were busy and Sean, like her, seemed to want to avoid eye contact. That was fine with Anna. Well, it was fine . . . but painful.

She got to the hotel five minutes before the meeting was scheduled to start, and instead of going to her office, she went directly to the conference room. To both her dismay and pleasure, Sean was already there. So were several other new employees, some she'd met and some she hadn't.

"Good morning, Miss Gordon," Sean said in a friendly yet formal tone. "There's coffee and treats back there."

She greeted him too, then distracted herself by fixing a cup of coffee and looking over the box of sweets from Elsie Dolce. Finally, after settling on a truffle because she knew it would be less messy, she took a seat next to a woman she hadn't met, pausing to introduce herself.

"Yes," the blonde woman nodded. "I've been eager to meet you, Miss Gordon. I'm Ellen Frost. Mrs. Newman hired me on Monday. I'll be second in command in housekeeping." She smiled. "I start work on Monday, and Mrs. Newman says I'm to report to you."

"I'm glad to meet you." Anna shook her hand. "Welcome to the team."

"I hear we'll be sharing an office," Ellen told her.

Anna tried not to register surprise. Mrs. Newman hadn't mentioned sharing her office, and already Anna had been making herself at home. "Of course," Anna said. "You'll be in charge of housekeeping when I'm not around."

"That's right." Ellen smiled. "During the slower part of the week. But our paths will cross on some days."

As Mr. and Mrs. Newman entered the room, everyone became quiet, taking their seats and waiting as the owners took the seats at the head of the table. "Welcome," Mr. Newman said. "It's good to see all of you in one room. I've had the pleasure to meet some of you, but not everyone. I think for starters, we will go around the table and introduce ourselves. Tell us the position you've been hired for and perhaps your last place of employment." He smiled at Sean. "Since you're head manager, I'd like you to start."

Sean stood up, introducing himself and telling everyone about the hotel he'd worked at in Ireland. "It wasn't nearly as grand as this one, but it was a great experience working there."

"Mr. O'Neil is too humble," Mr. Newman said. "He managed to turn the hotel around, increasing revenues by a very admirable percentage."

Sean just smiled, turning to the man sitting next to him. "This is our new assistant manager, Thomas Reed."

Thomas stood and introduced himself, telling about how he'd left a Hilton management job to come here. "I always dreamed of working in a smaller boutique hotel," he explained. "Such a different level of service." He smiled at Sean. "I look forward to learning all I can from Mr. O'Neil."

As they proceeded around the table, Anna couldn't help but notice that everyone's reference for their last place of employment was impressive. She cringed to think of how they would react when it was her turn. She tried to formulate the words to avoid as much embarrassment as possible.

"I'm Anna Gordon, head of housekeeping," she began in a clear voice. First she told them of her master's degree in business and hotel management. Then she quickly explained that she had been forced to take a job in her hometown to help her grandmother. "It wasn't a very impressive establishment," she confessed. "But I was head manager, and I did my best to keep it running smoothly." She smiled. "I can't begin to say how thrilled I am to work here." To her huge relief, no one seemed to think less of her. They simply nodded as she sat back down.

After they finished going around the table, Mr. Newman stood. "I plan to turn this meeting over to Mr. O'Neil, but not until I've had a few words with all of you." He looked around the table with a friendly intensity. "You are all here because my wife and I felt you were the best candidates for your jobs. You all have excellent references, personal integrity and intelligence, and perhaps most importantly, a solid work ethic. As you know, opening a new hotel comes with all kinds of challenges, and we need employees who are capable of facing new challenges with a positive can-do spirit, combined with gracious hospitality."

Mr. Newman looked around the table,

making eye contact with each of them. "I believe everyone here is up to the task, though it's no small task. I'm looking forward to working with all of you. I know you're all going to impress me as we forge ahead on this journey together. As you know, we will open just one week from tomorrow. We've made great progress in the past several days. Almost all the furnishings have been put into place. We still have plenty of work to do, specifically cleaning and setting up, but the end, or should I say the beginning, is in sight. I want to thank each one of you — some for the level of service you've already given and some for what's yet to come. You are all part of a very important and much appreciated team. Thank you!" As he sat down, everyone applauded.

Next Mrs. Newman stood. "I would reiterate everything my husband just said. I couldn't say it better. You're probably not aware that Mr. Newman and I have sunk everything we own into this business venture. And as you can see, we haven't exactly skimped either. But it's because we want the Rothsberg to be known as a place of excellence, quality, service, even splendor. If the Rothsberg goes under, we go under. I'm not telling you this to put on additional pressure, but simply to stress how important this is to us. This hotel is not a hobby business. It's not a tax write-off. It is our livelihood. Mr. Newman and I believe that our employees are the kind of quality staff that a hotel like the Rothsberg deserves. Yes, we have high expectations, but so, I believe, do you. We all will succeed together." She smiled warmly. "I thank you for choosing to go on this adventure with us." As she sat back down, they all clapped again.

Mr. Newman stood again. "I'd like to turn this meeting over to your fearless leader, Mr. O'Neil." He took his wife's hand, then nodded at Sean. "We'll leave you to it."

After the Newmans left, Sean made a short welcoming speech too. "But now I want to move on to practicalities. As Mrs. Newman mentioned, we will open in just one week, and there's lots to be done before then. That will be a soft opening. Our occupancy rate will be less than fifty percent those first few days, so you could get the impression that your workload is light. Just remember, that's only going to last a few days. It's everyone's opportunity to make sure that everything's done right. The real grand opening will be for the first weekend of July. Right now we're booked at eighty percent for that weekend, but I expect it to go higher. Everyone will have to be on their toes."

Sean went to his laptop now, and using PowerPoint on the big screen, he began to discuss work schedules for the upcoming weeks. "As you can see, head managers for every department are scheduled on Wednesday through Sunday, from 10:00 to 6:00. Night shift managers will work the swing and the night shift, but for the first month of opening, I want all my head managers on call 24-7."

Sean looked around the table. "If that's a problem for anyone, please speak up now." After no one said anything, he continued. "I realize that's a lot to ask, but at the startup of a hotel, it's necessary that one person knows everything that needs to be known about his or her department. Think of it as the buck stops here. Naturally, you head managers will be delegating appropriately, and eventually — as the machinery is oiled and running smoothly — you will no longer be on call like that." He smiled. "It's simply the price we all must pay for this opportunity to work at what we hope will one day become one of New York's premier boutique hotels."

Sean pointed back at the schedule. "As you can see, assistant managers will work

Friday through Tuesday — plus swing and night shifts. As you all know, the overlap is due to the peak busy days. No harm in having extra hands on deck, at least in the beginning. We will make adjustments to the schedule as needed later on down the line."

He continued talking and Anna tried to pay close attention, but at the same time she felt distracted by the sound of his voice, his profile, the way he paused now and then to make a joke or personalize what he was saying. Hopefully, she wasn't missing anything too important.

Finally, he was winding down and, like the Newmans, he finished on an optimistic note, telling them again how important they were and encouraging them with a "go-team-go" sort of pep talk. "I'll let you all get back to work now," he said as he gathered his laptop and things. "I know that you department heads have meetings with your own staff later in the day. I realize we're all going full bore until we open and that many of you are putting in extra hours. I sincerely appreciate that. Eventually, your efforts now will pay off with a smoother running machine on down the line." He grinned. "Carry on!"

Once again, they all clapped, and for a brief moment, Anna and Sean locked eyes.

Anna felt her heart pounding, but Sean, without batting an eyelash, turned to Thomas, quietly engaging him in conversation. Feeling slightly breathless and unsettled, Anna got her purse and hurried on out.

"Wait," Ellen was calling out. "Miss Gordon, can I walk with you?"

"Yes, of course." Anna stopped and smiled. "Feel free to call me Anna when there are no maids or guests around."

"Thank you." Ellen fell into step with Anna. "Are you feeling unwell?"

"What?" Anna turned to peer at Ellen. With her short blonde hair, serious brown eyes, and relatively plain features, she seemed like a dependable sort of person.

"You just looked like something was wrong at the end of the meeting. Are you feeling okay?"

"Yes, yes, I'm fine." Anna considered this. Were her feelings toward Sean that transparent? "I think I was just preoccupied toward the end. Probably thinking about the staff meeting with housekeeping this afternoon."

"Oh." Ellen nodded. "Is there anything I can help you with?"

As a distraction technique, Anna asked Ellen if she'd been given a tour of the hotel yet. When Ellen said no, Anna offered to give her a quick one. "It's important that you know where everything is and how long it takes to get from one place to another." Anna started by pointing out the public places that housekeeping was responsible for maintaining, describing the easily overlooked chores that Ellen should be cognizant of. Anna led Ellen into the lobby restroom. "I actually observed a couple of the maids making a mess in here," she said quietly. "They splashed all over the countertops and never bothered to clean it up."

"These maids are employed here?" Ellen frowned.

"For the time being." Anna sighed. "I'm still trying to figure out what to do about them."

"Why don't you let them go?"

"Mrs. Newman hired them."

"Ah . . ." Ellen's mouth twisted to one side. "That's tricky."

Anna told Ellen their names. "They gave me a hard time at first, but since then they've both been laying low. I suspect that despite their cheeky attitudes, they really do need their jobs."

"Then hopefully they'll work like they do."

Anna explained about Krista now. "She's a temporary assistant," Anna said quietly as they approached the housekeeping area.

"I've given her a desk in the storage room." Anna grimaced. "I feel a bit bad, but the girl is such a chatterbox, I couldn't really think when she was around."

Ellen chuckled. "I understand completely."

"As it is, I'm not keeping her busy enough to justify her position. I'm afraid I'll have to let her go. Unless you can think of a reason to keep her."

"Maybe you should wait until the hotel opens," Ellen advised. "Just to be sure."

"Yes, that would probably be fairer to her too. Give her time to prove herself."

Finally, they ended up at Anna's office — actually, Anna and Ellen's office. "I've already set up the filing system and am using most of the drawers in the desk, but I'll rearrange to make room for you. Or perhaps you'd like your own desk."

"I don't think I need my own desk. You'll be in charge of the suppliers and the housekeeping budget and all that." Ellen surveyed the small room. "I don't need much space. Just a spot for my personal things and a drawer or two."

Based on what Ellen had said during her introduction at this morning's meeting, Anna suspected that she was probably better qualified for Anna's position than Anna.

"You managed housekeeping at a Marriott — for twelve years?" Anna asked as she cleared out a drawer for Ellen to use.

"Yes. It was a good job." Ellen straightened a stack of papers on Anna's desk. "But I was tired of the big corporate feeling. I wanted something more intimate, something special. When I heard about the Rothsberg, I immediately sent in my résumé. That was months ago. I had actually given up on ever hearing back. I figured they'd already hired everyone. But then Mrs. Newman called me last week and, well, here I am, starting work on Monday."

"Well, I think you're going to be a great addition to housekeeping." Anna smiled. "To be honest, I'm more trained in hotel management than housekeeping."

"At least you have your degree." Ellen sighed. "That's worth a lot."

"I hope so. Still, I'm sure that there's a lot I don't know. Possibly things that you can help me with."

Ellen smiled. "I'm happy to. To be honest, I'm looking forward to a little less responsibility. And a little more free time."

"Oh yes, that's understandable." Anna started to sort the mail.

"What did you think of the head manager — Mr. O'Neil? Not bad looking, eh?"

Anna set the mail down and looked at Ellen. She was probably in her midforties and probably not truly interested in someone fifteen years her junior. Even so, Anna felt slightly irked by her observation. "Yes, Mr. O'Neil is nice looking enough. That's a good reminder for me for today's meeting. I want to go over the employee manual. I've been working on it all week, and it should be back from the printer before the hotel opens. In the meantime, the maids need to understand that there is zero tolerance for workplace romances. I plan to make that crystal clear."

"Good for you." Ellen nodded.

Even as she'd made this strong spiel, Anna felt guilty. Who was she to lecture others over workplace romance? What if they knew about her and Sean? And that kiss? She picked up the stack of mail again, flipping through and separating the bills. That was all behind her now. That day with Sean had been a one-time thing. And that kiss . . . well, it was just a fluke. Something she'd be best off to forget.

20

Even without the advantage of bakery goodies, Anna felt the housekeeping meeting was going well. So far, she'd covered most of her list, starting with the schedule for the next four weeks. She'd gone over floor assignments, maid partnering, and a list of other concerns. She started to wrap it up with a rather stern warning about the consequences of workplace romances. They'd already been in this meeting for an hour, and Anna could tell by the maids' expressions that their attention spans were lagging.

She didn't want to quit on a negative note, though, so in the same way the Newmans and Sean had done this morning, Anna planned to finish with some positive, upbeat encouragement. "I know you women are going to be a fantastic team!" She paused to look around the table, trying to make eye contact with all of them, although some —

like Bianca and Justine — made that difficult.

"I've already observed how hard you've all been working this week, and I'm so impressed. I expect we'll have all the rooms thoroughly cleaned and outfitted and ready for guests by Wednesday. That's when we'll take a little break of sorts with some training sessions. My goals are twofold. First of all, I want to make sure that we're all doing everything we can to accommodate our guests. Besides that, I want to ensure that everyone is working in a safe and sustainable manner."

She paused, realizing that she was losing them again. "But it's getting late!" She clapped her hands together, which seemed to wake them up. "For now, I just want to thank all of you for making such a great effort this week. A hotel is only as good as its housekeeping staff, and I think you women are the very best! Because we are so caught up with our work this week, no one will need to work on Sunday. You can all have the day off!"

They erupted into enthusiastic applause, and Anna told them to go home. "But come back ready to work hard tomorrow. Don't forget to punch the time clock on your way out. Some of you have been missing that. If you want to get paid, you must use the time clock."

As the maids were collecting their things and waiting to clock out, Anna noticed a woman in a dark suit slipping into her office. Thinking it might be Mrs. Newman, Anna went to investigate, but she was surprised to discover it was Marley. Dressed for work, Marley was casually leaning against Anna's desk with what seemed like a rather smug expression.

"Anna Banana," Marley said cheerfully. She used to call Anna that all the time back when they were kids, but this was the first time Anna had heard it in years, and it made her smile.

"Hey, Gnarly Marley," Anna shot back at her.

Marley laughed. "I was told I could find you back here." She glanced around the small office, taking it all in. "Cozy, huh?"

"Uh-huh, but it works." Anna set her briefcase on her desk. "What are you doing here? Looks like you're on your way to the airport. Night flight?"

"Yeah. Zurich to Bangkok to Los Angeles and home again, home again, jiggety jig. I'll be back midday Sunday."

Anna smiled. "Maybe I can nab your bed while you're gone?"

"Absolutely." Marley's brows arched. "And you'll never believe it."

"Believe what?"

"I found us an apartment!"

"You're kidding? This soon?"

"All morning I'd been cruising Craigslist. Then I even called everyone I could think of in New York. It looked hopeless, so I took a break and went out for a late lunch. On my way back to the apartment, I ran into Rodney, the super for our building. He's this bald, potbellied dude in his sixties, but he's a notorious flirt. Anyway, he was doing his usual small talk thing with me, so I mentioned how I was looking for a new place, and it just so happens that the Brewsters — that's this elderly couple on the third floor — are moving. Seems that Mrs. Brewster developed some health problems, and they just gave notice on their lease. Mrs. Brewster has already gone to Ohio to live with their daughter, and Mr. Brewster is packing up their place right now. Anyway, according to Rodney, the apartment will be available by the first week of July."

"Seriously?"

"Yeah." Marley nodded eagerly as she pulled some papers from her purse. "If you can fill out this application and give Rodney the advance sometime this weekend, he promised that the apartment will be ours."

"You're kidding!"

"I know — can you believe it?" Marley beamed at her. "Am I good, or am I good?"

"You're *great*!" Anna gave her a high five.

"An apartment in the same building. I could hardly believe it myself. I realize it's only a one bedroom, but that makes it more affordable. We can share the bedroom, or one of us can take the living room. Maybe we could get a sleeper sofa or a futon or something."

"Yes, whatever it takes. It'll be a huge improvement. At least for me."

"For me too. Going from one bathroom for four — I mean, five girls to just sharing one with you. I'll be in hog heaven."

Anna laughed.

"Anyway, I couldn't wait to tell you the good news. Just don't forget to get this back to Rodney." She tapped the paperwork. "The check too — I wrote the amount down there. We don't want anyone else to slip in and snatch it out from under us. Because I'm already a tenant in the building, he's not even asking for references from you. Easy breezy."

"Nice work." Anna nodded. "Impressive."

Marley's eyes lit up as she looked over Anna's shoulder, as if someone else was at

the door. "Hey there," she said enticingly. "What can we do for *you*?"

Anna turned to see Sean standing in her doorway. In his hand was an oversized envelope, but his expression looked slightly uneasy. "Sorry to disturb you. I, uh, I can come back later when you're not busy."

"Don't mind me." Marley peeled herself from the edge of Anna's desk, moving directly to Sean with a slightly catty-looking smile. "You don't even remember me, do you?" Her tone was definitely flirty.

Sean chuckled. "Of course I remember you. You're Max's kid sister Marley."

"Ooh, you're good, Sean O'Neil. Very good." Marley was standing extra close to him now, looking up into his face with undisguised admiration. "Do you know that my brother never even told me you were relocating to New York?" She jerked her thumb over a shoulder. "If not for Anna Banana, I wouldn't have heard about it at all. So tell me, Sean, are you Anna's new boss?"

Sean made a stiff smile. "Not exactly. I mean, housekeeping does report to me, but Anna's in charge of her own department. I have no reason to think she's not handling it impeccably."

"Thank you." Anna loosely folded her

arms across her front. "Did you need something from me, Mr. O'Neil?"

"Ooh, *Mr. O'Neil,*" Marley teased. "So formal and grown-up."

"It's policy," Anna said a bit stiffly.

"I, uh, I just wanted to give you this." Sean held out the white envelope. "It came to my desk instead of yours. Nothing important, probably, but I thought you might want to see it."

"Oh?" Anna took the envelope from him. "Thank you." She knew that Sean could've gotten this to her in a variety of ways. He certainly did not need to hand deliver it like this.

"I'll let you girls finish whatever you were do —"

"Actually, I was just leaving," Marley said quickly. "If you don't mind, I'll walk with you, Sean. This hotel is a bit confusing. I might get lost trying to find my way back to the lobby."

"Certainly." Sean gave her a congenial smile.

"Au revoir," Marley said to Anna as she looped her hand into the crook of Sean's arm. "See you on Sunday."

"Have a good flight, Marley. Thanks, Mr. O'Neil." Anna waved as the two left together, watching as they strolled down the hallway. They looked like a real couple. She glanced down at the envelope, almost expecting it to be something important — or perhaps something personal from Sean. It simply contained a bid from a linen supplier that had promised better quality for less money. No big deal.

As Anna closed the door to her office, she felt that deflated feeling coming over her again. Letting out a deep sigh, she was determined not to obsess over this. Instead she tried to focus on her lengthy to-do list, checking off the amazing amount of things she'd managed to accomplish this week. But there was still a nagging, pesky question — why had Sean gone to the trouble of bringing that insignificant piece of mail to her himself? Everyone knew how busy he was these days. Why would he set aside his work to act as a delivery boy? Even if he'd considered the letter important, he could've simply sent it by way of his assistant. Was it because he secretly hoped to see her? To talk with her privately? Her heart fluttered for a moment, and then a different kind of realization set in. Something she hadn't even considered.

Sean had probably observed Marley strolling into the hotel a bit earlier. Even from his office, he had full view of the lobby.

Looking so sleek and chic in her stylish flight attendant's uniform, Marley would've been hard to miss. Knowing Marley, she probably took advantage of her entrance. Anna could just imagine her striding into the hotel with head held high, perhaps striking a pose in the center of the lobby, pausing to ask someone for directions. Taking her time, making sure she was seen.

Sean was no dummy — he probably figured out that Marley was on her way to see Anna. Or maybe he overheard her asking for Anna. That had to be why he'd utilized the misplaced mail as his opportunity to make a connection with Marley. Really, what was wrong with that? It wasn't as if Marley and Sean had never met before. It was only a matter of time before their paths crossed again.

Of course, Marley had made the most of her "coincidental meeting." Why should Anna be surprised that Marley really turned on the charm? Why should she even care? Hadn't Marley made it clear from the start that she wanted to get her hooks into her brother's old friend? Why should Anna give this a second thought? Especially when she had so many other things to occupy her mind right now. She slapped the thick envelope onto her desk with a loud, irritated smack. Time to move on!

On Saturday morning, Anna stopped by the superintendent's apartment on her way to work to give him a check and her application. "Ah-ha," he said with what seemed approval. "So you're Marley's mystery friend?" He eyed her up and down. "She confessed that she'd snuck you into the apartment."

"I'm sorry," Anna said contritely. "Was that wrong? I'd really only planned to stay a week or two. Kind of like an out-of-town guest."

"Lucky for you, I got you girls a place." He tipped his head toward a closed door down the hall. "Mr. Brewster's in there packing right now. Movers will be here next Friday. Painters on Monday. All goes well, I should have you girls in there by July first."

"That's great." She beamed at him. "We really appreciate it. Thank you so much."

"Well, I like renting to stewardesses." He winked. "They pay on time and add some class to the place." He gave her a questioning look. "You're a stewardess too, right?"

She shook her head. "No, I work at the Rothsberg hotel. It's a boutique hotel in SoHo. Opening up soon." She frowned. "Hopefully that's not a problem. I mean, not being a flight attendant."

He grinned as he pocketed her check. "No, it's no problem. You'll class the place up just fine too."

She thanked him again, then, explaining her need to get to work, she told him to have a good day. As she walked to the hotel, she chuckled to herself. Rodney was probably perfectly harmless, but if he treated women like that in the workplace, he'd probably get accused of sexual harassment. Still, if Marley wasn't concerned, Anna didn't think she needed to be either. Even so, she'd probably keep a safe distance.

As usual, Anna used her employee key card to let herself in through the side entrance. She knew this wasn't necessary, but it was just easier than walking through the main lobby — running the risk of bumping into Sean. She'd gotten over her little jealous fit from yesterday. Oh, sure, it wasn't easy imagining Marley getting involved with Sean. But perhaps it would provide a good way for Anna to get over him once and for all.

Anna knew that was her only course of action. She had to get him completely out of her system or risk losing her job. Besides, she told herself as she put her purse away, Sean had obviously gotten over her. She didn't blame him for it either. It was the grown-up and responsible thing to do. She just wished that it was easier to do.

By late afternoon, Anna was pleased to see that more than three-fourths of the guest rooms were completely cleaned and outfitted and ready for occupancy. According to her calculations, with the maid staff she'd scheduled for next week, all the rooms would be done with plenty of time to spare for training. She felt happy and relieved as she waited for the elevator.

"Anna," Mrs. Newman said as the elevator doors opened. "Just who I was looking for. I was about to call you."

Anna smiled. "What can I do for you?"

"I know I told you to hold off on cleaning the penthouse suite that Vincent and I are using," she began. "Because the priority was to get all the guest rooms up and running. But I'd like you to send a couple maids up there ASAP. We're having a last-minute dinner party tonight — just a few friends — and I just realized that the whole place needs a thorough cleaning."

"Oh?" Anna tried not to look concerned. "You want it cleaned right now?"

"Yes, no one's up there. Vincent's at a meeting downtown and I'm on my way to pick up a few things for tonight. I don't expect to be back until after six. Our guests won't be there until 7:30." She checked her phone. "That should give them plenty of time."

Anna glanced at her watch, hoping that the last of the maids hadn't left yet. She'd told several of them that they could go home early since they were nicely ahead of schedule, and she was certain they'd spread the word. She'd have to catch a couple of them before they were all clocked out. "Yes, I'll see if I can round up someone," she promised.

"Thank you."

The elevator stopped at the lobby floor, and Mrs. Newman went toward the main exit as Anna hurried toward housekeeping. When she reached the maids' lunchroom and checked the time cards, she was dismayed to see that most of them had already clocked out. The only time card remaining belonged to Velma, but she had been a little negligent about her time card this week. That in itself was troubling, but Velma was such a consistently diligent worker that it was hard to hold her forgetfulness against her. Plus, she was the oldest of the maids and her presence always seemed to have a steady effect on the others. As a result, Anna had been punching out her time card for her occasionally and reminding her later.

Anna was just about to slide Velma's card into the time clock when Velma appeared. "What're you doing?" she demanded.

"I'm sorry." Anna handed Velma her card. "I just assumed you'd left with the others."

"Nah. I was just giving the lobby restrooms a wipe down. They weren't on my schedule, but Mr. O'Neil mentioned that the men's room needed a little TLC. So I just finished up." She started to put her card in.

"Wait, Velma," Anna put up a hand to stop her. "Can you stick around a couple more hours? I'll give you overtime."

"Sure." Velma removed her card. "What do you need done?"

"We're going to clean the Newmans' penthouse suite," she told Velma.

"We?" Velma frowned skeptically.

"You and me." Anna made a sheepish smile, then explained about the unexpected dinner party. "Hopefully it won't be too messy up there. I know they had maid service early in the week, but we've been so busy that, at Mrs. Newman's suggestion, I took them off the roster. As it turns out, they're having a dinner party at 7:30. But I'd like to get us out of there before six. Is that okay?"

"Okay by me." Velma nodded. "Overtime, you say?"

"That's right. You grab a cart and I'll go find the key card for the Newmans' suite." Anna knew that it was unfair for Mrs. Newman to throw this assignment at her last-minute like this, but she also knew that she was determined to bend over backwards if necessary, just to prove that the Newmans had not made a mistake in hiring her. Even if she had to clean their penthouse all by herself, she would do it — cheerfully.

21

Before long, Anna and Velma were inside the Newmans' penthouse, which unfortunately was more than just a little messy. "I'll tackle the kitchen," Anna told Velma. "You start in the powder room and the living room and work your way to the master bedroom."

"You sure?" Velma asked. "That kitchen looks like a pigpen."

"I know." Anna nodded grimly. "But I'm pretty good at kitchens. If you get done with your cleaning, you can always come back here and give me a hand."

Anna tried not to feel resentful as she cleaned up after the messy Newmans. For a seemingly organized couple, they sure weren't much use in the housekeeping department. *Note to self,* she thought as she touched something stubborn and sticky on the granite countertop. *Schedule the Newmans' suite for* daily *maid service start-*

ing on Monday.

With the dishwasher fully loaded and running — and more dishes left to hand wash — she went to work scrubbing the granite countertops. When was the last time someone had cleaned these?

"Hello?" a man's voice called from the living room.

"Hello?" she answered, hoping it wasn't Vincent. She wasn't eager to be discovered playing the role of a maid. With a dish towel in hand, she went out to investigate and was surprised to see it was Sean coming into the penthouse. His arms were filled with flowers: a big, clear, elegant vase of purple irises, as well as a huge container filled with peonies and other pastel-colored blooms.

"Anna?" He looked as surprised as she was. "What're you doing up here?"

She helplessly held out her hands. "Cleaning."

He set the vase of irises on the large dining table that Velma had already cleaned. "Why didn't you send some maids up to do this?" He peered curiously at her.

"I have a maid with me. The others were already gone by the time Mrs. Newman told me she needed help up here."

"Oh yeah, she said it was last-minute." He held out the other flowers to her. "These need to be arranged. A large one for the island in the kitchen and a smaller one for the powder room, but she wants them put into special vases. I'll get them."

As she carried the blooms into the kitchen, Sean went over to a wall of cabinets and began to search. Setting the pretty flowers in the sink, she tried not to think of the irony of this — Sean handing her a bouquet. What if it was really for her?

"I think these will work." Sean set an attractive round vessel made of thick, watery-blue glass on the counter she was cleaning and then a smaller cut crystal vase next to it.

"Need any help with that?" she offered meekly.

"I think I got it." He filled the aquamarine vase with water. "How about you? You need any help when I'm done here?"

"No," she said quickly. "I just need to get back to what I was doing." Yet she just stood there, watching as he carefully selected flowers to go in the vase, cut their stem bottoms with scissors, and dropped them in.

"My offer is genuine," Sean assured her as he reached for a pale pink peony. "I don't mind helping." He looked up with an open expression.

She returned his gaze and immediately

regretted it. The last thing she needed was to get pulled into those deep blue eyes and be captivated by that smile. "Really," she told him. "I'm fine." She returned to the countertop, scrubbing the granite like her life depended on it.

"I've been wanting to talk to you, Anna." He spoke quietly as he placed the flowers in the large vase.

She just kept scrubbing, wishing there was a way to do this differently but knowing there wasn't.

"I feel really badly for how things went with us that Sunday," he continued. "I never meant for it to go —"

"It's okay," she said quickly. Without looking at him, she rinsed out her cleaning rag. "There's nothing you need to say. *Really.*"

"But I wanted to tell you that I'm —"

"Please, Sean." She whirled around, locking eyes with him. "I mean, *Mr. O'Neil.*" She tipped her head toward where she could hear Velma running the vacuum cleaner in the master bedroom. "One of my maids is here with me. I can't risk her hearing this conversation."

"She can't hear us —"

"I fully understand the hotel's policy," she continued urgently. "Mrs. Newman has made it crystal clear to me. I'm to keep my staff from engaging in any workplace romances . . . uh, relationships. Any employee who doesn't comply with the rules will be immediately terminated. Period." She paused to watch him arranging a few of the flowers in the smaller crystal vase. He was actually pretty good at this. Not that she planned to mention it. Mostly she just wanted to get him out of here.

"Yes, I know all about the policy, Anna, but I —"

"There are no buts." She turned back to her feverish cleaning, bending down to scrub some drips from the face of a lower cabinet.

"Couldn't you just meet me somewhere away from the hotel, Anna — just to talk?"

She rinsed the cleaning rag again, determined not to get pulled in by him, although everything inside of her wanted to declare, *"Yes, Sean, I will gladly meet you anywhere. Name the time and the place and I'll be there."*

"Please, Anna, just hear me out —"

"Miss Gordon?"

Anna whirled around to see Velma standing behind Sean with a furrowed brow. "Yes, Velma?" Anna said nervously. "Do you need something?"

"I finished up everything you said to do.

Living room, powder room, master bedroom. What now?"

"How about the second floor?" Anna said eagerly. "Make sure it's presentable in case some guests go up there. Please check the other bedroom suite too."

Velma studied Sean and Anna with what seemed a knowing or perhaps even suspicious expression.

"Thank you, Velma," Anna said evenly. "You have no idea how much I value your help with this."

"Yes, Miss Gordon." Velma nodded in a subservient way. "Pleased to be of assistance."

"If you'll excuse me, Mr. O'Neil, Velma and I have work to do," Anna said crisply.

"Sorry to intrude," he said as he backed away. "Good evening, Miss Gordon."

Anna took in a deep breath, then muttered "Good evening" back at him. Without giving him another glance, she returned to her cleaning. As she scrubbed, she felt seriously aggravated at him. Why had he been so stubborn? Despite her warning him — practically begging him — to be quiet and just leave, he had persisted. She'd told him that Velma was here, that she might be listening, and yet he'd ignored her. It was as if he didn't even care. Maybe he wanted her to lose her job. But how could they fire her and not fire him? That wouldn't be fair.

However, Anna knew from experience that life was not always fair. It had often been her experience that life was completely unfair. And she knew it could happen again. She also knew that Velma was not stupid. She could put two and two together — and maybe already had. Then what? Anna could not afford to lose this job. Especially after having given Rodney that deposit check this morning. No, somehow she must do damage control with Velma. She must make her understand that there was nothing between Sean and Anna.

They finished up just a little before 6:00. "I'm so grateful for your help," Anna told Velma as she gave the sleek dining table one last swipe of her dusting cloth. It looked absolutely gorgeous with the tall vase of irises.

"Well, I appreciate the overtime," Velma said as she wheeled the housekeeping cart out the entrance, waiting as Anna securely closed the door. "My old man's been out of work for the last six years. I'm starting to think Marvin will never get back to work."

"Sorry to hear that." Anna pressed the button for the service elevator. "I know what it's like to be dependent on yourself . . .

your income."

"I expect you make more than a maid," Velma said a bit wryly.

"Well, yes. But I went to college for five years to train. And my job comes with a lot of responsibility."

Velma nodded as she pushed the cart into the elevator. "Yeah, I guess I wouldn't trade you for that. I'm not big on stress."

"I'm starving," Anna said as they went down. "I skipped lunch."

"Yeah, I just had some leftover soup. I'm hungry too."

"Want to join me for dinner?" Anna asked suddenly. "My treat since you helped me out. Or maybe your husband expects you home?"

"It's Marvin's poker night." She rolled her eyes. "Thank goodness, it's penny poker."

"I saw a cheeseburger place a couple blocks down. I've been dying to try it out."

"A cheeseburger sounds real good."

"Then come with me," Anna said as the elevator doors opened. "I'll even call ahead to see if we can get a table."

Velma nodded. "All right then. It's a date." She giggled as she wheeled the cart toward the storage room.

Anna told herself this wasn't exactly a bribe. It wasn't. It was simply her attempt to get to know one of her most dependable maids — and to thank her for her help this evening. Even so, she felt a tinge of guilt as she called the cheeseburger joint.

By the time Velma had changed and they'd walked to the restaurant, it was 6:45. Since Anna had made a reservation for 7:00, they hardly had to wait.

"This is fun," Velma said happily as they were seated at a colorful table. "Can't remember the last time I went out to eat at night."

"Well, I'm glad you could come." Anna picked up the menu. "I really don't enjoy eating alone." She told Velma about her four flight attendant roommates and how they came and went so much that meal planning was impossible.

"I think I'd like that." Velma sighed. "Every time I get home, Marvin looks at me like meals on wheels just arrived."

After they placed their order, Anna worked the conversation back to the incident between her and Sean. "It's interesting," she said. "Mr. O'Neil and I grew up in the same town. We've known each other since we were kids."

"Really?" Velma nodded. "I had no idea."

"Well, it's not something I'd go around advertising. I realize that we need to keep everything professional, but I'll admit it was a little awkward getting used to calling him Mr. O'Neil when I'd always known him as Sean." She laughed.

"I can see how that would be tough." Velma peered curiously at her. "For a moment there, I thought that maybe you two were involved. You know, like maybe you'd been dating?"

"No, no," Anna assured her. "I mean, we'd spent some time together before we started work at the hotel. But it was never anything serious. As a matter of fact, I think Mr. O'Neil is interested in my roommate Marley. She grew up in our hometown too. Her brother and Sean — I mean Mr. O'Neil — are old friends."

"Well, it certainly is a small world."

"I'm guessing that's what Mr. O'Neil wanted to talk with me about. He probably wanted my opinion on whether Marley would like to go out with him or not."

"Would she?"

Anna nodded. "Most definitely. She's been trying to get me to work on him for her. But I've been so focused on work, I suppose I forgot. Anyway, she came by yesterday, and she and Mr. O'Neil really seemed to hit it off." To change the subject, Anna told Velma about how she and Marley had managed to secure an apartment. "It was truly miraculous — right there in our same building. We get to move in the first of next month."

By the time they finished dinner, Anna felt certain of two things. One, Velma was convinced that there was absolutely nothing besides old friendship between Anna and Sean, and two, Anna could trust this older woman. As they parted ways and Anna walked home, she decided that she would choose Velma to be head of her shift. Besides her having more experience than the other maids, Anna knew she could count on her. And Velma probably wouldn't mind getting a small raise.

Anna had intended to work a full day on Sunday, mostly because she knew she'd accomplish more with no maids around to distract her. But as she walked to work she realized it was a beautiful day and her last free Sunday before the hotel opened. By the time she reached the hotel, she had decided to quit early. She was only accountable to herself on this, and she knew that housekeeping was already ahead of the game and in great shape. So why not?

As usual, she let herself in the side entrance, careful to punch in the security code lest she trigger the alarm system. She knew that some workers might be around today, but for the most part, the hotel would be quiet and empty. She turned on a hallway light and went to her office, going straight to work on the projects that seemed most pressing.

It was close to 1:00 by the time Anna was turning off the lights and locking the door to her office. She wasn't even sure what she'd do with this slightly unexpected time off, but she intended to do something. As she turned around, she ran smack into someone.

"Sean!" she exclaimed. "I mean, Mr. O'Neil — you scared the life out of me!"

He made an apologetic smile. "Sorry, didn't mean to startle you."

She steadied herself, putting her purse strap over a shoulder. "I was just finishing up," she said. "Just leaving."

"So was I," he said brightly. "Why don't we leave together?"

"Um . . ." She looked around, worried that someone might be watching. "What about the security cams?" she whispered.

"It's okay, Anna. We're simply co-workers, exiting through the side door. Don't act suspicious and no one will suspect." He nodded in the direction of the exit. "Let's go."

"Okay." She tried to act natural as they walked together. "Sorry, you just caught me off guard. I sort of forgot anyone else was in the building."

"It's pretty much evacuated," he said as he opened the door and punched in the security code. "It will be a much different place by this time next week."

"Yes." She nodded as they stepped out into the bright sunlight. "Exciting, isn't it?"

"Yeah." Sean securely closed the door, testing it to be sure.

Anna reached in her purse for her sunglasses, slipping them on partly to shield her eyes from the sunshine and partly to mask the surge of emotions running through her. "Well . . . have a good day, Mr. O'Neil."

"Come on, Anna." He tilted his head to one side. "You don't have to call me that when no one's around to hear."

"It's a good habit to stay in." She started walking in the direction of the apartment, although she was not really sure that was where she wanted to go. Of course, Sean continued walking with her.

"I'm really sorry about saying what I did yesterday," he began. "I really didn't think the maid was listening."

"Well, she was," Anna snapped back at him. Oh, she regretted her tone, but maybe it was for the best.

"I'm really sorry about that, Anna. I just felt so desperate to talk to you."

"Don't worry. I did damage control with Velma. Took her out for a cheeseburger and told her we were old friends." She glanced over at him. "I also told her you were dating my roommate."

"Dating your roommate?" His brow creased.

"Yes." She nodded firmly, feeling stubborn and still a little vexed. "Marley would love to go out with you, Sean. I thought perhaps you two might have already set something up by now."

"Would that make you happy?" He frowned.

She shrugged. "It would make me happy to remain gainfully employed."

"I get that, Anna. But it seems like you're being a little extreme about this."

"I'm being extreme?" She stopped walking, staring up at him. "I feel like I've risked everything to get this job. I realize I was lucky to get it. It could be a huge opportunity for me to finally get a good reference. Plus I've placed a pretty big deposit on an apartment. I feel like my whole life is riding on this right now. I can't afford to blow it, Sean. Do you get that?"

He pressed his lips together, exhaling through his nostrils like he was holding back whatever it was he had wanted to say.

"If that's extreme," she continued, "well, then I suppose I am being extreme. But I honestly don't know how else to be."

He slowly nodded. "I understand, Anna."

"Thank you." She let out a sigh and started to walk again.

"The reason I've been kind of stalking you lately —"

"Stalking me?" She blinked, turning to stare at him.

He grinned. "Well, not exactly stalking. But for the last week I've been trying to get a chance to have a word with you in private. You should've seen how many times I tried. Most recently in the Newmans' penthouse yesterday. I guess I was just so eager to speak to you that I threw caution to the wind."

She felt an unwanted surge of hope. He had made that much effort just because he wanted to talk to her — in private? "What did you want to speak to me about?"

"I just wanted to tell you I was sorry."

"Sorry for what?"

"For letting things get carried away . . .

on that day we spent together. I felt bad then and I've felt worse ever since. I knew about the hotel's policy, Anna. I should've been more careful."

"Oh." She simply nodded. "Okay, I accept your apology."

"I was really hoping we could still be friends."

She looked up at him, then quickly looked away. She couldn't bear to look into those eyes. He wanted to be friends? Really? "I, uh, I don't know, Sean. I mean, it's tricky being friends with fellow employees, you know?"

"But we could —" He stopped talking as someone approached.

Anna looked over to see that it was Max, just emerging from Elsie Dolce. He had a big smile and was coming directly toward them. "Just who I wanted to see." Max clapped Sean on the back. "I was about to call you, buddy."

"Hey, Max," Sean said with a smile.

Max looked at Anna now. "How's it going, Anna?"

"Good." She forced a big smile. "Great weather, huh?"

"I'll say." Max turned to Sean. "Elsie wants you to come to dinner tonight, Sean."

Before Sean could respond, Anna decided

to use this opportunity to excuse herself. "You guys have a great day," she said as she waved, hurrying off. On one hand, she was thinking it was a little rude to invite someone to dinner when someone else was just standing there. On the other hand, she was relieved to escape. Besides, she reminded herself as she strolled in the sunshine, Max and Sean's manners had improved greatly since adolescence. She remembered a time when she and Marley had made a batch of chocolate chip cookies, and while the treats were cooling and the girls were preoccupied with something else, the boys had gobbled them all up. And they never even said thank you. Maybe some things never changed.

22

Anna spent her afternoon walking around Greenwich Village and SoHo — much like she'd done before, only today she took the time to browse in the shops and even bought a few specialty grocery items. She stopped at Washington Square Park to listen as some classical musicians performed. It was really a lovely afternoon . . . except that she felt lonely. Compared to that other Sunday in New York, despite the ongoing blue sky and sunshine, the day felt gray and dismal. Really, it was more fun being drenched in a thunderstorm with someone you liked than being all by yourself on a warm sunny day.

It was nearly 6:00 by the time she got back to the apartment, and she was just putting away her groceries when Marley burst in. "What a day!" she exclaimed as she kicked off her shoes. "We got stuck in LA for three hours!" she declared as she grabbed a bottle of water from the fridge. "Three freaking hours just sitting on the tarmac. It was stinking hot, and we couldn't even run the AC most of the time. Talk about a nightmare. The passengers were furious. Like it was the flight attendants' fault for not taking off." She pressed the water bottle against her temple and sighed. "I'm beat."

"Sorry it was such a bad day," Anna said as she folded a bag. "Hopefully you can kick back and take it easy."

"No way. I've got a big date tonight." She glanced at the stove's clock. "Yikes, I better get ready."

"Big date?"

Marley's eyes lit up. "Well, sort of. You see, I texted Elsie last night — or maybe it was this morning New York time. Anyway, I begged her to throw an impromptu dinner party for Sean . . . and for me too. She's going to serve it on their rooftop terrace with all her pretty lanterns and stuff. It's really romantic up there. You should see it."

"Uh-huh." Anna acted nonchalant, like she hadn't already heard about this little soiree. "That sounds nice."

"Yeah." Marley looked slightly concerned. "I would've had her invite you too, Anna, but I didn't want it to be uneven, you know? Like a fifth wheel. Hey, that reminds me, I found a guy for you."

Anna cringed to think of Marley dragging in some weary, bedraggled businessman from her LA flight. "A guy for me?"

"Yeah. He's a pilot. Really good looking. And single. And fun."

"Then why aren't you interested in him?"

Marley smirked. "Because *I'm* interested in Sean, silly girl. Remember?"

"Oh . . . right." Anna turned away, trying to hide the emotions churning inside.

"Anyway, I told Warren — that's the handsome pilot — I told him all about you when we were in Bangkok and he is dying to meet you."

"What on earth did you tell him?"

"Just that you look like Nicole Kidman's younger sister." Marley tweaked a strand of Anna's hair. "And that you're really sweet and nice."

Anna rolled her eyes.

"Well, if you'll excuse me, Anna Banana, I need to go shower and make myself beautiful, and I'm just not sure I can accomplish all that by 7:30."

Anna smiled. "I think you already look beautiful, Gnarly Marley."

Marley laughed. "Yes, well, I need to *feel* beautiful too."

Anna made a point to stay out of Marley's

way as she beautified herself for her "date" with Sean. Okay, Anna knew it wasn't actually a date. Not really. But then it might turn into a date before the night was over. Anna wondered what it would feel like with the lanterns and things Marley had described. Would it be romantic enough to inspire a relationship between Marley and Sean? Why was Anna even allowing herself to go there?

"What do you think?" Marley asked as she finally emerged wearing a short red dress that showed off her legs as well as her curves.

"You definitely look hot." Anna thought perhaps she looked a little too hot — like she was showing off a bit too much. But no way was Anna going to say that.

"Thanks, dahling. Hopefully Sean will think so too."

"Have fun." Anna felt slightly sick inside as she said this. Because honestly, the last thing she wanted was for any of them to have fun tonight. Yet that made her feel even worse.

"You look tired," Marley said as she slipped on a pair of high-heeled sandals. "Which reminds me, you can have Tia's bed tonight." She laughed. "Imagine — Anna Banana, the bed-hopper — who back home would believe it?"

"Hopefully no one," Anna said dryly. "Since it's not really true."

"My little straight stick." Marley patted Anna on the cheek as she reached for her small glittery purse. "That's why you'll make such a good roommate for me. I know you'll never do anything regrettable. Good night, Anna Banana."

"Good night, Gnarly Marley."

As Anna sat down on the love seat, she wondered about what Marley had just said. *Anna would never do anything regrettable. The little straight stick.* Oh, she knew Marley meant no harm, but it stung just the same. It was like being told she was no fun. Like she didn't know how to be spontaneous, or that she was a wet blanket. Maybe it was true. Maybe Anna was all of those things. But Anna had learned long ago that it was dangerous to take risks. She'd seen both her parents make horrible, stupid mistakes with no care for the future — theirs or hers. She refused to repeat them.

For the next several days, Anna was determined to block out everything but work. Her plan was to keep her nose to the grindstone and do everything within her power to ensure that the opening of the

Rothsberg hotel was a huge success. Or at least a success on her end of the hospitality chain, because even if it killed her, housekeeping would be run like a well-oiled machine.

By Wednesday afternoon, all the rooms were set up and ready for guests. All the linens were impeccably in place, the soaps and toiletries were arranged on their sleek metal trays, beverage bars were stocked, everything in each of the rooms was shining and clean . . . perfect.

On Thursday morning, Anna distributed the maids' uniforms, explaining what was expected of them as far as appearances went. Then she spent the rest of the day doing training sessions. Oh, sure, the maids already knew how to make beds and hang towels and fold a proper point on the toilet paper. She wanted them to start practicing efficient time management, to take turns with various cleaning tasks to prevent injuries, and to help each other in flipping mattresses or moving heavy furnishings to clean more thoroughly. More than any of this, she wanted to impart to them the importance of practicing real hospitality.

"I know the guests who stay here will be strangers to you," she told them at the end of the day. This was their last meeting before the big opening tomorrow, and she'd even provided treats to sweeten up her final pep talk. "I want you to pretend that these guests are your most respected family members. Imagine that the guests you're caring for are your beloved grandparents. Make their stay at the Rothsberg as special as you can. That means smiles and polite greetings. If they ask for something, you make sure they get it ASAP. I expect every guest here to be treated like royalty. Is that clear?"

She looked at the maids and could see that some of them, like Bianca and Justine, were not really getting this. "Imagine that this hotel is your home and that you're entertaining important dignitaries — people you want to treat with great care and respect." She paused for emphasis. "I don't want this to be your motivation, but a hotel of this caliber — a boutique hotel — is known for having guests who leave generous tips."

Okay, now she had gotten their attention. "I have mentioned this before, but my policy is that your tips are yours to keep. If you've serviced the room well enough that a guest leaves a tip for you and your partner, then you've earned that tip. If you've serviced a room for a full week or longer, then you need to share your tip accordingly with the maids who serviced the room when you weren't working." She paused again, making sure they were still tracking with her. "I expect you all to be fair about this, and I do not plan to monitor your tips. Understood?"

There were a few questions and some discussion, and then she told them all good night. Being the head of housekeeping felt a bit like being a parent. At least she assumed it was like a parent might feel. She wanted her maids to do their best. She wanted them to take pride in their jobs. She didn't want them to bicker or do anything to embarrass her — or the hotel. Yet she knew that they were only human. They would probably make some mistakes. It would be up to her to fix them.

As Anna walked home, she felt a real sense of anticipation. Tomorrow would be the first big day. Sure, they wouldn't have full occupancy, but according to the Newmans at yesterday's staff meeting, they were nearly 75 percent full. That was impressive.

"There you are," Marley said as Anna came into the apartment. "Don't you ever check your phone?"

"It's been a pretty busy day." Anna reached into her bag, extracting her phone only to discover it was dead. "Looks like I need to charge it."

"Well, Elsie enjoyed our little dinner party last week so much that she's planned another one for tonight."

"Oh." Anna nodded absently. "But it's not even the weekend."

"I know. It just worked out better for Elsie and some of the other guests."

"Well, it's a lovely evening. I'm sure you'll all have a good time."

"You're invited too."

Anna was surprised. "Really — I'm invited?"

"Yes, and since I couldn't get ahold of you, I went ahead and accepted on your behalf."

"Oh, you did?"

Marley grinned. "Hey, it's free food. Elsie is a fabulous cook. I already got a jar of fabulous olives for us to take — as a hostess gift, you know. It's an expensive Greek brand, but I think it will go nicely with the Greek food that Elsie is making."

"What time is this little shindig?"

"Seven thirty. I already had my shower, and the other girls are gone, so you can have a completely uninterrupted shower."

"Wow, this is a special day." She paused on her way to the bathroom. "Is this supposed to be a dress-up event?"

"Sort of. I mean, I plan to wear a dress and you should too. Hey, while you're in the shower, maybe I can find something for you."

"Knock yourself out," Anna called. "You know the limits of my wardrobe."

It was a little past 7:00 by the time Anna and Marley were getting into a taxi to take them over to the Bronx where Max and Elsie lived. "It takes about twenty minutes," Marley explained to Anna after she told the driver where to go. "Unless there's traffic. In that case, we'll be elegantly late."

"I don't know about this dress." Anna looked down at the light blue sundress that Marley had finally proclaimed as "perfect." "It feels a little short and skimpy to me."

"Oh, Anna, you're such a little old lady. In fact, that dress is so much better on you that I'm giving it to you. Consider it my contribution to banishing the old lady."

Anna frowned at the uncomfortably familiar words. Marley had been calling her an old lady for most of her life. She didn't think it amusing at thirteen and perhaps even less now.

"Besides, that dress is longer than this one." Marley smoothed her red-and-white striped dress. "It's been a hot day and it'll be a warm evening. We'll be outside with no AC. You'll be glad you went with a cool dress. Just relax."

"I am relaxed," Anna told her. "I'm just not used to showing this much leg."

"Well, with your legs, you should show them more often."

Anna laughed nervously. "Who all is coming to this party anyway?"

Marley held up two fingers. "Vincent and Denise, for starters. Elsie wanted to have this tonight as a celebration for tomorrow's opening."

"The Newmans are coming?" Anna asked in alarm.

"Yeah. What's wrong with that? Max and Vincent are good friends. Elsie had been wanting to have them over."

"I know they're friends. I just didn't realize my bosses would be there tonight." Anna frowned down at the gauzy blue dress, wondering if it looked more like a nightie than a dress. "I just hope I'm dressed appropriately."

"Oh, Anna!" Marley shook her head. "You look like a Greek goddess." She held up the bag with the olives in it. "You'll go with the Greek olives *and* the food." She laughed.

"So . . ." Anna braced herself. "Who else

is coming?"

"Well, Sean, of course. And a few others."

By the time they got to the Bronx, Anna felt like a bundle of nerves. Why had she agreed to come tonight without asking about the guest list first? As it turned out, they were elegantly late. Denise and Vincent, looking comfortable in summery clothes, were already there, chatting casually with Sean and Max. Greetings were exchanged and Anna tried to act calm, but she felt like it was a thin veneer that everyone could easily see past.

Anna went to look for Elsie, finding her busily arranging some interesting concoction involving grape leaves. "Can I help?" Anna offered.

"Thanks, Anna, but most everything is done."

"It looks amazing," Anna told her.

"It's called grape leaves Aleppo," Elsie told her. "Hopefully it will taste amazing too."

"This terrace is absolutely beautiful," Anna said. "The lanterns and flower boxes and everything. It's perfectly charming."

"We love it too," Elsie said. "Everyone in our apartment building has helped make it special up here. We all take turns using it, and since no one had reserved it for tonight,

I thought, why not?" She lowered her voice. "Besides, I kind of owed the Newmans a dinner. Thought this would be a good way to celebrate with them."

"Great timing."

Elsie called out to Max. "Time to check those kabobs." Elsie set the grape leaves plate on a little table that already held some other things, including a pretty platter of colorful veggies and olives and a large bowl of hummus. "Appetizers," Elsie called out, and the others drifted over. Anna filled an appetizer plate for herself, but after briefly greeting the Newmans and Sean, she casually wandered over to the edge of the terrace, pretending to check out the view as she was actually attempting to gather her wits. Just exchanging those few words with Sean had been unnerving. Looking into his eyes was almost painful. She knew she was being silly, and that she had to get beyond this. Taking several deep breaths, she reminded herself that she was a grown woman — not a schoolgirl.

"Are you all ready for the big day tomorrow?"

Anna turned to see that Sean had joined her. "Yes," she said crisply. "I am."

"That's great." He made a congenial smile. "It must've been no small task to put all those rooms together as well as to get your housekeeping staff ready."

"It's certainly kept me busy." She turned away, looking out over the other rooftops as if they were extremely interesting.

"I feel really good about the staff I've hired."

She turned to look at him, knowing that he was probably making small talk for the sake of the Newmans and feeling irritated by it. "Excuse me," she said curtly. "I need to speak to Elsie about something." She walked away. Okay, she knew it was rude and immature, but it was simply a survival tactic on her part.

Before Anna made it back to Elsie, Marley came over with a tall blond guy in tow. "Hey, Anna, I want you to meet Warren. Warren, this is my good friend Anna."

"Warren the pilot?" Anna immediately regretted her words. How juvenile. At least she hadn't said "the handsome pilot," although he was handsome enough. Besides that, he was a good diversion — a good excuse to keep a distance from Sean.

"Some people call me that." Warren grinned as he shook her hand. "Pleased to meet you, Anna." He winked at Marley. "You didn't exaggerate. She does look like Nicole Kidman."

Anna waved her hand. "Marley always says that. You'd think I paid her or something."

Marley laughed. "Now there's a thought."

As Anna and Warren stood there visiting, Marley eventually slipped away, going over to join Sean and the Newmans. Anna realized now that it was a smaller group than Marley had insinuated earlier. Just eight people and, it seemed rather clear, *four* couples, since Marley had obviously partnered Anna with Warren. When it was time to sit down for dinner, they were placed next to each other, with Marley and Sean directly across.

It wasn't as if Anna minded being with Warren. Certainly he was pleasant enough. And not hard to look at either. But somehow, seeing Marley sitting next to Sean and chatting so intimately with him — well, it was still rather irksome. Anna felt like she'd been duped. Even so, she did her best to keep a smile pasted on her face, making her best attempts at table talk and looking forward to when this evening was over.

Fortunately, a number of talkative personalities were present and Anna didn't have to be overly chatty. Much of the talk centered on the opening of the Rothsberg tomorrow. Several toasts were made to the success of the hotel. But as the evening progressed, Anna found herself saying less and less, and although she tried not to, she was subtly studying Marley and Sean, trying to gauge their interest level.

Sean, as always, was being the perfect gentleman — attentive and personable and thoughtful. Marley was clearly infatuated with him. If Sean made a joke, she laughed, perhaps too loudly. If he asked for something, she was the first one to jump for it. Anna wondered if Marley realized how silly she looked.

Anna did her best to make polite conversation with Warren when there was a lull or if he asked her a question — and he asked her a lot. She could tell he was probably a good guy, but she didn't feel any serious interest in this relationship. Yes, he was good looking, but he was not her type. She could feel it deep inside of her. Despite his attentiveness, she had no intention of leading him on. When Elsie stood to start clearing the table, Anna quickly offered to help. Efficiently stacking an armload of plates, she followed Elsie over to the makeshift outdoor kitchen.

"This must've been a lot of work bringing everything up here," Anna said as she set the dishes in a plastic tub of soapy water.

"Max did most of the packing up the stairs, and he promised to pack it back down." Elsie smiled. "I'm just the cook."

"And an excellent one."

"Thanks. Want to help me get dessert?"

"Absolutely."

"I left it in the apartment," Elsie said as she led the way back downstairs, "so the ice cream wouldn't melt. Plus I chilled the plates."

"I barely saw your apartment when Marley and I got here earlier, but it looked really cute."

"I love it," Elsie said as she opened the door for Anna. "I've lived here about six years. Max had another place, over in the Village, and we could've lived there, but I just couldn't bear to leave here. Not only is this apartment bigger, but we've got the terrace. I don't mind riding the subway. It gives me a chance to chill and catch up on my reading. So Max sublet his apartment to a friend, and that's where Sean is staying right now."

"That was handy." Anna looked around the charming apartment. "You have a real knack for decorating, Elsie."

"Thanks!" Elsie handed Anna a carton of vanilla ice cream and a metal scoop. "How are you at making ice cream balls?"

"I'll do my best." Soon she was dipping relatively round ice cream balls and setting them next to generous servings of baklava. She watched as Elsie artistically drizzled strings of honey over the whole concoction. "That looks yummy." Elsie placed four servings onto a tray, and Anna offered to take them up.

"Great. I'm going to make some coffee."

"I'll come back for the other four," Anna told her.

"Oh, that's okay. You stay up there and enjoy the others."

"I'll come back and get the other desserts first," Anna insisted. The truth was, she was enjoying this break from the other diners. She needed a chance to breathe and compose herself.

As Anna was serving the first round of desserts to the Newmans and Marley and Sean, she caught Sean watching her closely. In fact, it seemed more like he was staring at her. She was determined not to reveal how nervous he was making her. She hoped that he wasn't looking at her with disapproval due to the skimpy sundress, although Marley had been right that it was rather comfortable on this warm, balmy evening. Trying to avoid Sean's steady gaze, she focused her attention on not dumping an ice cream ball in anyone's lap. Then she went back for the next tray. Before long they all had their desserts and coffee and were visiting happily.

As the sun dipped below the horizon of the rosy sky, the terrace grew even more lovely. The lanterns and hurricane candles glowed in a magical way, and strains of Greek music that Max had put on added to the amazing ambiance. Anna could see why Marley had called this place romantic. It was so delightful that Anna could almost imagine falling in love with Warren the pilot. Except that she knew it was hopeless. She'd already taken one fall this summer. One fall too many.

23

Although it was opening day, the hotel was eerily quiet by midday on Friday. That was only because check-in wasn't until 3:00. Anna had held a meeting with the maids on duty, checking their uniforms, hair, and makeup. To her relief, everyone looked fine. Even Bianca and Justine had pinned up their hair just like Anna had instructed. And to Anna's delight, the special packaged chocolate mints had come in. Wrapped in gold foil with the hotel's insignia embossed on top, they were to be placed on the pillows of freshly turned down beds in the evening. As she gave a box to each of the maids, she pointed out that she'd written a date on top of the box to remind the maids of how long the quantity of mints should last. Not that she didn't trust them, exactly. But she knew how easy it was for a few small things to go missing . . . and before long it was a lot of small things.

Anna was just making a final walk-through of the lobby and public areas of the hotel, inspecting to make sure that everything was perfection, when she noticed Mrs. Newman approaching. She looked sleek and stylish in her cream-colored jacket and skirt with a loose pastel-colored scarf draped around her neck. "Good afternoon, Anna," Mrs. Newman said. "Do you have a minute?"

"Certainly." Anna nodded.

"My office," Mrs. Newman said.

As they walked, Mrs. Newman was reading her phone and saying nothing. For some reason, Anna was starting to feel nervous. Was something wrong? Had Anna forgotten something? Had someone on her staff made a mistake?

Mrs. Newman opened her door. "Your suit looks very nice on you, Anna."

"Thank you." Anna made an uneasy smile. "I was just admiring how chic you look today, Mrs. Newman."

"Thank you." She pointed to a chair. "Take a seat."

Anna sat down on the edge of the chair, keeping her back rod straight. Waiting.

"Vincent asked me to speak to you, Anna."

"Oh?"

"He's quite concerned about something." She looked evenly at Anna. "It's about you and Sean."

Anna felt her throat getting dry. "Yes?"

"Vincent said that he observed you two last night, and something he saw bothered him."

Anna pressed her lips together, waiting.

"In fact, he said it wasn't the first time he'd been worried that something was amiss."

"Really?" Anna took in a shallow breath, bracing herself.

"Yes. I told him it might be his imagination, but he was so insistent that I speak to you. He made me promise to deal with this before we opened today."

Anna barely nodded. "What seems to be the problem?"

"Vincent is convinced that you are harboring some deep dark resentment toward Sean."

"What?" Anna blinked.

"Yes, I know it sounds a bit silly. But Vincent thinks that because Sean was hired for the position you had hoped to get, you are holding that against him."

"No, that's not true at all. I honestly believe that Sean — I mean, Mr. O'Neil is the perfect one for the job. I have absolutely no resentment."

"Yes, that's what I told Vincent last night.

Then he suggested that it might have something to do with you two growing up in the same town. Perhaps something happened to drive a wedge between you. Something that's made you feel disrespect toward him."

"No, there's nothing at all like that," Anna assured her. "I've always had the utmost respect for, uh, Mr. O'Neil. Honestly, he was a really great guy back in Springville. I mean, he's *still* a really great guy. I do respect him."

"Then why is Vincent so certain there's something between you two?"

"I don't really know." Anna felt a mixture of relief and fear.

"Vincent refuses to employ managers who don't get along, Anna. I must agree with him there. For our hotel to succeed, we need all our managers to be on excellent terms with each other. Good communication is crucial in a business like this. If you have trouble communicating with Sean, it will set us up for problems. Can you understand that?"

"Absolutely. I have no problems communicating with Sean — I mean, Mr. O'Neil. We've had frequent conversations."

Mrs. Newman studied Anna now, as if she was trying to make heads or tails of this. "I have to admit, it is perplexing. Vincent actually has really good instincts about people." She frowned. "So do I."

"I think I know what the problem is," Anna said cautiously. Somehow she had to straighten this mess up, and that would require honesty. She didn't have to spill all the beans, but she needed to spill some.

"Really?" Mrs. Newman leaned forward with interest.

"You see, I've been lecturing my maids about not getting involved with other employees. I've told them to avoid even casual friendships with the opposite sex. I know, that's probably extreme, but I've seen how quickly these relationships can develop in the workplace, and I'd hate to see any of my maids lose their employment."

"Yes, and I appreciate that."

Anna made a crooked smile. "Maybe I've been acting overly cautious myself. I suppose I thought I was setting some kind of example. Perhaps I simply took it too far."

Mrs. Newman held a finger in the air. "That must be it, Anna. It makes perfect sense. I told Vincent last night that you were a very serious worker, very diligent, and I thought perhaps he'd misread your work ethic as hostility toward Sean. But you were simply being careful."

"Yes." Anna nodded eagerly.

"Well, from now on, I want you to treat Sean like a friend, Anna. You're both important managers. We need you two to communicate. In fact, I would recommend that you schedule regular meetings. Perhaps even daily for the first few weeks of operation. Can you promise to do that?"

"Certainly."

"I'll inform Sean of this too."

"Great." Anna forced a big smile. "That will actually be helpful. A way to make sure we're always on the same page."

"Exactly." Mrs. Newman stood. "I'm so glad we cleared the air on this, Anna. I can't wait to tell Vincent that he was wrong." She laughed. "That doesn't happen a lot." She looked at her watch. "Say, have you taken your lunch yet?"

"Not yet. I was about to."

Mrs. Newman reached for the phone receiver, hitting an extension number and waiting. "Oh good, Sean, you're still in. Have you had lunch yet?" She waited. "Well, I have Anna here in my office. I want you two to take your lunch break together. A meeting of sorts. I'll call down to the restaurant — they're not open until this evening, but I'll tell them you're there to do a managerial inspection. I'm sure they can throw something together for you." She paused. "Yes, I'll send Anna now." She smiled with satisfaction as she hung up. "There. You can go meet with him right now."

"Uh, thank you." Anna stood with uncertainty.

"Hurry along," Mrs. Newman waved as she picked up the phone again. "I'll let the restaurant know."

Anna felt slightly dazed as she walked back toward the lobby. A forced lunch date with Sean? So that they could communicate better? To placate Mr. Newman's concern that they were at odds? How perfectly ridiculous. However, as she got closer, she could see the sensibility in this plan. Perhaps it was just what she needed. If she started having daily meetings with Sean, it might help to make her more comfortable. Get her past these troubling feelings. Help her to move on.

"Anna," he said cheerfully as they met in front of the restaurant. "I hear we're going to play spies in there."

"Something like that."

He gave her a curious glance as he opened the door. *"Entrez, s'il-vous-plaît."*

"Merci beaucoup."

"I want to make sure we don't step on

any toes." Sean excused himself to go to the kitchen to speak to the chef, and Anna wandered around the beautiful restaurant. Everything, like the rest of the hotel, was old-world elegant perfection. Seeing the doors to the courtyard and sunshine pouring in, she couldn't resist going out there. The fountain was bubbling and the flower pots looked even fuller and prettier than the last time she'd been out here.

"There you are," Sean said as he joined her, handing her a lunch menu. "Hey, why don't we eat out here? That way they won't have to reset a table in the dining room."

"I'd love to eat out here," she told him.

"I'll go let them know."

As Sean went back inside, she found a table in dappled sunlight, sat down, and took a deep breath, attempting to calm herself. This was simply a business luncheon, she told herself as she skimmed over the menu. The beginning of a good healthy business relationship between her and . . . Mr. O'Neil. Nothing more.

"What's going on?" Sean asked as he sat across from her. "Why did Mrs. Newman set up this little tête-à-tête?"

Without beating around the bush, Anna retold the whole story in detail, only pausing as a waiter came out with water and table settings and to take their orders. After he left, she continued spilling the whole slightly embarrassing tale.

"I'm afraid it's my fault," she said finally. "It seems I was being a little too cool toward you." She explained what she'd told Mrs. Newman, about being overly cautious as an example to the maids.

"She bought that?"

Anna nodded. "Absolutely."

"That still doesn't explain why we're here, having lunch together."

"Mrs. Newman decided that you and I should have daily meetings. This is our first one."

"I'm down with that." He grinned.

"So am I. Managers need to be in communication. It makes perfect sense."

His eyes twinkled. "So we're friends then?"

She stuck out her hand. "Totally."

He grasped it for a moment, then shook. "Good. I missed your friendship."

As she extracted her hand from his, she tried to ignore the electric tingles that were running up her arm. This was business. "You're all set for opening today?" she asked as she laid her napkin in her lap.

"All set." He pursed his lips. "Trying not

to think this is just the calm before the storm."

"You don't really think there'll be a storm, do you?"

"Well, there are bound to be a few kinks and wrinkles. You have to expect that. But we'll iron them out."

"Yes, we will."

They continued to talk about the hotel and their expectations. As they ate, they discussed some of the challenges with some of their employees, offering suggestions to each other. By the time they finished, Anna actually felt better. Like they really were friends — members of the same team, working for the same thing.

"Thank you," she told him as they were leaving.

"Why are you thanking me?"

"For making our first business meeting go so smoothly."

"We can both check our calendars for the best time to keep on meeting. I assume that it won't always need to be this long." He chuckled as they paused in the main lobby. "Though I'll admit it was pretty nice."

"I'd think fifteen to twenty minutes would be sufficient."

He nodded. "Sounds good to me." He glanced at his watch. "We have a couple of guests checking in early today. I should probably get back to my staff. Good luck today, Anna."

She smiled. "You too."

As she walked back to her office, Anna held her head high, thankful that was behind her. Really, it hadn't been so bad after all. In fact, she felt as if she'd won a small victory. Over herself.

The opening of the hotel went surprisingly smoothly. Oh, there were a few kinks and wrinkles like Sean had predicted, but nothing significant. Anna couldn't have been more pleased with the quality of her maids' service. She had warned them that she'd be doing pop-in inspections, but each time she popped in, she'd been pleasantly surprised. Everyone — even Bianca and Justine — seemed to be on their best behavior.

By Sunday afternoon, after most of the weekend guests had checked out, Anna felt confident that housekeeping was off to a solid start. Still, she knew she'd have to be diligent. She told the maids that pop-in inspections would continue for the next few weeks. What she didn't tell them was that they would probably continue indefinitely. She did tell Ellen. "Well, it's the official changing of the guard," Anna said as she got ready to go home. "I know everything is in good hands until I get back on Wednesday." Already Ellen had been working the later shift, and Anna had no reason to believe this woman wasn't completely efficient. Perhaps even more efficient than Anna, although Anna wasn't ready to admit that to anyone.

"I have your number if there's any kind of emergency," Ellen reminded her. "Go home and enjoy your days off."

"Well, it's certainly good timing." Anna explained how she and Marley would be moving into their new apartment on Tuesday. "This will be the first time I've had two days off in a row since I started working here."

"You deserve it." Ellen was looking over the notes Anna had made for her. "So far everything seems to be running like clockwork. You've done a great job."

Anna thanked her, then gathered her things and left. Ellen was right: their department had been running smoothly. Even Anna's morning meetings with Sean had gone surprisingly well. So much so that she began to think that all her stress and agony over him was simply a product of her imagination. At least that was what she kept telling herself. She hoped that over time she would convince herself of it. Until then, she would continue her brainwashing techniques.

It wouldn't hurt having a couple days off. She was looking forward to getting their new apartment set up. She'd already gotten a sneak peek at it and couldn't wait to actually move in. The painters were supposed to be finished by Monday afternoon, and already Anna was making plans for where things might go. Not that she had any furnishings. Marley didn't seem to really care as long as she had a comfortable bed to sleep in and a bathroom only shared by two. But Anna wanted more.

Although she was trying to be cautious with her savings account, her precious nest egg, she also knew that payday was right around the corner. She thought maybe she could splurge a little, just this once. After all, she'd never really had a place of her own before. Well, it was hers and Marley's, although so far, it felt more like Anna's since she'd made the deposits and Rodney had informed her that the lease was in her name. That was fine. She needed some housing references of her own. This would only help.

Anna had made a list of some furnishings and household goods that she thought would be nice for the apartment. She was longing to feel settled in and at home. She hoped that it would provide just one more good distraction for her heart. Because Anna knew she was going to get over this — in time.

24

Anna got up earlier than necessary on Monday morning, but only because she was so excited over the prospect of shopping for her new apartment. She'd slept in Sophie's bed last night, and it wasn't a very comfortable one, so she was determined to shop for a good bed. She and Marley had decided that since the single bedroom was relatively good-sized and even had two closets, it would be better to share it with twin beds. Besides, Anna was tired of sleeping on couches.

No one in the apartment was up yet, so Anna decided to use this opportunity to take a nice long shower, and then she packed up most of her things so that she'd be all set to move tomorrow. Seeing that the kitchen was a mess — as usual — she decided to show her appreciation one last time by giving it and the living room a thorough cleaning. She wasn't sure that anyone ever appreciated her housekeeping skills, but it made her feel better. As if she was paying her dues.

When she was done, she realized she was hungry, and since she hadn't had time to get any provisions lately, she decided to hit the nearest café and then continue on her shopping expedition. She was just going out the door when her phone started ringing inside her bag. She fished around for it, not sure who it might be. She didn't think it was her grandmother since they had spoken at length last night, and she hoped it wasn't the hotel with some sort of emergency. To her surprise, it was Sean.

"It's time for our meeting," he said.

"It's my day off," she told him.

"Yeah. Mine too. But I was hoping we could still meet."

"To talk business?" She frowned as she walked.

"Of course. I was just on my way to get a late breakfast. Want to join me? You can just get coffee if you've already eaten."

"Actually, I was on my way to get a late breakfast too," she admitted.

They arranged to meet and Anna tried not to get herself worked up over this as she entered the Little Red Hen Café. This was a business meeting. That was all.

"Hey, Anna." Sean waved from a table by the window.

Anna greeted him as she sat down, then pretended to be captivated by the menu posted on the wall.

"This is great," Sean said after the waitress took their orders. "I really didn't feel like eating alone today."

"You said this was a business meeting," she reminded him.

He beamed at her. "It is. I just wanted to say great job with everything, Anna. Your housekeeping team is the best."

"The best?"

"Absolutely. We even had several guests compliment the quality of maid service."

"Really?"

"Yep. I thought you should know."

"Well, thanks." She paused as the waitress set down their coffees. "That's very nice to hear."

"See?" He spooned sugar into his cup. "This is a business meeting."

"Well, if we're dispersing compliments, I should tell you that I'm very impressed with how well you've managed everything, Sean. The opening was amazingly smooth. It's obvious that the hotel is in very good hands."

"Thank you." He picked up his phone

with a slightly uneasy expression. "I just hope that Thomas isn't having any problems."

"It's a Monday," she reminded him. "The hotel is less than thirty percent occupied. It's probably totally dead there right now."

He made a sheepish grin. "Yeah, I know. It just feels kind of like being a new parent and leaving your baby alone with the sitter for the first time."

She laughed. "You know, I've had the exact same feeling."

They chatted as their food was served, and when there was a lull in the conversation, Anna asked him something she'd been curious about for a while. "What was it that got you interested in hotel management? I mean, you seemed like the kind of guy who could do anything. Obviously, you could've gone into your family's tire business. Why hotels?"

"First of all, I could never have worked in the family business. I hate the smell of tires." He wrinkled his nose. "Always have."

She nodded. "I know exactly what you mean. I took my grandma's car to get new tires last year, and I nearly got sick in the waiting area. The smell of rubber was so strong. I had a headache all day."

"When I was nine, my dad took me to

Chicago with him. He was going to some tire convention and it was my birthday, so he offered to take me along. Or maybe Mom made him. I can't remember."

"Ugh, a tire convention — that must've smelled pretty bad."

He laughed. "Actually, I can't even remember what the convention was like. All I remember is being totally blown away by the fantastic hotel. It was a huge glass building, right by the river. Everything was so shiny and clean and beautiful — I was just in total awe." He sighed. "You see, my mom wasn't much of a housekeeper. To be fair, she had six kids and did the bookkeeping for my dad, so she was pretty busy. But she never really cared if the place was a mess." He shrugged. "With six kids . . . well, you can probably imagine."

"Interesting." Anna was surprised. She'd always assumed that Sean O'Neil's home was perfection.

"Seeing this immaculate, amazing hotel just blew my mind. I remember waiting for my dad inside the hotel. I was standing in the lobby, and he was outside tipping the valet or something. I had leaned my face against the window — you know how kids are — and suddenly I realized I'd left this nasty smudge on their clean, shiny window.

We'd probably just had lunch and I'll bet my face was greasy. Anyway, I used my hand, trying to wipe it off, and naturally, that just made it worse. I'm standing there feeling bad for making a mess when this big guy in a black suit walks up with a totally serious expression, and I'm thinking, oh no, he's going to arrest me and throw me in the hotel jail."

"Like there's a hotel jail." Anna laughed. "Although that's not a bad idea for some places. So what happened?"

"The guy reaches into his pocket, and I'm thinking it's going to be handcuffs or a gun. But he pulls out this little tiny spray bottle." Sean showed the size with his fingers. "He gives my smudge a couple of squirts, then pulls out a handkerchief and instantly wipes it clean. Then he turns to me and says, 'Presto change-o,' and he pats me on the back with a big grin."

"What a guy."

"Yeah. It sounds silly, but it had an impact on me. I thought, when I grow up, I want to work in a place like that. Where everything is clean and orderly and the men wear cool suits and have good manners." He chuckled. "Pretty weird dream for a nine-year-old boy, huh?"

"I think it's sweet."

"What's your story? Why did you choose hotel management?"

Anna was still so touched by his story that she knew she had to tell him the truth, something she'd managed to avoid doing when she got asked this question back in college. "Well, in some ways my story's not all that different than yours, although your parents were functional, whereas mine were not even close. I already told you about how messed up my parents were, and our living conditions were awful. Sometimes we'd get thrown out of a place, and a couple of times, when we had nowhere to stay, someone would put us up in a motel. I'm not even sure who. Maybe it was a church or the mission or something." She paused to sip her coffee.

"I can still remember that first moment of going into a clean and neat motel room. Sure, it was a cheap motel, but to me it was like the Ritz compared to what I was used to. I went around examining everything and wishing we could just live there always and that we could keep it looking nice and tidy. It got messy right away, and even though I'd try to clean it up, my parents didn't care. I know it sounds pathetic, but I think that's when I got the hotel bug."

"That's not pathetic," Sean said with a

sad expression. "Although it is a little heartbreaking."

"Sorry." Anna forced a smile. "Didn't mean to break your heart over waffles."

"Thinking of a little girl feeling like that." Sean shook his head. "That's hard."

"Well, fortunately I got out of there." Anna decided to change the subject by telling him about the new apartment. "I'm shopping for a few furnishings and things today." She felt her face lighting up. "I can't wait to get started." She glanced at her watch. "The stores should be open by now."

"Want any company?"

"You're kidding." She frowned. "You'd want to spend your day off looking for household items with me?"

"Hey, don't let this get around, but I took an interior design class in college and I happen to have pretty good taste in home décor." He made a sheepish grin. "For a straight guy."

She laughed.

"Seriously, just ask my oldest sister. I helped her with her first house." He pointed at her. "What's your style?"

"Style?"

"For your apartment. Are you a shabby chic girl? Traditional? Old-world? Contemporary? Midcentury modern?"

"Wow, you really do know your stuff."

"I wouldn't lie to you."

She thought about it. "I actually kind of like midcentury modern. But not the shiny plastic, metal, and glass sort of furnishings. Maybe I'm modern and traditional. Clean lines, but comfortable."

"I like that." His brows arched hopefully. "Do I get to come?"

She shrugged. "Well, if you really want to —"

"I do!"

"Okay, but I give you the right to bow out at any point."

"I'll keep that in mind."

By the end of the day, Sean had not only refused to bow out but had shown great endurance too. Perhaps even better than Anna's. Plus he'd been extremely helpful with decision making, which wasn't Anna's forte. He knew how to barter too. She was amazed how many items he'd gotten reduced. He'd even suggested they borrow the hotel's shuttle van to pick up some of the larger pieces on Tuesday.

"As long as I replace the gas, no one minds," he told her as they rode home in a taxi that was heaped with bags and boxes.

"I'll help you get your stuff inside," Sean

said as she paid for the taxi.

With an armload of bags, Anna nodded toward what remained on the sidewalk. "How about if you watch this while I run inside to see if the painters have finished? Maybe I can just leave everything inside there for the night."

When she got to the apartment, Rodney was just locking the door. "The painters finished about an hour ago," he told her. "Looks pretty good too. Wanna see?"

"If it's okay, I'd like to put some things inside tonight." She explained about the things still outside on the sidewalk.

He grinned as he handed her a key. "It's all yours, Anna."

"Thank you!"

"The painters used a low-VOC paint, so it doesn't even smell too bad."

Anna unlocked the door and peered inside to see all the walls looking clean and fresh and white. "It looks great," she told him.

"Tell Marley she can pick up her key tomorrow." He peeled off a strip of blue painter's tape that had been missed above the door. "Enjoy!"

"Thanks." Leaving the door open, she hurried out to tell Sean, and together they hauled the rest of the stuff up the stairs and into the vacant apartment, piling it all in the center of the living room.

"Hey, this isn't bad," Sean said as he walked around examining everything. "Not bad at all."

"I know." Anna ran her hand over a windowsill. "I've never had a place of my own before. I mean, I realize it's Marley's too, but she doesn't seem that interested in fixing it up. That's fine by me. Marley's most excited that the bathroom will only be shared by two of us." Anna went into the kitchen, which was similar to the one upstairs. "I know there's not much space in here, but I'm looking forward to cooking again."

"Do you like to cook?"

She nodded eagerly. "My grandma does too. Fortunately, she taught me a lot of things while I was growing up, although she usually did most of the cooking." Anna could feel Sean standing behind her, almost as if he was just inches away. She could imagine him reaching out to her, pulling her toward him — and just the thought of this made her slightly dizzy. She leaned forward, holding onto the edge of the sink.

"Are you okay?" he asked with concern.

"Yeah," she said slowly. "Probably just tired."

"And hungry," he added. "We haven't

eaten since this morning."

"Yeah." She nodded. "I got kind of light-headed. Maybe it's low blood sugar."

"Come on," he urged. "Let's run and get an early dinner. If we hurry we can beat the rush."

Anna knew she should decline, but after spending the whole day with him and having such a great time, it was as if her resolve had dissolved, so she agreed. As they walked, he made a phone call, securing them a table somewhere. She felt a little uneasy as they walked past the hotel, as if she was doing something wrong, although she knew she wasn't. In fact, she was doing exactly what the Newmans had encouraged her to do — developing a stronger friendship with Sean. At least she hoped that was what she was doing.

"Here we are," he proclaimed when they reached the same little restaurant where they'd first shared a meal together, on Anna's first Saturday here in New York. "I asked for a sidewalk table," he said. "Hope that's okay."

"Perfect."

It was perfect — the food, the conversation, the company. To Anna's relief, Sean didn't even argue when she insisted on paying. "It's my way of thanking you for all your help today," she said as she clung to the bill like a lifeline.

As Sean walked her back to her apartment, she knew she was treading on thin ice. She knew she needed to guard her heart more than ever right now. She could not afford to fall in love. She would not allow it.

"Thanks for everything," she told him as they lingered at the foot of the steps.

"Thank *you* for letting me hang with you all day," he said brightly. "It was a great distraction from worrying about the hotel." He held up his phone. "They never called once."

"Your darling baby is just fine after all," she teased.

"At least for now. I'll stop by the hotel tomorrow morning to see if anyone's using the shuttle van. If it's free, I'll give you a jingle. Okay?"

"Sure, if you don't think it's a problem."

"If I thought it was a problem, I wouldn't have offered."

She nodded as she moved a couple steps up the stairs. "Yes, I know you wouldn't." She knew she was trying to put a comfort zone of space between them. Not because she was worried about Sean either. "Talk to you tomorrow," she called as she continued on up. "Thanks again!"

When she reached the top step, she imagined she was home free. She pushed the security code, then hurried inside, but instead of going on up to the other apartment, she let herself into the new one. After all, Rodney had said it was all hers. Well, hers and Marley's. But for tonight, it was just hers.

25

Anna spent a couple hours opening boxes, unloading bags, and basically playing house. Okay, it was a bit of a challenge to play house without any real furnishings, but it was fun to imagine how it might look by this time tomorrow. Thanks to Sean's shopping savvy, she had made some fabulous finds at several furniture thrift stores. Thanks to Sean's persuasiveness, telling the salespeople that because of her job, Anna couldn't purchase anything that couldn't be delivered tomorrow, it was all scheduled to come on Tuesday.

In the meantime, she did get the kitchen and bathroom thoroughly cleaned and somewhat set up. She felt a tiny bit selfish taking over like this all on her own, but she knew that Marley had no real furnishings to contribute besides her bed, not to mention no real interest in playing house. That's what she had claimed, anyway. But by eight o'clock, Anna felt guilty, so she went upstairs to confess to Marley what she'd been up to.

"Marley got called in for a sick flight attendant this afternoon," Tia told Anna. "She won't be home until Thursday night."

"Oh, okay." Anna explained what she'd been doing, and since Tia didn't seem particularly interested, Anna decided to take her packed bags downstairs and start putting one of the closets to use.

"You can have Marley's bed tonight," Tia told her. "Unless you're sleeping down there. Do you even have a bed?"

"Not yet," Anna confessed. "I've got bedding, though. I might try camping."

Tia laughed. "Well, you're one tough cookie, Anna. I can't believe how you've gone from couch to bed to couch and no place to hang your clothes — and you never even complained."

Anna shrugged. "Well, I'll admit that I'm looking forward to having my own bed for a change."

"Thanks for cleaning up around here," Tia called as Anna was leaving. "I know we seem like a bunch of ungrateful slobs. But we did appreciate it."

"I appreciated you letting me stay here," Anna said. "It was a huge help to me for getting and keeping my job."

"Hey, that's New York karma. Someday you'll probably be helping some other girl out. What goes around comes around."

As Anna went downstairs, she considered that. "New York karma" sounded like a good thing to her. Kind of like hospitality. She took her time hanging up her clothes in the closet on the left side of the room. Marley had already put dibs on the right side since Anna didn't really care. Besides that, the left side was closer to the door, which meant she could slip out more quietly if Marley was asleep. It was perfect.

At the bottom of her big suitcase, Anna discovered the MP3 player speakers that she'd gotten in college. Suddenly longing for music, she set them up in the living room, and before long she was rocking out. Okay, she wasn't really rocking out since it was an old Sarah McLachlan song and not even turned up too loud, but she was certainly enjoying it.

Anna considered unpacking the bedding and pillow she'd purchased today, but although the hardwood floors were good for dancing, they didn't look too inviting for sleeping. With all she wanted to get done tomorrow, she probably needed a good night's rest, so she turned off the music and turned out the lights, and as she locked the door, she told the sweet little apartment good night.

Anna got up early on Tuesday morning. She knew none of her deliveries would come this soon, and she didn't expect Sean to call until around 10:00, but she could use this time to stock the kitchen with some staples. Armed with a rather long shopping list and several shopping bags, she trekked down to the closest grocery store.

"You moving in?" the elderly Asian woman asked as she put a bag of jasmine rice into the second bag.

"Yes. Into a new apartment," Anna told her. "I've been in New York a few weeks now."

"I can tell you are new." The woman held up a jar of cinnamon. "By what you buy."

Anna cringed to look at the running total. "It's kind of expensive, isn't it?"

"Yes. But it's not so bad if you cook. If you cook, you will save lots of money."

"Yes," Anna said eagerly. "That's what I hope."

"Too many kids don't cook. Waste money on restaurants. That's no way to live."

Anna smiled. "My grandma taught me to cook when I was a girl."

"That's a smart grandma. All girls should learn to cook."

Anna paid for her groceries, then hoped that she could manage to carry everything. She already knew that New Yorkers had to be tough, but she hadn't planned on lugging fifty pounds of groceries home. At least that's what it felt like. Fortunately, the grocery store was only a few blocks from her building. By the time she was unloading her purchases in the kitchen, her hands were throbbing and she had broken a sweat.

She had just finished putting the perishables in the fridge when she heard her door buzzer ringing. She looked out to the street to see a big white truck from the mattress store. Her bed was here! She was so excited that she raced down to let the delivery men inside, staying out of the way as they carried in and set up her twin bed and bookshelf headboard as well as a bedside bureau. It all seemed to take less than ten minutes, but before they could leave, she stopped them. "Do you suppose I could entice you to help me move another twin bed from upstairs?" she asked hopefully.

They didn't seem to mind, and before long Marley's twin bed was set up on the wall opposite from Anna's. "Thank you!"

Anna gave them a generous tip.

Anna opened the front window in the hopes that she would hear if another big truck pulled up while she was putting the bedding onto her new bed. She didn't want to miss a delivery, and she didn't want to keep them waiting. Of course, now she realized that she would need to stick around the apartment all day. At least until the last of the deliveries. She couldn't complain — this was starting to feel a lot like Christmas!

Sean called, as promised, a little before 10:00. "I've got the van — just leaving the hotel. Ready to go?"

She explained her concern about missing a delivery. "Marley can't be here because she's on flights until Thursday."

"No problemo. I'll swing by and get your receipts and pick up the stuff myself. As I recall it was only three stores, right?"

"That's right. I owe you big-time, Sean O'Neil."

He just laughed. "Well, I'll have to think of some way you can repay me."

She remembered what the woman had said about young people and cooking. "How about some home-cooked meals?" She told him about lugging home groceries.

"All right! Sounds like a plan."

Of course, after she hung up she instantly

questioned the sensibility of her spontaneous offer. Was she setting herself up for problems? She remembered what Mrs. Newman had said about friendships. Didn't friends cook for friends? Besides, she could make sure that Marley was around if and when she did cook for him. No big deal.

Besides, she didn't have time to obsess over this because one of the thrift store trucks had just pulled up. Before long she had a cream-colored sleeper sofa and a pair of lemon yellow chairs in place — and they looked great. Just like a real living room, albeit a small one. She was just admiring them when she heard another vehicle honking down below. Seeing it was Sean, she grabbed the bundle of receipts and ran them down to hand them off.

"Thanks," he said. "Better go, I'm double-parked."

"Thank you so much!" she exclaimed happily.

About an hour later the second thrift store truck arrived. The first thing they brought in was a tall painted dresser that Anna thought she and Marley could share in the bedroom. What she was most anxious to see was a set of Danish modern furniture that Sean had discovered. They had just been unloading the pieces into the shop, and

Sean claimed they were just like some that his grandmother used to have. "I think they might be valuable," he'd whispered. "If you decide you don't like them, you could always resell them on eBay for a profit."

She wasn't really sure about that, but as she saw the teak dining set being carried in, she was certain that she liked it. Next came the coffee table and end tables, and they looked perfect with the couch and chairs.

"The console table will go here by the door," Anna said as they were going back for the next load. "The bookshelf, over there next to the window." After the last of the Danish modern was put into place, Anna knew she owed Sean a great deal of gratitude. These pieces were perfect. Knowing that her grandma would appreciate them, she took a bunch of photos.

Sean arrived just before noon. Hearing the horn beep, she ran down to help him carry in lamps, rugs, decorative throw pillows, a set of dishes, pots and pans, and several other bulky items. "Wow, this is looking great," Sean said as he paused by the door. "I'd stick around, but I promised to have the van back before noon, and I'm cutting it close."

"Yes, do get the van back on time," she urged. "Thank you so much!" After Sean left, Anna worked to get the large area rug in place in the living room. She'd fallen in love with it at the first store they'd gone to, but with its shades of orange, moss green, and yellow, she couldn't quite imagine it in the apartment. Sean had encouraged her to get it, saying that it would be like a cornerstone for the rest of the furnishings. "Everything you pick out, just imagine it with that rug," he'd told her.

Of course, he was right. The rug was perfect. She took her time getting lamps and some other decorative pieces into place, but it just kept getting better and better. She was so excited to see it coming together that she felt like dancing. And that reminded her of the MP3 speakers, and before long she had them set up on the teak bookshelf with a selection of west coast jazz playing.

As she wadded up the various packing materials and trash, stuffing them into one of the biggest cardboard boxes, she couldn't remember when she'd ever been happier. It almost seemed wrong to feel this happy. But it was as if she couldn't help herself. Since she didn't have her key, she left her door cracked open as she took the box of trash down to the Dumpster, but when she got back, her door was closed. She looked up and down the hallway, thinking perhaps

Rodney had been by, but no one was around. Had Marley gotten home early and gone in? Anna pounded on the door, and to her surprise it swung open and Sean was inside.

"What —"

"Sorry," he said. "The super let me into the building, and I saw your door open and assumed you were in here."

"That's okay," she assured him. "Did you look around?"

His face lit up. "It looks fantastic, Anna!"

"I know." She went inside and closed the door. "I can't even believe this is my place. It's amazing."

"If we ever lost our jobs at the hotel, we could probably go into business setting up apartments for people."

She laughed. "That wouldn't be too bad."

Sean went around admiring everything with almost as much enthusiasm as Anna. "There's just one thing missing," he said.

"Huh?" She looked around, trying to figure out what she'd forgotten. "What?"

"Hold on and I'll get it." Sean headed back toward the bedroom.

"What are you doing?" she demanded.

"Just wait," he called. "I need to get something."

Feeling slightly dumbfounded and on the

verge of vexation, Anna waited. What on earth was he doing in the bedroom?

"Okay," he called out. "I've got it."

Sean came out carrying what looked like a stretched canvas, but he was holding the front of it toward him.

"What?" she cried out. "Where did you get *that*?"

He chuckled. "I stashed it in there while you were out."

"What is it?" She came over curiously, but he held up a hand like a stop sign.

"Not so fast."

"I don't remember buying anything like that. What is it?"

"It's a housewarming gift."

"A painting?"

"It's not an original." He grinned. "That would be a little out of my reach. But it's a pretty good reproduction."

"What is it?" she asked. "Can I see it?"

"Not yet." His eyes twinkled. "First of all, I know that it's wrong to buy someone else artwork. I mean, it's very personal what you hang on your wall. Chances are you won't even like it."

"How will I know if I can't even see it?" she asked impatiently.

"I want you to know that I understand," he continued. "I'll only let you see it after you promise to be honest."

"Honest?"

"If you don't like it, you have to tell me. It won't hurt my feelings. In fact, I asked at the shop and they said you can even return it, as long as it's within twenty-four hours."

"How do I know I want to return it when I haven't even seen it?"

"Promise you'll tell me if you don't like it?"

She held up her hand. "I solemnly swear."

"Okay." He turned the canvas around so she could see.

Anna's hand flew up to her mouth as she stared at the scene. It was obviously a Manhattan street, with tall buildings on each side and taxis and cars moving down the road. The sky was cloudy and the air was misty, lights glowed from the buildings' windows like illuminated amber, and the pavement of the street and sidewalk glistened in the rain.

"So . . . ?" Sean waited.

"Oh my." Anna felt close to tears and couldn't even explain why.

"You don't like it."

"No, that's not it." She swallowed against the lump in her throat.

"I can return it." Sean leaned it against the sofa, then came around to look at it himself, rubbing his chin thoughtfully. "Or maybe I'll just keep it."

"No," she said suddenly. "I mean, I *really* do want it, Sean. I love it."

He brightened. "You do?"

"It's just so . . . so wonderful . . . I think it literally took my breath away." She couldn't stop staring at it. It looked just like that Sunday when they got caught in the thundershower outside of St. Patrick's Cathedral.

"It's nice, isn't it?" he said happily. "It's called *Rainy Day New York.* Painted by Alexei Butirskiy. He's a Russian artist just a little older than us."

Anna couldn't stop staring at it. "It's so beautiful, Sean. I really do love it."

He lifted it up above the sofa now. "You could hang it up here."

She nodded. "That's perfect." Tearing her eyes away from the image, she headed for the kitchen. "I have some nails and a hammer I borrowed from the super."

Before long, they had the picture centered and hung above the sofa, and Anna was still staring at it in wonder. "I don't think I'll ever get tired of looking at it," she told Sean.

"I couldn't agree more," he said quietly.

But when she glanced at Sean, he seemed to be staring at her. Feeling her cheeks growing warm, Anna returned the hammer to the kitchen and, pausing in front of the sink, attempted to steady herself.

"Hey, Anna," Sean called. "You hungry?"

"Yes," she called back. "I thought I'd try out this stove and some of my new cookware. You game?"

Sean came into the kitchen. "Seriously? You're going to cook something?"

She smirked. "Well, it won't be anything fancy. But if you're interested —"

"I'm in," he told her and stood there, watching and waiting.

"Why don't you go sit in the living room," she suggested nervously. "Take a break . . . put your feet up."

He looked slightly reluctant but left anyway.

Anna looked in the fridge and in the food cupboard, and after some deliberation she finally decided to just keep it really simple by making one of her favorite lunches. If Sean didn't like it, he could always duck out to a nearby deli. She hummed to herself as she bustled about the tiny kitchen. It was fun getting out the new things she'd just purchased and using the moss green pots and pans. Sean was being so quiet out there, she wondered if he'd fallen asleep. She quietly set the Danish table with sleek white sandwich plates and bowls, laying the smooth flatware in place. She was tempted to take a photo, but her iPhone was in the other room and she didn't want to disturb Sean. It would be sweet if he was enjoying a little nap on the comfy sofa. She remembered how her grandpa often took a nap while her grandma was cooking.

26

Anna was just flipping the grilled cheese sandwiches for the second time when she heard the buzzer for the front entrance of the building. "Hey, Sean," she called out. "Can you see who that is?"

When he didn't answer, she went out to discover that Sean was gone and she was alone in the apartment. When she checked to see who was outside, Sean answered.

"What're you doing out there?" she asked as she pushed the button to let him into the building. She opened her door and there he was with a small bunch of flowers arranged in a Mason jar. "What?" She tilted her head to one side.

"For the table," he explained. "It just seemed like it needed something."

She couldn't help but smile as he carried the sweet arrangement of daisies, small sunflowers, lavender, and some bright green button flowers over to the dining table and set it down. "There," he said. "How's that?"

"Perfect." She pointed to a chair. "Take a seat. I hope the lovely table will help make up for the rather simple meal." Feeling slightly giddy, Anna ladled out their soup and set out the sandwiches. "Oh, I forgot something." She hurried back to get the little dish she'd put some pickles in. "Can't have grilled cheese without sweet pickles."

She sat down, looking at him expectantly. "I hope you like it, but if you don't, I'll understand."

"Like it?" He beamed at her. "This is one of my all-time favorite lunches. Mind if I say a quick blessing?"

She felt her heart give a happy lurch. "I'd love that."

They bowed their heads and Sean prayed. "Dear heavenly Father, we thank you for your provision, and we ask you to bless this meal and the hands that prepared it. We also ask your blessing on Anna's new apartment. We thank you for your goodness to us. Amen."

"Amen," Anna said in a slightly husky voice. "Thank you, Sean."

He lifted his spoon. "Thank you!"

As they ate, they talked about the apartment and the painting and the music that was playing. They talked about work and their plans for the big grand opening coming up. And although Anna's heart was singing a different kind of song, Anna's head kept telling her, *We are friends . . . just friends . . . that's all.*

Sean insisted on helping to clean up the lunch dishes, and eventually they wandered back to the living room where they both just stared at the painting again. "It reminded me of that Sunday," Sean said slowly.

"I know . . . ." Anna pressed her lips together, trying to think of something to say to move them on from this place. "You know what this apartment needs?" she said suddenly.

"What?" he asked with interest.

"A pet."

He looked surprised. "Seriously — a pet in here? What about when you're at work?"

She laughed. "I'm not thinking of a cat or a dog. Nothing with hair. But I do think a goldfish in a nice round bowl would look lovely right here." She pointed to the console table by the door. "My grandpa got me a goldfish when I was nine. It was my very first pet. I named her Ariel — you know, like the Little Mermaid." She laughed. "Not terribly creative. But I managed to keep that fish alive for several years."

"Let's go get a fish," Sean exclaimed.

"Yes! I noticed a pet shop about six blocks from here." She grabbed her purse.

It felt good to be out in the sunshine. As much as Anna loved the new apartment, she had felt the walls closing in on her — on them — and she was relieved to escape. Outside, they were walking briskly, making jokes and laughing. This was what friends did.

"I'm sure it's down this street," Anna told Sean after they'd walked for what felt like more than an hour and going around in a circle. She paused to pull out her walking map, trying to determine where they were.

"You're not lost, right?" He jabbed her with an elbow as he pulled out his phone. "How about if I check my GPS?"

"Do as you like," she said, turning the map around. "Which way is north?"

Standing on the street corner, they bantered playfully, but eventually, with the help of his phone, Sean figured it out. "Two blocks that way." He pointed down the side street.

Sure enough, there was the pet shop. As they went inside, Anna wondered how she'd missed it, but she quickly forgot all about that as she knelt down to look at some fluffy brown puppies. "Oh my!" She reached in to caress their soft fur. "It's a good thing I'm only shopping for a fish today."

They went around looking at all the animals, holding the kittens, playing with the puppies, chatting with the birds, and staring at the creepy creatures, until they got to the fish section. Anna picked a medium-sized fishbowl. "Not too big, not too small, just right." She also got some nice black rocks for the bottom of the bowl, a little ceramic arch for the fish to swim through, some fish flakes, and even drops to remove chlorine from the water. She set these up by the cash register and informed the young man that she was ready to choose her fish.

"Now to pick out just the right one." Anna went over to the big tank of goldfish, squatting down to see better. "I want a midsized one," she told the clerk as he prepared a plastic bag, then dipped his net into the tank, causing the fish to scramble. She pointed to an interesting fish. "Can you get that one? The one with one black spot?" It took several attempts, but eventually the fish was caught.

"Nicely done," Sean told him. "If only you could figure out how to do that with a marlin."

The fish things were loaded into a box, which Sean insisted on carrying. This time their walk, thanks to Sean's GPS, really was only six blocks. In the apartment, Sean watched as Anna rinsed out the fishbowl as well as the rocks. She arranged the rocks and the arch and filled the whole thing with tap water. She carefully followed the instructions for the chlorine drops, then set the fish, still in the bag, down into the water in the bowl, opening the top of the bag to allow in some fresh air.

"Looks like you know what you're doing," Sean observed.

"I told you I had goldfish experience." She grinned. "One of my chores was to clean the fishbowl on Saturday. But I didn't have these handy drops." She put the bottle in a kitchen cabinet. "I had to fill up pitchers of water to sit overnight."

"You never got to have any other pets?" he asked as he leaned against the counter. "Even though you proved yourself a responsible pet owner?"

"No. My grandpa had allergies."

"I see." He nodded. "You've told me a lot about your grandma but not much about your grandpa. What was he like?"

She considered this as she reached for a new dish towel, using it to dry and polish the outside of the bowl. "He was a quiet person. A very traditional man. He liked everything just so. He went to work and Grandma stayed home to cook and clean. Their roles were very clear-cut. I suppose I was kind of afraid of him at first. He was so serious and somber. I guess I was worried that he might decide he didn't like having a kid around, you know, and if I did something wrong, he might send me off somewhere."

"That must've been hard."

"It was at first, but as the years passed, I began to understand him better. I realized that his heart had been broken by my mom . . . when she left . . . got in trouble . . . and then died. I think he was afraid I'd follow in her footsteps."

"But you didn't."

"That's right. Eventually my grandpa realized that I wasn't going to. Then things got better between us. He seemed happier." Anna checked the temperature of the fish water. "I think the fish is acclimated," she announced, tipping over the bag and allowing the fish to swim freely.

"He's pretty," Sean said as he bent over to see better.

"How do you know it's a he?"

Sean laughed. "I'm not sure. He just seems like a he to me."

"I think I agree." Anna nodded as she

picked up the bowl, carrying it out to place it on the console. "There," she said, stepping back to take it in. "Isn't that much better?"

"I do believe you're right."

"There's something nice about having a living thing in a room."

"Yeah." He nodded.

"I wonder . . ." Anna looked at him. "What if there were fishbowls in the guest rooms at the Rothsberg?"

"Fishbowls in the guest rooms?" He rubbed his chin thoughtfully.

"Yes. I mean, imagine you were staying at a hotel by yourself for a few days. Wouldn't it be nice to share your room with a bright shiny fish? Maybe I'll mention this to Mrs. Newman. It seems like something she might like."

"Interesting."

"I think it would make the hotel rooms feel more homey. Perhaps each fish would have a name. There could be a little sign by the bowl, introducing the guest to a new roommate, the fish." She laughed.

Sean pointed to her fish. "Does he have a name?"

She thought for a moment. "Gordy."

"Gordy?"

"That was my grandpa's nickname. Gordy

Gordon."

"I like it. Gordy the Goldfish." Sean looked at his watch. "I think I may have worn out my welcome."

"What makes you think that?"

"I promised myself I wouldn't make you sick of me today," he confessed. "Plus I have laundry to do."

"Well, thanks for all your help," she said as she walked him to the front entrance. "I still owe you some real meals."

"Hey, lunch was a real meal."

She smiled. "Yes, but you still get a couple more." She wanted to add "when Marley is home," but at the same time, she didn't.

"I'm looking forward to it."

As much as Anna loved her apartment, she was glad to get back to work on Wednesday morning. There was plenty to be checked on and plenty to be done as they prepared for the grand opening party on Saturday. As she and Sean met for their morning meeting, she could tell that he had much more on his plate than she did, yet he still seemed calm and congenial and competent. The Rothsberg couldn't have hired a better manager.

On Thursday, when Anna got to work, she overheard Bianca complaining in the maids' dressing room. "As if we don't have enough to do," she was growling to someone. "Now we have to clean up fishbowls too?"

"Fishbowls?" Anna asked as she went into the room. "What are you talking about?"

Bianca looked up from buttoning the front of her uniform. "Yeah, didn't you hear the news? A bunch of the guest rooms are getting their own fishbowls. We're supposed to feed the fish every day and clean out their bowls on Wednesdays." She made a face. "I didn't sign on to be handling slimy fish."

"Seriously?" Anna frowned.

"Yeah," Cindy confirmed. "Mr. O'Neil got this big old fish tank installed in the back of the storage room. It's swimming with fish."

Anna felt curious as well as slightly indignant. After all, that had been her idea, and she had intended to tell Mrs. Newman about it. But Sean had run ahead and done it himself. Okay, she knew she was being silly. Especially considering all that Sean had done to help her. It wasn't as if she owned the idea of fish in fishbowls anyway. Perhaps the best thing was to just let this go. Besides, it was a good idea. For Sean to actually try it out was a rather nice compliment to her. Then why did she feel slightly irked?

When she got to her office, she had a message saying that Sean couldn't meet with her this morning. Fine, so he'd stolen her idea, then blown off their daily meeting. No big deal. Even as she thought this, she knew she was being juvenile. She didn't have time to be childish this morning. There was too much to be done. Sean wasn't the only one who was busy.

Anna felt bone tired by the end of the day, but as she walked home, she suspected that her weariness wasn't as much a result of hard work as it was of not having crossed paths with Sean today. She hadn't seen him once, not even in passing. That wasn't surprising since the grand opening was only two days off and taking up everyone's time. Sean's to-do list was probably much longer than hers. She needed to get over it.

As Anna got closer to the apartment building, she felt a happy rush. At least she had a wonderful place to go home to. That made up for everything. As Anna let herself into the apartment, she knew that Marley might be in there already. According to Tia, Marley was expected to get home from her globe-trotting sometime tonight. Anna really hoped that she wasn't there yet. "Hello?" she called out tentatively.

To her relief, everything was just as she'd left it, except that it was hot and stuffy.

There were no signs that Marley was back yet, and selfish as it was, Anna had been enjoying having the place to herself. Just her and Gordy. She opened the front window and went to change out of her work uniform. Since it was so warm, she decided to put on the pale blue sundress Marley had bequeathed to her — her contribution to getting rid of Anna's "little old lady."

Feeling cooler in her bare feet and sundress, Anna went to the kitchen, where she intended to make some angel hair pasta. She'd been craving pesto pasta all day and had picked up some pesto sauce and mozzarella during her lunch break. While the pasta was boiling, she went out to put on some music, and then, thinking she might get some air flow going, she decided to open the front door. Much better. She took in a deep breath of fresh air, assuring herself that the business with Sean and the fish was behind her now . . . just the way life happened and nothing to get upset over.

27

Anna was just pouring the pesto onto the angel hair when she heard someone in the apartment and remembered she'd left the door open. "Marley?" she called out as she grabbed the wooden spoon. Brandishing it in front of her as she peeked out into the living room, she was ready to scream if it was an intruder. "Oh, Sean!" She lowered the spoon in relief. "What are you doing in here?"

"Rodney was out front having a cigarette." He made a sheepish smile. "He told me to go on into the building. Then I saw your door was open . . . again." He frowned. "Sorry to just walk in, but when I called out your name and you didn't answer, I got a little concerned."

"Oh, the music was probably too loud." She closed the door. "I just wanted to let some air flow. It was stuffy in here."

"Understandable." His brow was still

creased. “Just don’t forget this is a big city, Anna. You’re not in Springville anymore.” His countenance softened.

“Yeah, maybe that wasn’t too smart. I meant to close it before now.” Anna turned down the volume of her MP3 player. “I sometimes forget.”

“Well, my apologies for just barging in.” He looked slightly uncomfortable, standing there in his stylish gray suit with his hands in his pockets. “I didn’t really mean to intrude.”

She pointed her wooden spoon at him. “Well, what are you doing here?”

He made a funny face. “I was, uh, homesick.”

“Huh?”

He waved his hands toward the living room. “I kept remembering how nice this place looked and, okay, I know it sounds pathetic, but I just wanted to see it again. I’m sorry to intrude like this. I’ll get out of your hair now.” He turned.

“Wait,” she said quickly. “Are you hungry?”

“Are you kidding?” He sniffed the air. “Do you realize how good it smells in here?”

“Why don’t you take off your jacket and tie? Relax while I finish this up.”

“Seriously? You don’t mind me crashing

in like this?"

"Not at all. Remember, I owe you a meal or two for all your help." She opened the fridge, taking out a leftover green salad she'd made last night. If she added another tomato and some cucumber and pepper, it would probably be enough for two.

As she set the table, this time putting down the moss green placemats, she was glad to see the flowers Sean had brought her on Tuesday still looked nice. Before long, they were both seated at the table, and once again, Sean offered to say a blessing.

"It's a pretty simple meal," she said as they began to eat. "If I'd known you were coming, I'd —"

"Do not apologize, Anna." He looked at her sternly. "This is great."

"Oh . . . good." She forked into her salad.

"I missed our meeting this morning," he said.

"So did I." She took a bite.

"I really wanted to talk to you. As you know by now, I used your idea to put fishbowls in the rooms. The Newmans loved it."

She bristled as she chewed.

"I'm sure you read the memo about how we'll do it," he continued obliviously. "Guests will have the option for fish or no fish. I realize some guests might not be overly fond of fish."

"Some of the maids aren't overly fond either," she admitted. "But I think they'll come around."

"Anyway, I told the Newmans it was your idea, Anna, and they were —"

"You told them it was my idea?" She set her fork down. "Really?"

"Of course. You don't mind, do you? You mentioned you were going to tell Mrs. Newman. We were in a meeting and it just kind of came out. I hope that was okay."

"Sure." She smiled. "That's great."

"They were so pleased to hear that you and I have become better friends. It was kind of like a win-win."

She felt guilty for having doubted him but inexplicably happy that he had not betrayed her. "I'm so glad we can be friends." She lifted her water glass. "Here's to friends."

He looked slightly reluctant as he picked up his glass, clinking it against hers. "To friends."

"Well, what have we here?"

They both looked to see Marley standing in the living room, staring at the two of them with an expression of disbelief. "Marley!" Anna jumped up, going over to her. "You're home. *Welcome!*"

"Hey, Marley." Sean stood politely. "How's the world traveler?"

"Tired." Marley glared at Anna.

"Are you hungry?" Anna asked her. "I'm sure there's enough for one more."

"I don't know." Marley narrowed her eyes as she peeled off her jacket. "It looks like three's a crowd."

"No, it's not," Anna insisted. "We were just celebrating our friendship. The Newmans had complained that we weren't getting along too well and —"

"Looks like you're getting along pretty well to me." Marley reached over to finger a strap of Anna's dress with a suspicious look.

"Sean just happened to drop by," Anna continued quickly. "I was already making pasta. And I owed him a thank-you dinner." She waved her arms around to indicate the apartment. "He helped me put this place together. Isn't it amazing?"

"Amazing," Marley said wryly.

"Come on," Anna urged. "I'll go fix you a plate. Get yourself comfy and come join us, okay?"

"Well, I am hungry."

Anna hurried to the kitchen and began fixing a third plate. Fortunately, there was more than she realized and plenty for a makeshift meal. "Here you go," she said as she set it in front of Marley. "What do you think of the place?"

Marley looked around, then shook her head. "I can't believe you did all this without even asking me."

Anna felt like she'd been slapped. "I did ask you. Remember, you said you didn't care."

"Yes, but you didn't take into account what I like and don't like. Seems like I should've had a say."

"You don't like it?" Anna felt even more crushed now. "Really — you don't like it at all?"

"I don't like being left out."

"You can blame me too," Sean said. "I encouraged Anna to go for it. We had our days off on Monday and Tuesday, and we just went kind of wild." He looked around. "I think it looks fabulous."

Marley shrugged. "I suppose." She pointed to the table. "I'm not really a fan of this wooden furniture, though. I think it looks cheesy. I like glass and metal better."

"I looked up the maker's marks on these Danish modern pieces," Sean told Anna. "They are very collectable — and valuable. If you decided you didn't want them, you could easily sell them."

"I don't want to sell them," she said

quickly. "I love them."

As they ate — and Anna's appetite dwindled — Marley continued to make sharp little jabs. Anna knew it wasn't really about the furniture. It was about Sean. Finally, after Sean left, Anna assured Marley that her relationship with Sean was strictly business. "Just friendship."

"I don't know . . ." Marley curled her feet under her as she sat on the sofa. "Looked like there were some sparks flying when I showed up."

"If I got involved with Sean, *I would lose my job,*" Anna said plainly. "Sean and I are just friends, Marley. That's all it can be."

"You're sure about that?" Marley narrowed her eyes.

"Besides the fact that my savings account has shrunk significantly, I have to get some good work references to ensure my future. I cannot afford to risk everything. I cannot afford to lose my job. Period." She sighed. "I doubt Sean would want to risk his position either. He's doing an excellent job."

"Even so," Marley persisted, "if you really fell in love with him, wouldn't you be willing to take that kind of risk?"

Anna didn't know how to answer that question.

"I know I would." Marley nodded firmly.

"Are you in love with Sean?" Anna asked, instantly regretting it.

Marley's mouth twisted to one side. "In love . . . ?" she said slowly.

"Really, it's none of my business."

"But you asked." Marley studied Anna closely. "The truth is, I suppose I'm not *in love* with Sean, but I wouldn't mind giving it a try. He's awfully good looking and a truly nice guy."

"Uh-huh."

"I'm surprised you don't throw caution to the wind and just go for him yourself, Anna."

"Really? How would you feel if I actually did that?" Anna frowned. "Not that I ever would. But wouldn't you be upset?"

"If you guys were meant to be, well, I suppose I wouldn't mind too much."

Anna didn't know whether to believe her or not, but to distract her and reroute the conversation, Anna began to tell her about the upcoming grand opening. Since the big gala on Saturday night was an open house, Anna invited Marley to attend. "Max and Elsie will be there too."

"Ooh, that does sound fun. I don't have another flight until Sunday afternoon."

"Great. I'll put your name down." Anna slowly stood, looking at the painting of the rainy day behind Marley and sighing. "It's been a long day. I think I'm going to call it a night."

"Thanks for getting my bed moved down for me," Marley called as Anna headed for the bathroom. "Sorry I was such a witch tonight. I think I must be really tired."

"It's okay," Anna paused by the bathroom door. "I'm sure it's exhausting flying all over the world the way you do. I understand."

"The truth is, this place looks great, Anna. Nice job."

On Friday morning, the hotel was bustling and filled to near capacity. All of the staff were on their toes just trying to keep up, plus there were preparations for tomorrow night's celebration. The last thing Anna needed was the memo she got from Mrs. Newman, informing her that she was to dismiss one of her maids. Not only that, it was one of her most dependable maids — second in line to Velma. In fact, she was Velma's sidekick, Cindy. Anna knew that she had no right to question Mrs. Newman on this. Yet it seemed that as Cindy's boss, she did have the right to know what she had done wrong.

Because she was scheduled to meet with Sean — although he'd blown off their last two meetings and she doubted he'd be there now — she decided to find out what he knew first. Or else she'd have to stop by and ask Mrs. Newman. To her surprise, Mrs. Newman was already in Sean's office, and her face looked grim.

"Good, you're here," she told Anna. "I only have a few minutes. I'm sure you got my memo by now."

"Yes." Anna sat down. "I felt a bit blind-sided, though. Cindy is one of my best maids."

"I know, and that's a shame. Especially when we're so busy. But rules are rules."

"What did she do?"

"You don't know?" Mrs. Newman's fair brows arched.

"No. I haven't had a chance to ask anyone."

"Cindy was discovered with Arnie, the night doorman," Sean said in a flat-sounding tone. "In a full embrace."

"Oh dear."

"They both must be dismissed." Mrs. Newman looked at Anna. "Let's not let this lesson go to waste. Use Cindy as an example for the other maids. Make them see that we mean business. Here today, gone tomor-row." She snapped her fingers. "If they value their employment, they won't mess around."

"Right." Anna avoided Sean's face.

"Take care of it ASAP," Mrs. Newman told them. "And get them replaced."

"I'm on it," Sean told her.

"Yes." Anna stood. "So am I."

"Good." Mrs. Newman smiled. "I'm glad I can depend on both of you."

As Anna left, she felt as if storm clouds were gathering. Or as if she were walking into a dangerous minefield. She reminded herself that she had done nothing wrong. Sure, the friendship she shared with Sean felt like it could bloom into something more. But not if she nipped it in the bud. Okay, maybe it was more than just a bud by now. But she would nip it. She would not allow her feelings to derail both her and Sean. In the meantime, she had to go fire someone.

The grand opening party was well attended, and it seemed that the Rothsberg was well on its way to becoming SoHo's next big success story. Anna was glad to see Marley there, dressed to the nines and looking like a million bucks. Marley divided her time between the Newmans and Max and Elsie, as well as the who's who of Manhattan. As Anna watched from the sidelines, she was slightly surprised to see that Marley was such a good schmoozer. No one would ever have guessed that Marley, like Anna, was from a small town like Springville. Of course, Sean shared their humble origins too, but he always seemed so at ease, so comfortable and in his element, that Anna sometimes forgot how similar their roots really were.

With everyone looking all glamorous and glittery tonight, Anna felt like a small-town bumpkin. Especially since she was dressed in her serious black work suit. However, she reminded herself, she *was* working. Although Sean was working too. Yet he was wearing a stylish tux and doing just as much schmoozing as Anna's congenial roommate. Anna tried to watch discreetly from the sidelines, admiring how Sean skillfully worked the crowd. He was hard to ignore — so handsome and debonair, so outgoing and friendly. Almost like a celebrity.

Her spying was spoiled when she witnessed Sean and Marley clinking their glasses of champagne together — visiting and laughing like old friends . . . or much more. Anna knew it was childish, but she couldn't take it. She returned to housekeeping. After ensuring that everything was under control, since Ellen was still there and Anna's shift had been over for a couple of hours, Anna went home and went to bed.

With the hotel at nearly full capacity, Sunday was just as busy as Saturday had been, and when quitting time came, Anna was thankful to call it a day and looking forward to two blessed days off. She was also thankful to come home to a vacated apartment, because she knew that Marley was going out tonight and then flying to Amsterdam and who knew where else tomorrow morning. Anna would have the place to herself for a couple of days. A couple of days to think some things through.

By Monday morning Anna was painfully aware of two things. One, Sean had been all business ever since that night when Marley had popped in unexpectedly and made her insinuations. Two, Anna was hopelessly in love with Sean. There was no denying it.

As hard as it was to admit these things to herself, Anna knew it was time to face them head-on. For one thing, Anna was worried that she might be getting an ulcer, especially after having to fire Cindy. For another thing, Anna was worried for Sean's sake because Velma had been fit to be tied. Oh, she didn't really think that Velma would go to Mrs. Newman or tell her what she had observed that night in the Newmans' penthouse. Besides, what *had* she observed? An awkward conversation? A stilted apology? That was all. But what if Velma did tell? What then?

Anna suspected that Sean had experienced similar concerns. That was probably the reason he'd played it cooler than ever these past few days. He had obviously reached the place where he realized that pursuing a relationship with Anna — even if they called it "just friendship" — would ultimately put his job at risk. Like her, he probably could not afford it.

Pacing back and forth in the small apartment, Anna was trying to come up with a solution. She knew that if she quit the hotel now, she would probably get a fairly decent reference from Mrs. Newman. For the next job she sought, though, she would probably be questioned about why she'd quit after only one month on the job. Such a short stint at such an up-and-coming hotel would be a red flag to her next employer. But if she stayed, she might risk getting fired. Whether it was from her own carelessness, or Sean's, or even a vindictive Velma, Anna could easily lose her job. Then where would she be? With her nest egg dwindled away, her only recourse might be to go back home to live with Grandma.

Anna stopped pacing and looked up at the

Rainy Day painting and let out a long sigh. Why did life have to be so complicated? How could something so good turn out to be so wrong? She went over to check on Gordy, crumbling a couple flakes into his bowl and watching as he gobbled them up. If only her life was as simple as his.

28

By Tuesday evening, which happened to be the Fourth of July, Anna had made up her mind. She told herself that since it was Independence Day, she would exercise some independence by making a decision that would ultimately set her free. Okay, maybe she didn't really want to be cut loose and set free, but if it would preserve Sean's job and hopefully get her a decent recommendation, it would be worth it. Besides that, it seemed like the right and decent thing to do. As head of housekeeping, she just plain couldn't fall head over heels in love with the manager of the same hotel, and she knew that's what she'd done. To be fair, it seemed that it was partly Sean's fault too. Didn't it take two to fall in love? Or was that two to tango? But since their relationship didn't seem to unnerve him quite the way it did her, she figured it was her responsibility to move on.

Anna had spent the afternoon cruising job sites on the internet and had already made a short list of places she planned to check out. She knew she had to give the hotel two weeks' notice, but it wouldn't be too soon to start putting in applications.

As she fixed herself a light dinner of soup and salad, she began to feel better about the situation. Sure, it wasn't ideal, but at least she was taking the bull by the horns, as Grandma would say. Even if her references weren't stellar, she knew that she could prove herself . . . again. This time she would stick with the job for at least two years. She might even promise her new employer as much. Really, what choice did she have if she wanted to be taken seriously?

After dinner, she called her grandma, but instead of telling her of this decision, she kept the conversation light and happy. She didn't want Grandma to concern herself with Anna's problems just yet. After she got resettled in a new job, she'd spill the beans.

"Are you going to watch the fireworks?" Grandma finally said. "I've heard they're really something out there in New York City. You'll have to take some photos to send me."

"I'll see what I can do," Anna told her. "I think I might even be able to watch them from the apartment."

"I showed my bunco group the photos you sent me of your apartment, Anna. They were so impressed. You're such a big city girl now. Go figure."

It was fun to hear the pride in Grandma's voice. Just one more reason not to tell her about the job situation before she was squared away.

After Anna hung up, she thought about going outside to see if there was a good spot in the neighborhood to watch the fireworks. But the way she felt tonight, well, she just wasn't in a festive firecracker sort of mood. Oh, she was resolved and even experiencing a tiny bit of relief, but she wasn't feeling celebratory. Knowing she had work tomorrow, she was thinking she might just call it a night.

She was just turning out the lights in the living room when she heard the buzzer for the front entrance. Thinking it might be Marley coming home early and unable to locate her key, Anna answered the intercom, saying, "Who is it?"

"It's me. Sean."

"Sean?" She felt a flutter in her chest.

"Yeah. I've been trying to call your cell for about an hour. I finally decided to just stop by and see if you were here."

"Why?"

"To take you to the fireworks."

"Huh?"

"Come on, Anna. Don't say no."

She pushed the button to let him into the building, then waited at her door. "What on earth are you doing?" she asked, trying not to be pulled in by his hopeful smile.

"Taking you to see the fireworks." He looked at her scruffy shorts and stained T-shirt. "That what you're wearing?"

"No." She frowned. "I mean yes. I mean —"

"Hurry, Anna, go change."

"But I —"

"This is our first Fourth in New York, Anna. We have to see the fireworks."

Feeling slightly lost but also slightly giddy, Anna ran to the bedroom and quickly changed into khakis and a blue-and-white striped T-shirt. Grabbing up a navy cashmere cardigan in case it got cool, she hurried back out.

"Beautiful," he said appreciatively.

"Well, I don't know about —"

"Come on." He grabbed her by the hand. "Let's go."

"Where are we going?" she asked as they hurried out of the building.

"You'll see."

It didn't take long for her to realize he was headed for the hotel. "What are you doing?" she demanded as he slid his employee card into the side entrance door.

"You'll see."

"Sean," she pleaded, "this is going to look suspicious. You can't —"

"Shh," he hissed. "Come on." He led her directly to the service elevator, inserted his card again, and pushed the top button, which had to be for the rooftop terrace, although she'd only seen it once.

"Sean, this is crazy. The Newmans are using the private terrace for their party tonight."

"I know."

"We can't go up there. They'll see us and —"

"Relax, Anna. I've got this under control."

"But it's nuts, Sean. You're asking for trouble."

He turned to look at her. "Just trust me, okay?"

"It's your funeral." She sighed, thinking it would be hers too. So much for giving her notice and making a graceful exit. If they got caught together, they'd both be going out like the fireworks — with a big boom!

The elevator opened into a little room that led out to the terrace. As they went outside,

Anna's heart was pounding. Had Sean lost his mind? She could see flickering lights off to one side. She heard the sounds of voices, music, and laughter, obviously the Newmans' party. Surely Sean didn't intend to crash it.

To her great relief, he led her in the opposite direction. Using a little flashlight to guide them around various lumps and bumps on the roof, he turned a corner, and there in a quiet nook was a pair of chairs, a small table with a hurricane candle burning bravely, and what appeared to be a picnic basket.

"What is this?" she asked as he led her over.

"Our personal fireworks show." He helped her to sit in a chair, then knelt down to open the picnic basket. He removed a plate with cheese and fruit and crackers, setting it on the table. Then he proceeded to open a bottle of sparkling apple cider, fill a pair of glasses, and hand her one. "Here's to us, Anna." He clicked his glass against hers as he sat down next to her.

She was too stunned to even speak. On one hand, she was over the moon thrilled. This was so beautiful, so romantic, so unexpected. But on the other hand, she was terrified. What if they were discovered by the Newmans? How could they not be discovered when they were only twenty or thirty feet apart?

"I'm toasting to *us,* Anna," Sean said with an urgency.

Anna just sat there, staring dumbly at him. Had he lost his mind?

"Aren't you going to toast me back?" he asked.

"To be honest, I'm in shock," she told him. "I don't even know what to say to you."

He laughed. "Yes, I'm sorry about that. I suppose this seems pretty extreme."

"You could lose your job," she said quietly, concerned that someone from the party might wander this way and overhear them.

"I'm not worried."

"Well, you should be. I mean, I plan to give my notice tomorrow, but you —"

"Give your notice?" He looked alarmed. "Why?"

"Because I think it's wise. For your sake as much as for mine."

"You'd quit your job to protect me?" He reached over to touch her cheek. "See, Anna, that's just one more reason to love you."

"Love me?"

"Of course." He leaned over and kissed her forehead. "But you knew that all along, didn't you?"

"But I . . ." She felt light-headed, like she was afraid to breathe, like this might all just evaporate.

"I know it's been a whirlwind romance, Anna. Not at all like I planned it should be. And not very convenient — at least where our jobs are concerned. But when something's right . . ." He shrugged. "What can you do?"

"I, uh, I don't know." She studied him, still trying to determine if this was for real or just some weird, happy dream.

He held up his glass again. "To us?"

She nodded, clinking her glass against his. "To us."

They each took a sip and then, just as a giant burst of fireworks exploded over the river, Sean leaned over and kissed her. There was no doubt this time that the kiss was intentional. It was long and intense and passionate — and the fireworks exploding inside of her were far brighter and louder than the ones exploding over the river. When he finally stopped kissing her, she was totally speechless.

"I love you, Anna," he said quietly. "I've known it for a full month now. Remember when I invited myself to eat dinner with you at the outdoor café near the hotel? Well, right then and there, I knew that I was falling. Oh, I tried to convince myself otherwise, but it was useless."

"I love you too," she acknowledged. "I wanted to deny it. I pretended it wasn't true. But I fell for you on that first Sunday we spent sightseeing together. I think I knew it for sure when we were at Ellis Island. I tried to tell myself we were just friends, but deep inside I knew it was more."

"I've never felt as connected to someone as I do to you," Sean confessed. "I know it sounds corny, Anna, but it feels like we really were made for each other."

She laughed. "It doesn't sound corny to me. I've felt the same way. I mean, how many times have we both liked the same things, expressed similar thoughts, finished each other's sentences? It's like we've known each other for ages."

"Well, we did grow up in the same small town." He ran his fingers over her cheek.

"So did Marley," she pointed out.

He chuckled. "So much for that theory. I mean, Marley is nice and all, but she is not you, Anna. Not even close."

As the fireworks continued exploding, Sean kissed her again . . . and again. Finally, as much as she was enjoying this magical evening, Anna knew there were questions that demanded some answers.

"What about your job?" she said during a lull between explosions. "I mean, I do plan to give my notice tomorrow, but I'd like to get a good recommendation before I move on." She glanced nervously over her shoulder. "What if the Newmans discovered us up here tonight?" She jerked her thumb back toward the area where their party was still going on. "We'd both be toast and you know it."

"Maybe not."

"Maybe not?" She shook her head. Had Sean lost his senses? "You heard Mrs. Newman the other day. 'Rules are rules.' No exceptions."

"That's right." He nodded. "But are you aware that the rules have a provision for married couples?"

"What?" Anna wondered if she'd heard him right.

"Because Mr. and Mrs. Newman are married, they decided to put in a provision saying that married couples can work at the Rothsberg."

"I've never seen that in the employee manual." Anna blinked. Was he saying what she thought he was saying?

"That's because it's a new rule. I just spoke to Mr. Newman this afternoon, explaining our situation and —"

"You told Mr. Newman about us?"

He nodded. "I think honesty truly is the best policy."

"Oh." She felt slightly breathless now. Had Sean really just mentioned marriage?

"He talked to Mrs. Newman about it, and they have agreed to change the rules to allow married couples. It makes perfect sense. Married employees are usually the most dependable."

"We're not married, Sean."

"Not yet." He leaned over to kiss her again. "Anna, will you do me the honor of marrying me?"

"Yes," she said without even stopping to think about her answer. "I most definitely will."

As another big display of red, white, and blue explosions burst over their heads, lighting up the blackened sky, they kissed again.

ABOUT THE AUTHOR

Melody Carlson is the award-winning author of over two hundred books, including *The Christmas Pony, A Simple Christmas Wish,* and *The Christmas Cat.* Melody recently received a *Romantic Times* Career Achievement Award in the inspirational market for her books. She and her husband live in central Oregon. For more information about Melody, visit her website at www.melodycarlson.com.

The employees of Thorndike Press hope you have enjoyed this Large Print book. All our Thorndike, Wheeler, and Kennebec Large Print titles are designed for easy reading, and all our books are made to last. Other Thorndike Press Large Print books are available at your library, through selected bookstores, or directly from us.

For information about titles, please call:
(800) 223-1244

or visit our Web site at:
http://gale.cengage.com/thorndike

To share your comments, please write:
Publisher
Thorndike Press
10 Water St., Suite 310
Waterville, ME 04901